CIRCUMSTANCES OF WAR

ROBERT JOHN GARDNER

Disclaimer:
This is a work of fiction. All characters, locations, and businesses are purely products of the author's imagination and are entirely fictitious. Any resemblance to actual people, living or dead, or to businesses, places, or events is completely coincidental.

CHAPTER ONE

Springfield Illinois October 8, 1933

Stacked snowbanks in front of St. Joe's church had turned sooty black and rock hard in short order after the early October ice storm had abated. The white steeple of the old, but grand, Catholic Church pierced the gloom above. The street was empty save for a handful of cars parked diagonally. Barren trees stretched out like skeleton arms.

Inside the ornate church capable of holding five hundred or more sat a sprinkling of perhaps fifty parishioners.

Two boys stood at the foot of the altar, facing away from the assembly, hands folded. Mo and Max Gordon, identical twins, were Father Fraley's favorite servers. They could not be distinguished by their features, the only difference being Max was a half inch taller than Mo. Other than that, they were bookends.

The tall, strikingly handsome priest, spoke in Latin. He completed his blessing and moved toward the marble communion rail with his jeweled silver chalice filled with communion wafers, known as hosts to Catholics.

As the priest passed the twins, the taller of the two turned and followed, holding a flat silver platter with a handle, called a communion-plate, to catch a host should the hand to mouth delivery go awry.

The faithful knelt at the communion rail waiting for

Father Fraley to reach them, while the other twin, Mo, went to the side of the altar where a hard, wooden chair awaited. Mo sat with hands folded, the black altar boy cassock unable to hide his right leg as it bounced up and down in what seemed to be perpetual motion. Mo was already thinking about Kelso and his gang. He knew they'd be waiting for Max and him on the way home.

When the priest had delivered communion to the last kneeler, he took Max's communion-plate, turned deliberately, and strode up the altar steps. The twins, perfectly synchronized, came together in the center and stood at attention, hands folded, facing the huge wooden cross with the Christ hanging which loomed behind the altar. Their pressed cassocks allowed for well-worn hard brown shoes to show below. But that didn't matter here at St. Joe's. This parish in North Springfield was populated by industrious factory workers just happy to have a job. Times were tough.

CHAPTER TWO

Springfield Illinois October 8, 1933

The twins bounded down the stairs from the Sacristy at the rear of the church.

"You wanna race home, Maxie?"

"No. It's too icy."

Playfully punching his brother in the arm, Mo continued his needling. "C'mon!"

Jostling each other, Mo let Max get him in a headlock, but resisted when Max started to give him a noogie.

Breaking away, Mo laughed. "No noogies."

The twins walking home from St. Joe's on Sundays were a familiar sight, their house on Black Avenue only a long block away. As the boys walked down the middle of the pock-marked blacktop street talking and laughing, ice-cold air made every exhalation obvious. Snow banks on each side of the road matched the blackness of the church snow, while traces of crushed salt showed white on the roadway.

As usual, both boys wore the same outfits: farmer's jeans with suspenders, white sweatshirts and those brown shoes.

Getting almost halfway home, Mo and Max eyed the group of boys on the porch of the house owned by the White family.

"Oh, oh, there's Kelso" said Max.

"I knew they'd be waitin' for us Maxie."

Max turned to his brother with a worried look.

"Let's just ignore them, Mo".

Mo was silent as they neared the gang. The tallest boy on the porch had a sly smile on his face as the little group of thugs watched the Gordons draw close. When the twins were directly in front of the house, the tallest yelled out.

"Look guys. There's the Gordon idiots. Been at the church again? Aren't you holy!"

Max looked at his brother. "C'mon Mo."

The two continued to walk ahead, when Kelso shouted again.

"Tryin' to make up for that criminal old man'o yours got himself killed?"

Stopping in his tracks, Mo turned around.

"Shut up, Kelso!"

"Who's gonna make me, Gordon?"

Up on the porch, Kelso's boys were gleeful at the escalation in these challenges.

Max turned to Mo. "C'mon Mo. Let's just go home."

"I'll kick your butt any day, Kelso."

"Right now, then" shouted Kelso as he started down the stairs followed by his wild-eyed batch of punks. Some of these same boys had been picking on Max for years at the school.

Max tried to grab Mo but he broke away. As Kelso and his gang reached the curb, Mo walked right up to Kelso, taller than Mo by a few inches. "Kelso, you got the ugliest face of anybody I've ever seen."

Kelso lunged at Mo, grabbing him as they tumbled to the ground. They rolled on the wet pavement, punching at each other.

Kelso's gang and Max watched as the fight raged. Kelso was getting the better of the fight, but Mo continued, punching furiously, and Kelso had blood on his mouth.

From the porch where the gang was waiting, Mr. White hurried down the stairs toward the mayhem in the street.

"You two stop fighting now! All of you boys, get out of here!"

As he pushed Mo away, Kelso got up, his face scratched and bleeding.

"We're not done, Gordon."

Mo jumped up, face red and puffy, fists clenched.

"Oh yeah? Well you're done growin' Kelso an' I'm still gettin' bigger!"

Kelso started off down the street as his gang followed. A couple of the boys turned around to look at Mo. Mo glared back, causing them to quickly turn away.

"You know Momma told you not to fight with Kelso, Mo."

"Couldn't back down Maxie. After he said what he did about Poppa? And he had his whole gang with him. Now none of those punks'll mess with me."

CHAPTER THREE
Munich Germany October 8 1933

Cold damp fog dripped mist, engulfing the rows of shops on both sides of the street. Immune to the gloom, people went about their business. Bakeries, delis and sidewalk cafes teemed with activity on this day, unusual in these times.

Older bearded men and younger ones unable to muster facial hair all dressed in similar outfits. Long pants either black or grey, black shoes, white collarless shirts and black coats. They all wore the Jewish head covering, known as a kippah or yarmulke.

Two younger boys walked together. One boy, taller and thinner, carried a violin case. His skin was white and his kippah covered only a small part of his thick curly black hair. The other boy carried a much smaller case. They entered one of the shops.

On one wall hung bolts of material. Not fancy material or bright colors. Only material for basic garments. The windows that faced the crowded street were old, the paint chipping off the wooden frames, but the glass was spotless. A counter on the back wall was filled with boxes, books and baskets. A table in front of the last remaining wall on the left had two old sewing machines being worked by a man and a woman.

The man, thin and pale, moved fabric through his

machine effortlessly with enormous hands. He was the taller boy's father, Abraham Gittelsohn. The woman, who looked much younger than the man, was the mother, Golde. Without looking up, Abraham spoke.

"Where have you two been? I expected you here much sooner." Aaron Gittelsohn answered his father.

"Father, Asher and I took the long way back. The German boys want to hurt us when we take the short way home. Last time, we ran faster than them, but now they wait and try to trap us."

Abraham glanced over at his wife, their eyes quickly meeting before she looked back down. Abraham stopped and looked back at the boys.

"Well then, you are smart. Better not to go where ruffians give you trouble. These are dangerous times. There is much hate."

As he stood, Abraham stretched taller than he appeared behind the machine. He put a hand on each boy's shoulder as he spoke.

"Go in back and practice your music. When I finish, I will come to teach the English language and art history. Today we study Josef Chelmonski, a great Polish artist."

Looking up from her work, Golde gave the boys a smile.

"Aaron, Asher. Fresh bagels are in the cupboard. You may both have one. Asher, take four to your mother when you go home."

The mood lightened, and both boys smiled. "Thank you, mother. We are hungry."

"Thank you, Mrs. Gittelsohn. My mother will be thankful also."

As the boys went into the back room, Golde and Abraham looked at each other, their faces reflecting concern.

Since Hitler had assumed full power in Germany,

organized attacks on Jews happened more frequently. Democracy had been obliterated by the Nazis. Germany was a police state, getting more brutal by the day.

Abraham's tailoring business once thrived with Jewish and German customers. Now the Jewish neighborhood considered itself lucky when no Nazis stood outside their businesses, intimidating would-be customers.

CHAPTER FOUR

Gloucester Harbor Massachusetts October 8 1933

The sun shone brightly and the sky was mirrored on the placid blue waters of the bay. Men scurried about a private dock, making ready an exquisite seventy-five-foot motor yacht. Senator Russell Royce had commissioned the ship builder to replicate a downsized version of Hoover's Presidential Yacht. As the Senator regularly said to his guests, "Just like the Sequoia, but shorter. But then, a Senator's yacht shouldn't be as long as the President's, should it?"

He would always neglect to mention that when Hoover had used a photo of the Sequoia on the official White House Christmas card, it helped seal the sitting President's doom. Apparently, starving Americans didn't give a damn if Hoover used only a one-hundred-foot yacht instead of a ship three-hundred feet long. Hoover seemed out of touch with America, and his election thrashing at the hands of FDR was a predictable result. Hoover's loss was of little consequence to the Senator, as he was a strong supporter of the new President, who he had known personally for quite some time.

On this unusually calm and warm October afternoon, Senator Royce was preparing to entertain a younger colleague from Congress, and he wanted everything perfect.

Four impeccably dressed deckhands loaded large cases

as Captain Charles Rose stood at attention next to the ramp, facing toward a stately white two-story mansion fronting the harbor. Decks wrapped completely around the bottom floor, with a wide grand staircase descending to the sprawling lawn, still green for this time of year. Indian summer had been late and favorable to Massachusetts. The Senator knew opportunities for this kind of excursion would not last long. The weather could turn any day. Winter would not be denied much longer.

Four term Massachusetts Senator Russell Royce stepped out onto the deck. Somewhat pudgy, the Senator was stylish in pressed white slacks, white shoes and white shirt under a blue blazer matching the color of the bay. He sported a wide brimmed white hat. As he cupped hands around his mouth to create a bullhorn effect, the Senator's voice boomed to the Captain below.

"Charles, the women seem to be holding things up. We'll be down in short order."

Standing up a bit straighter, saluting, the Captain yelled back just as loudly. "Fine Sir. We're almost finished loading."

The Senator returned the Captain's salute. Behind him, coming out onto the porch emerged a handsome young boy, TR Royce, the Senator's fourteen-year-old son. He already towered over his father, and appeared fit and athletic.

"Looks like you're ready TR. Good! Now if we can just get the women out here."

"Father, I'm hoping I don't have to go today. I need to be at the polo field. It's one of our last matches and the team depends on me. They can't afford to have their number one not show up."

"TR, today's ride in the bay is very important. One day you'll understand, I promise. I'm entertaining the new young Congressman from New York. He's sure to go far in politics.

Maybe even become President. I want you to meet him. Now, go see what's holding up the others. The Congressman and his wife will be here any time now."

Somewhat distraught, but seemingly not too upset, TR headed off as he heeded his father's wishes.

CHAPTER FIVE

Springfield Illinois October 8, 1933

The Gordon house was the biggest on the street. Two stories constructed of heavy split face stone with a steep roofline of dulled green shingles. A wide staircase with six risers led up to a long porch which stretched across the front of the house and wrapped around on the side leading to the front door.

Purposely avoiding the shovelled walk, the two boys enjoyed the scrunching noise of the snow as they walked in the yard. As they ascended the steps, Mo was the first to speak.

"Maybe everybody's back in the kitchen."

"It's not gonna make any difference. Momma's gonna see your face."

As the boys walked into the vestibule, everyone was in the living room, just to the right. Sitting on the couch were their older sisters Olga, Della, Anne and Cecilia. The twins were the babies of the family with Mo the real baby. Max was born fifteen minutes before Mo. Mo had problems at childbirth, and almost died. The age difference was stark, the boys being almost eight years younger than Cecilia, the youngest and prettiest of all the girls.

In her usual spot, a large cushioned chair next to the stand-up radio, was their mother, Mary Gordon.

A handsome man who appeared to be in his early thirties

stood in the center of the room, Edward Vernon. Edward rented one of the bedrooms upstairs and had become like a family member in the few years he had lived in the house.

As the twins walked in, all conversation came to a halt as everyone spied Mo, whose face and clothes bore the aftermath of his encounter with Kelso.

"My word, Mosie, what have you done to yourself?" said Cecilia.

Before Mo could say anything, Max answered. "Mo got into a fight with Tommy Kelso down the street."

"Mo, I told you to stay away from that Kelso boy" scolded his mother, Mary.

"Mama, Kelso was makin' fun of Maxie an' me in front of his whole gang. Then he said somethin' bad about Poppa. Nothin' I could do 'cept give him a wallopin'."

At this statement, Edward Vernon did his best to hide a smile as he chimed in. "Who gave who a 'wallopin'? That face is pretty puffy boy."

"Eddie, Kelso was bleedin' too. I got him good. He won't be botherin' us any more, I tell ya."

Cecilia got up off the couch and went over to Mo, inspecting the damage to his face. "Well, come on into the kitchen. Let me clean you up young man." As Cecilia took Mo into the kitchen, Mary looked over toward Max. "You go on too now Max. Go wash up."

"Yes Momma."

After the boys and Cecilia had left the room, Edward finally let his smile come full.

"Don't be too hard on Mo, Mrs. Gordon. If he doesn't do what he did, that gang down the street only gets worse for those two."

"I know Edward. I've been trying to do the right thing by them since Poppa has been gone."

"They're good boys. Don't you worry about them. With you and their sisters, how can they go wrong?"

"Edward, you've been so good with the boys. They look up to you."

"Mrs. Gordon, you know I care about those boys a bushel. I think I'll go in and see if Cecilia needs help cleaning up Mo's face."

As Edward left the room, Anne and Olga looked at their mother, rolling their eyes. They all knew Edward was nuts about Cecilia. Della kept her eyes trained on Edward as he went to the kitchen.

CHAPTER SIX

Gloucester Harbor October 8, 1933

The outer harbor was filled with pleasure craft. Everyone realized this to possibly be their last chance to get out on the water.

A light breeze created small crests on the sparkling bay as Senator Royce's yacht cruised slowly in the protected waters.

Shielded from the bright sun by the floor of the top deck, Senator Royce and his guest, Congressman William Tucker, lounged in plush wicker chairs. They both enjoyed a glass of aged scotch, and each had a fat cigar.

Although there was a generation between the men, they were enjoying one another's company.

"And so that's why I made sure to put cushions on all my chairs, William. There's nothing worse than those damned wooden deck chairs with no cushions. Before you know it, your whole ass is numb!" Both men laughed as they lifted their glasses to drink their scotch. Senator Royce sat back further in his chair, exhibiting his comfort level, puffing on his cigar.

"William, I've known your family for years. I remember when you were ten years old. Seems like yesterday. Hell, that was a couple years before TR was even born. Now here you are, seventeen years later and a newly elected Congressman."

"Senator, you've always been Dad's best friend. I still

remember the two of you letting me sit in on your political discussions. I learned a lot by osmosis."

"I wish your mom and dad could have made the trip today. New York will never have a better Senator than your dad."

"Dad wanted to come, but with mom under the weather...you know."

"Yes, I know." Taking another drink, the Senator continued. "I never heard anyone debate like you. When you led your debate team to the Championship in high school, you used more logic than Hoover ever did."

"Thank you, Senator. Dad's always said arguing with me is like wrestling a pig in the mud. Pretty soon you come to realize the pig is enjoying himself."

Both men had another laugh.

"William, on a serious note, what do you make of the little fanatic taking over in Germany? You just got back from England. Do we have anything to fear from him?"

"It seems most people I spoke to in England are worried about the state of affairs. Germany is getting strong, and Hitler is getting away with building up his military. He's an ambitious man."

"William, I feel the same way. The problem is, now it's not popular to bring it up. We have a nation of idiots with their heads buried in the sand." The Senator stopped for a moment, puffed on his cigar and then took a drink before he went on.

"People think since we have an ocean between us and Europe we've got nothing to worry about. We're not as isolated as people think."

"I agree Senator."

"William, take my advice. Keep those ideas about Hitler to yourself. Don't air unpopular opinions right now. They might come back to haunt you in the next election. I guarantee, the day will come when we are forced to stand up to Germany, and we'll need you in Congress when we do."

As the Senator finished talking, TR came down the stairs from the top deck, his face flushed from the sun, relentless for anyone on top.

"TR, excellent timing my boy. Come on over for a minute."

When TR reached his father's side, Senator Royce reached out and put his arm around his son's waist, looking up at him as he spoke.

"You know, the day might come when you two both work together."

TR looked at Congressman Tucker, a man almost fifteen years his senior, then gave his father a quizzical look.

"I'm a boy. What can I work on with Congressman Tucker?"

Smiling as he spoke, the Congressman addressed TR.

"TR, you're fourteen. You know, in only twelve more years you'll be old enough to be a Congressman too. If that happened, we could be working together, and on important matters."

Senator Royce had a broad smile as he took a puff of his cigar and pulled his son a little closer. TR, doing a little bit of age math in his head, then answered the Congressman.

"I'd like that, Congressman Tucker. Us working together."

CHAPTER SEVEN

Munich Germany October 8, 1933

Abraham Gittelsohn meticulously folded the garment he was working on, then looked over at Golde who was still concentrating on her sewing.

"I'll complete this later. I don't want to keep the boys waiting. Asher must get home before dark."

As he finished folding and put the material on one of the shelves, two men with brown uniforms barged through the door. One man held a piece of paper in his hand. They were wearing holsters with German Luger pistols in them, and both had stern and hateful looks. The one with the paper spoke.

"Abraham Gittelsohn?"

Golde looked up with alarm as Abraham answered calmly.

"I am Abraham."

The man began reading from the paper. "All Jewish shop owners in this district will now pay an additional fifteen percent tax for all work performed. Collection will occur once per week. Failure to pay will result in the closing of the business and confiscation of this building. Any attempt to cheat will be punishable by incarceration. We collect every Saturday. Be here with your books or face prosecution."

The men turned and walked out, leaving the door open to the cold fog outside.

Abraham went over to the door, closed it slowly, then turned to face his wife.

Golde had a hopeless look.

"Now they want fifteen percent of what we make over what we already pay? Abraham, we are hungry. Now this?"

"We'll give them what they want. We have no choice. Their evil knows no limits. They know what they do, collecting their ransom on our Holy Day."

As he walked over to the door leading into the back room where the boys waited, Abraham turned once more to Golde.

"Golde, don't worry. There are others much worse off than us. Pray for them. We will make it work, and in a few years we shall join my brother in America."

CHAPTER EIGHT

Springfield Illinois Seven Years Later 1940

From street view, the front of the Gordon house was a well-maintained home. Hedges on both sides of the opening leading to the sidewalk up to the porch were trimmed to perfection. On the right side taking up a full corner of the yard was a Hibiscus bush as big as a small tree, in full bloom with hundreds of giant red flowers. Oversized bumblebees helped themselves to the fragrant blossoms. The grass was green, trimmed and edged. The porch had Adirondack chairs with cushions matching those of the swing on the far-right end of the porch. Edward Vernon's shiny 1938 Ford Model 82A was parked in the driveway just to the left side of the yard. Only a few households on Black Avenue could afford an automobile.

Inside the house, Edward was sitting on the couch in the living room. Mo and Max, now handsome young men, were sitting in two chairs, one on each side of the couch. Max looked natty in his civilian suit and tie. Mo wore a clean and pressed army uniform and hard black shoes spit shined. The three had a conversation going.

"Eddie, you gotta level with me. Can I ask you a really tough question?"

"Sure Max. What's on your mind?"

"Now that Mo's back from basic, he's gonna ship out

pretty soon. I'll be leaving for law school. You'll be the only man in the house."

Max paused before he continued.

"Are you ever going to ask Cecilia to get married?"

Sitting on the opposite side of Edward, Mo nodded.

"Yeah Eddie. We've been expecting a wedding for a long time."

"Boys, you both know I love Ceil. But with Della gone and married and the other two out of the house and hankerin' to get married, Ceil's the only one left to take care of your Ma. Mary's getting on now, and Ceil feels like she's got to stay here."

Eddie got up off the couch and walked to the center of the room. Mo and Max had their eyes trained on him.

"Listen here fellas". Edward turned and looked at the men.

"I'm not going anywhere, believe me. Ceil will always be the gal for me. And I care a lot about your mom, too. Things are taken care of around here and neither of you two need to worry about home while you're both off doing what you got to do."

Still sitting in his chair, Mo leaned forward and looked at the floor for a moment, then looked back up.

"Eddie, you're a hell of a guy. Max and I owe you everything. You've been like a father to us all these years."

"Yeah Eddie. Mo and I want to thank you."

As Edward turned away from the two, he reached into his trousers to retrieve his handkerchief, dabbing at his eyes before he turned back. "You fellas never need to thank me for bein' here. I always figured I was the one gettin' the best end of the deal havin' you two boys around. You know, your Poppa was a good man. I knew him for the first three years I boarded here at the house. All he cared about was his family, and he worked real hard to take care of all of you best he could. Wasn't right what happened to him, and to you boys. I know your Poppa would like to know I stayed on to help bring you up."

As Edward finished his words, Cecilia's voice could be heard from the top of the stairs. "Eddie honey, are you ready to go?"

"Yes Ceil. I'm just sitting here with the guys waiting for you."

Hollering down again, Ceil answered.

"I'll be down in a couple of minutes. I just need a little rouge on my cheeks and lipstick."

"OK. No hurry."

"Well, Eddie, you and Cecilia have a good time tonight. Max and I are heading downtown to the SoHo Grill across from the Capitol Building. Maybe this uniform snags us a couple of girls."

"You fellas need a ride down there?"

"Nah. Max's rich buddy Deuce Bunding from Oak Knolls let him use his new Cadillac Sixty Special for a whole week while he's out of town. His dad owns that big insurance company downtown."

"It's still gonna cost you a bundle at the SoHo. That's where the politicians go after they're done at the State House. And when Capone was in town a couple of years ago that's where he ate dinner."

Reaching into his pocket, Edward pulled out his gold money clip and peeled off a few bills. "I'm treatin' tonight boys."

"Eddie, Mo and I have enough money with us. Put your money away."

"Now listen, I insist. You boys don't know it yet, but I just got a big raise down at the Sangamo plant. I'm in charge of the whole tool and die division. Sangamo just got its biggest contract ever from the United States Government."

"Eddie that's great," answered Mo. "What kind of contract?"

Edward lowered his voice as if he were being overheard.

"It's on the QT, so keep this to yourselves. Two big things. We're working on parts for anti-submarine sonar equipment and communications equipment, radio parts. It's like the plant is on total war production, but we aren't even in the war."

"Eddie, that's why I joined the army now. We will be in the war real soon, and me joining before we're in means I could be a sergeant or something."

Edward paused as a more serious look overtook his face.

"I know Mo, but the advantages of rapid advancement and promotion during wartime also has its share of drawbacks."

"Yeah, I guess it could, but I don't plan on bein' a part of the drawbacks part."

As she walked into the room, Cecilia looked beautiful. The last seven years had been good to Cecilia. Her figure was still like a teenage girl and her face was fresh. Max let out a catcall whistle as Mo spoke up.

"Take a look at our big sister Max. What a knockout!"

Smiling at the two boys she had basically raised, Cecilia revelled in the compliments. "You boys are sweet to say that."

Edward was still holding money in his hand. "Ceil, the boys are going out on the town tonight, and I want to treat them, and they're giving me a hard time about taking the money."

"You two just let Eddie treat you. He just got a big raise."

"I guess we better, Max. Big sister says so."

"OK" as Max let Edward hand him the money. "Thanks Eddie. Now you two go on and have a great time yourselves."

"Bye bye, boys". Cecilia grabbed Eddie's arm as they headed toward the door. When they reached the bottom of the stairs in the vestibule, Cecilia yelled up the stairs.

"We won't be too late Mama. Bye."

From up above Mary's voice was heard.

"OK honey, have fun. Bye Eddie."

Narration

Dark forces have waged battle for control of earth since the beginning of existence. Never had they been closer to eclipsing the light than during the reign of Adolph Hitler.

War is a terrible and most unfair atrocity, and many lives are taken. Soldiers have the honor of losing life on the field of battle. Civilians are collateral damage.

Worse than war is genocide. The devastation of millions of innocents who perished during this most horrific period on the planet was an abomination. Lives ruined. Families destroyed.

Unspeakable cruelty and wickedness unleashed on humankind, causing heartbreaking sadness. All this caused by the power of evil, which runs rampant over the material world.

Such was the Holocaust.

CHAPTER NINE

Ten miles outside Munich Germany Seven Years Later 1940

The truck that Abraham, Golde and Aaron Gittelsohn had crowded into with so many other Jews came to a jarring halt. German soldiers pulled back the tarp at the rear of the vehicle, as the prisoners got their first look at Dachau.

Wire fences stretched between tall posts which curved in toward the center of the compound. Strands of barbed wire were strung tightly along the top of the fence circling the camp. Tall towers were placed on all sides and corners of the fenced area, manned by guards with machine guns. Row after row of one-story barracks sat silently waiting for their occupants. Intermittently inside the fences, along the outside edges and corners of the camp were platforms raised about two feet off the dirt. Tall wooden posts on each side were connected by horizontal wooden beams. The Jews would learn the purpose of these platforms.

Over the main gate was an inscription, written in German. "Arbeit macht frei" which translated to "work will make you free." The Germans at the back of the trucks started yelling at the Jews to unload. Most of them pointed their machine guns menacingly. There was much weeping and lamenting from the masses being treated worse than cattle.

Men, women and children climbed out as quickly as they could, fearing the German wrath. Some stumbled or fell to the ground, which merited a rifle butt to the head or back, or a kick to their ribs by the German soldiers as they screamed and swore at the prisoners.

Abraham and Aaron sat on each side of Golde, Aaron closer to the back of the truck. As it was their turn to disembark, Aaron jumped nimbly onto the ground, then helped his mother, keeping her from feeling the guard's wrath. He then assisted his father and anyone else he could until one guard cursed him and pushed him away from the truck, telling him to line up with the others.

Aaron saw a long line of trucks waiting to drop off more unfortunate souls. The Germans only became more fierce in their screaming, exhorting people to move faster.

A row of tables was set up outside the fences near the gates, German soldiers sitting behind them. Ledger books were in front of them as Jews filed by so they could be processed. Soldiers with machine guns strolled about, pushing and prodding people with their weapons.

As the lines streamed forward, Aaron watched as families tried to stay together, the Nazi soldiers having no interest in letting them do that. The men behind the tables looked quickly at the person standing before them, and motioned one direction or the other. Younger and fitter men, women and some children who looked able to work were sent forward to enter through the gates. The very old, very young or anyone with any sort of infirmity were turned back and forced to load back into the very trucks they just vacated. As the Gittelsohns watched families being broken apart, they heard crying and wailing as babies and grandparents became separated from their loved ones. They wondered what would happen once they reached the table.

One young woman refused to release her baby. As a guard began to wrestle her baby away, she struggled mightily as best she could, clinging to her child. Another German soldier wearing a higher-ranking uniform walked quickly to the table where the commotion was taking place. The officer screamed for her to release the baby, as her husband urged her to obey, give up the baby, and go with him through the gates. Crying, while cursing at her husband, she refused. When the officer ruthlessly ripped at her arm in an attempt to take the baby away, the woman turned and spit in his face. An enraged look overtook the Nazi as he wiped the spittle from his cheek before he reached into his holster, pulled out his Luger pistol and shot her point blank in the face.

As her body hit the ground, still clutching the baby, the officer turned to dumbstruck onlookers.

"Any disobedience will be immediately dealt with. We have no time for this!"

He then looked at two stronger males in line, and still holding the pistol in his hand, commanded them.

"Pick up this woman and baby and put them in the back of that truck!"

As the men moved the body, others had no choice but to step through her blood as they moved in front of the man behind the table who would determine their fate.

People clutched one another, knowing it might be the last time they ever saw or touched their loved ones. Sobbing and crying only grew louder. When the Gittelsohns reached the table, Aaron stood next to his mother. At twenty-one, Aaron had grown into a thin, lanky, yet sturdy young man. There was no doubt he was destined to stay and work. The soldier at the table looked at Abraham and Golde, appraised them, then motioned for them to move back to the trucks.

Golde looked at Abraham and Aaron in a state of shock.

Before they could be led away, Aaron spoke out to the German behind the table.

"My father and mother should be allowed to stay here and work. He is an expert tailor."

Looking again at the two, then back down at his ledger, the soldier behind the table answered.

"I've made my decision."

Then looking at one of the machine gun wielding guards he gave instructions.

"Move these two into the trucks. This one stays to work."

Aaron spoke up again.

"You must let them stay. They are strong."

Hearing Aaron's protests, the officer who just shot the woman came over to the table.

"You did not hear what he said? Those two will go where they are told."

"But sir", Aaron began to protest.

The officer began to reach for his Luger once more when Abraham spoke up. "Aaron. Be quiet. Golde and I shall do what they say."

Just as Abraham finished, another officer, obviously higher ranking, walked over. The surrounding guards as well as the officer who just shot the woman clicked their heals, stood at attention and gave the Heil sign.

"What is going on here, Lt. Klein? Why did that woman get shot?"

"She would not obey, Herr Commandant. Everyone must know we do not tolerate defiance."

He then turned to Aaron before he spoke.

"Why then do you try to get shot?"

Showing no fear, his voice strong and confident even surrounded by Germans with guns, while he looked the Commandant directly in his eyes, Aaron answered.

"Sir, my father and mother have many talents. He is a fine tailor and a scholar in Art History."

Hearing this, the Commandant studied Abraham and Golde.

"This is true? You know of Art History? And a fine tailor also?"

"Yes, I have devoted my life to the arts, and have taught my son."

Abraham then continued. "I made my living as a tailor. We had our own shop in Munich."

Turning toward Aaron, the Commandant looked him over carefully before he spoke. "You too know art?"

"Yes."

"Do you have other talents?"

"I play violin."

The Commandant paused, scratching his chin.

"I see."

The Commandant turned to Lt. Klein and the soldier behind the table, both still standing at attention. He surveyed the guards around the area. "This family is to be kept together. The woman stays with her husband and son. No harm comes to them or someone will answer to me. Put them in the building closest to the gates near the villas. Give them amenities. I have use for these talents."

The Commandant glared at the soldiers. "Do you all understand me quite clearly?"

"Yes, Commandant" they all chimed, except for Lt. Klein, who had a frown to accompany his defiant body language. As he turned back to Abraham and Aaron, the Commandant addressed them.

"You two will be brought to my home this evening. We will see about your talents."

"Lt.Klein, see to it. Have them brought to me at seven tonight."

Shrugging, with an angry look, Klein answered.

"Yes Commandant."

CHAPTER TEN

Springfield Illinois

The SoHo nightclub in downtown Springfield was always filled with well-heeled and well-connected Illinois elite. Directly across from the State Capitol Building, the SoHo was the watering hole for politicians, lobbyists and an occasional downstate mob boss. More deals had been struck in these booths than the halls of the Capitol.

Max wheeled the shiny new Cadillac Sixty Special up to the curb in front of the SoHo where four valets waited. One valet opened the passenger door for Mo. Another raced around the back of the car to open the door for Max, who stepped out and gave a silver coin to the young man.

"Take good care of this baby" Max smiled at the fresh-faced kid.

"Yes Sir! Thank you!" The doorman opened the door into the club for the two men as they went inside. The door was thick with wood paneling on the outside and leather padding on the inside. Mo and Max got their first glimpse of the legendary Springfield supper club.

Larger than it appeared from the outside, the tables were packed. You could cut the air in the room with a knife because of smoke from cigarettes.

Even now in their twenties, the twins were impossible to tell apart. Tonight, however, Max wore a civilian suit while Mo stood out in his crisply pressed army uniform. As they walked in, they raised eyebrows from patrons, an occurrence to which they had grown very accustomed.

A pretty young girl in the corner of the room played piano and sang at a piano bar, surrounded by people on stools. It was a happy crowd, with drinking, singing and laughing.

At the long bar taking up the back wall of the establishment, the men spied two seats unoccupied on the end. Their seats afforded them a perfect view of the young entertainer across the room.

The short, burly and bald bartender, wearing a white shirt and tie, approached the twins.

"Looks like you two know each other."

Max glanced over at Mo, then turned back to the bartender.

"Never laid eyes on this guy before."

Mo pointed back at Max, "Don't know this guy."

At that, the bartender and both men got a laugh.

"Well, what'll it be tonight fellas?"

Mo answered first. "Scotch, straight up."

"You got it soldier." Then back at Max. "How about you?"

"I'd like the piano player." Looking at the young girl playing the piano, the bartender then turned back around to Max.

"You gotta fend for yourself pal. I'm the drinks guy here. But we look out for that little gal, so behave, you hear?"

"Oh I will, don't worry. In the meantime, bourbon rocks."

"That I can do. Back in a minute, men."

His eyes trained on the pretty girl surrounded by patrons across the room, Mo turned toward Max.

"Max, I'm afraid you're gonna be out of luck with the piano player."

"Why do you say that?"

"Because that's the girl I'm gonna marry" Mo answered very matter of factly.

"Says who?"

"Me, that's who. I'm marryin' that girl. She's the most beautiful thing I've ever laid eyes on."

With an exasperated look, Max stammered. "Dammit Mo. We came down here to meet a coupla girls for the night, have some fun, and you go all bonkers for the piano player?"

Even more serious, Mo reached over and put his arm around Max's shoulder.

"Hey, you can still meet a gal, Max. Look, there's some unattached ones here. But when I get my drink, first person who gets up over at that piano, I'm gonna go park myself on the closest stool I can near her."

CHAPTER ELEVEN

Cambridge Massachusetts Seven years later 1940

As he sat next to his wife and family in the front row of spectators in the Sever Quadrangle, where graduation degrees would be conferred, Senator Russell Royce looked over his program for commencement day at Harvard University. The family had moments before been escorted from the Alumni spread in the yard, a Harvard tradition when families enjoyed food and drink at tables under the trees. For every year since TR had been in college, the Senator had been a large donor for the Alumni spread. This year, the college itself generously paid for the cost of the affair.

The Senator's youngest daughter, a pretty girl of fourteen, leaned over and whispered to her father. "When will they get here?"

Smiling, Senator Royce leaned way back, allowing him to pull the chain of his gold watch from a small pocket near his large waistline, then looked at it before answering. "Should be any time now. The procession is coming from Massachusetts Hall. Just sit tight. This will only happen once in your brother's life. We don't want it to get over with too quickly."

The Senator didn't get many chances to spend time at his beloved Harvard, being among the most famous of the University's alumni, especially the living ones.

As he glanced to his right, the Senator spotted one of his old friends and classmates, Bill Dwyer, sitting on the aisle.

"I'll be right back. I'm going to say Hi to Bill Dwyer."

Without looking up from her program, the Senator's wife motioned slightly with her hand. "Fine dear."

As he moved toward his friend, Bill noticed the Senator, and stood to say hello.

"Long time no see, Russ. I didn't spot you at the spread."

"I don't know how we missed each other either, Bill, but it's great to see you. Quite the afternoon, isn't it?"

"It sure is. Couldn't have ordered a better day. I know you're as proud of TR as I am of Bill Junior. Our boys have turned into men."

With the wistful acknowledgement of time racing by and a helplessness to slow it down, the Senator responded.

"That they have Bill, that they have. Now that Bill Junior is done here, what's his plan?"

"He wants to work in the family business and I'm damn glad about it! He's going into the Engineering Program next year at MIT. How about TR?"

"Looks like we have a couple of cases of the apple not falling far from the tree, Bill. TR's going for his law degree. Then into politics."

Smiling, Bill Dwyer slapped the Senator on his arm as only a longtime friend would do. "Well, I'll sure as hell vote for him, Russ. Listen, let's visit some after the ceremony. Bar's open. We'll have a quick drink and I'm buyin'! Can't stay too long though, you know. We all have big parties planned."

"That we do, Bill. And I'll take you up on that drink. Chance for us to catch up a little. Enjoy the graduation."

CHAPTER TWELVE

Dachau Concentration Camp Germany

German soldiers, all with machine guns at the ready, herded men, women and children of working age into the rows of barracks behind the tall fences of Dachau. Loved ones clutched onto any family member with them, trying not to be separated during the process. Most people had only the clothes on their backs, while some carried some sort of small bag. The floors were a mix of bricks and compacted dirt. Short, cramped wooden bunks lined the building. The Nazis took pleasure in prodding and aiming their weapons menacingly, then laughed after intimidating their captives. When a barracks became full, a guard turned to yell orders.

"Tomorrow you will be issued camp clothing and your hair will be cut. Be ready at sunrise. Those not cooperating will be dealt with accordingly."

The Gittelsohns had their own two guards as they moved past rows of barrack buildings, heading to the rear of the prison. Upon reaching a smaller building directly in the back corner, next to a pair of gates leading out of the camp, the guards stopped. "This is the building where you stay. The first room is yours. You are lucky. This is better than where others are kept, and your family stays together. This building is for Jews who work with us."

The guards left the three of them standing in front of the building as they walked away.

Golde went to the door, opened it and walked in. Abraham followed, as Aaron stood outside studying his surroundings. Two guards just outside the gate looked at him with disinterest, while the two in the looming guard tower at the corner of the camp glowered down when he looked up. He turned and went inside the building.

The room had four stiff wooden beds, two on each side of the room. The beds had thin mattresses, two coarse blankets and a small pillow. The floors and walls were old wood plank, and there was a square wooden table in the center with four old wood chairs.

As she sat at the table, appearing too weak to stand any longer after the ordeal the family had been forced to endure, Golde was the first to break the silence.

"May Hashem forgive us if we stay here while the others are kept like animals in those other buildings. I do not want to be a Jew who works with these Germans."

Taking a chair next to Golde's, Abraham put his hand on hers as he spoke.

"Golde, we must have patience. We may be able to do more good by staying alive and being here. Maybe we help others stay alive."

"Father's right, mother. If we had refused that officer, they would have put you and father back into the trucks. Who knows where they were taking the ones not allowed to stay here."

Golde was silent as she stood, walked over and put her small bag on one of the beds.

CHAPTER THIRTEEN

Springfield Illinois

Mo and Max nursed their drinks at the bar. Two patrons on stools closest to the piano player dropped a tip into the jar that sat on the piano and got up to leave. Mo and Max grabbed their glasses and hurried over to fill the stools, Mo taking the closest. The young woman playing the piano smiled at both as they seated themselves. As she played the piano, talking with the patrons and singing, it was obvious that she did not need to look at the piano keys.

"Hi fellas."

Eagerly, Mo was the first to answer.

"Hi. We've been listening to you sing and play. You're great."

"Yeah" says Max. "I can't figure out how you know the words to all these songs."

"Thanks. When I hear a song I like, I learn it. Playing piano and singing are what I do."

"My name is Mo Gordon. This is my twin brother Max." Still playing without missing a note, the piano player continued the conversation. "You guys are twins? I would never have guessed that."

"Yeah, it was probably Mo's uniform that threw you off."

"Your Ma must be proud to have two identical handsome sons."

"You know our names, but we don't know yours" asked Mo.

"Janey Ryan, and it's nice to meet you both."

From the other side of the piano bar, a man appearing to be in his fifties sat next to a woman who could be his wife. Obviously feeling the effects of his drinks and sounding like it, he spoke up.

"Janey, I've come up with one you won't know. I've got a good tip for you if you surprise me."

"Walter, you and Mitzi have been trying to stump me all night long and you haven't yet."

"This one will, young lady. Just came out last year. Fred Astaire. 'Nice work if you can get it'."

Hearing this, Janey smiled and started right into the song as she said "I'm glad you asked for that one. I love that song."

Janey proceeded to play and sing the entire song, as Mo, Max and everyone else at the piano bar sat in amazement.

CHAPTER FOURTEEN

Dachau Germany

With no warning the door into the Gittelsohn's room opened, revealing two German soldiers, machine guns ready, and a third in an officer's uniform, a Luger sidearm in his holster. He stepped two feet inside the room before speaking.

"The commandant wants the two men to report to his villa. The woman stays here."

Afraid to leave Golde alone, Abraham addressed the officer.

"I would like my wife to come with us."

"My orders are only the two of you. No harm will come to your wife while you are gone."

Golde looked at Abraham and Aaron. "Go with them. I am not afraid."

With a worried look but helpless to do anything but obey, Abraham walked to the door. "Very well, Golde. Come Aaron."

The air was cold and damp as the soldiers led the men to the gates outside their building. The guards on the other side hurriedly opened them, giving a heil salute to the officer as they stood at attention while they passed.

As the men walked the wide dirt road toward the homes of the Nazi officers, the road surface transitioned to cobblestone. Walking perhaps one-half mile, the area began to become well lit. They heard laughter and music coming from a building which they took to be a restaurant ahead.

They passed many soldiers with machine guns on patrol. Coming to the largest and nicest home, the officer led them around to the rear of the building.

"This is the Commandant's villa. You will always enter through the back."

The two soldiers with machine guns stood at the ready on each side of the door and stayed outside as the officer took Abraham and Aaron into the home.

In a large kitchen area, two cooks prepared gourmet food, nothing like the subsistence supplies which had been brought to the Gittelsohn's room earlier.

The officer led the way down a hall into a room filled with artwork. Oils were on the walls while other works sat on the floor propped up against furniture. He then instructed Abraham and Aaron.

"We wait here until the Commandant arrives. Remain standing."

After almost ten minutes of standing in silence, the Commandant arrived in the room, smoking a cigarette. He looked at Abraham and Aaron as he smiled, and then waved off the waiting officer.

"You may leave us now. Please, stop in the kitchen and have them feed you and the men while you wait in the back." Happy at hearing this order, the officer straightened up stiffly, giving the Heil salute.

"Thank you, Herr Commandant. You are most kind."

The officer hurried out of the room.

The commandant managed a perfunctory heil in response to his subordinate, then turned back to Abraham.

"I trust your room suits you rather than the barracks? And the food I instructed my men to bring?"

Answering, Abraham asked, "Thank you for food, but how can this be happening to our people? How can we accept special treatment when others suffer?"

With a troubled frown, the commandant took a long drag of his cigarette before exhaling the smoke toward the ceiling.

"Germany is at war. The Fuhrer feels that anyone who might cause us problems now must be kept in camps. When we have won the war, you will all be allowed to return to your homes. Everything will be back to normal, so the best thing you can do is keep yourselves strong and alive."

"And there is something my son and I do for you which gets us special treatment?"

Holding his cigarette between his fingers as he gestured around the room, the commandant answered.

"Look around this room. Surely this collection which I have assembled means something to you, does it not?"

Abraham slowly walked among the artwork, scanning with his eyes. He stopped in front of one painting, bending down to study it. He moved to a second, then a third. "You have indeed quite a collection. A fortune in paintings in this room alone I would say. Over there is a Matisse, this one a Chagall, and a Paul Klee over there."

Abraham pointed at another painting.

"That is one of Franz Marc's earliest works."

His eyes ablaze, the commandant spoke.

"Yes, yes. You do know art. Excellent! This is not all of my collection, just some I had brought in as a test, which you have passed beautifully."

"And you need an authenticator?"

"No, no. I know they are authentic. I know a real Matisse. I would like to know the history. Do you have this type of knowledge?"

"I do."

"Good! Then you will be my personal curator. When I entertain dignitaries and friends, you shall select and organize the art to be displayed and research and catalog my collection. I will supply you any materials you need."

The commandant walked over to a desk where he put out the cigarette butt getting short between his fingers. He opened a lacquered box on the desk and reached in to get another cigarette.

"Would either of you like a cigarette?"

Abraham replied. "No."

Up until this moment, Aaron had been silent.

"No."

"Very well. Suit yourselves." The Commandant continued, looking at Abraham. "Your skill as a tailor will also be valuable. I always want to look my best." He paused as he lit his cigarette with an ornate silver lighter on the desk, then took a long draw.

"I can make things easy for your family, but I think that is not what you want. I can help you to help others of your choosing with food, medicine, clothing. You can do well for your people by working for me. I know that must appeal to you, does it not?"

Without waiting for an answer, the commandant turned to Aaron.

"You play the violin? I would like to hear you play."

"I have no violin. It was taken from me."

Going to shelves on a bookcase, the commandant picked up a violin case with a bow, then handed them to Aaron.

"If you do indeed play, then these will be yours to keep. And you may practice as much as you want while you are here. Take advantage of your time. Please, play something."

Aaron opened the case, carefully taking out the violin, admiring it as he looked over at his father, who nodded. Taking the bow, he tuned the instrument. Aaron then began to play "Claire de Lune" brilliantly like the prodigy he was.

When Aaron finished, the commandant applauded.

"Bravo. That is my favorite by DeBussy. I would like you to teach my son and daughter to play. You will be their teacher."

"I have never taught, only played. I never had a teacher."

"Then in that case you are a musical genius! Show them what you know. Work with them. I want music in my house. I want to surround myself with art and music. I want to surround my family with beauty."

CHAPTER FIFTEEN

Cambridge Massachusetts

Senator Royce had the ballroom at the Hotel Commander reserved for over a year. He wanted TR's graduation celebration to be a memorable one. Banners of crimson, white and blue combined Harvard's school colors with the Senator's chosen patriotic theme. A full dance band played while guests enjoyed the dance floor. Waiters strolled about with platters of hors d'oeuvres, and the champagne flowed.

Senator Royce was by himself at the head table observing festivities when TR spotted him.

"Dad. Thanks for this party. I couldn't ask for any better graduation day."

"You're welcome, TR. You've worked hard to get to this point in your life. You deserve it."

"Dad, I've been thinking a lot about something."

"What's on your mind?"

"I want to postpone law school."

A look of concern came over the Senator.

"Why would you want to do something like that, TR? You've already been accepted."

"Well, it's because of what you've been saying all along. We need to stop Hitler. He's taken Poland. I should join the service, and be ready to protect the country."

A sense of urgency in his voice, Senator Royce began to plead his case.

"TR, listen. I know I've been saying we need to stop Hitler. But we're not even in the war. We'll get in eventually, but I don't know when. Right now, public sentiment is for America to stay out of the war. A young man like yourself will help us more as a leader, not some foot soldier."

The Senator paused before continuing.

"I tell you what. Go to law school and do the V12 Naval Training at Harvard while you're studying."

"I don't want to go Navy, Dad. I want to be in the Army."

"TR, coming from law school, even if your studies are only partially complete, I can make sure you get into officer's candidate school. As a commissioned officer, you'll make decisions, not just take orders. You need to be smart about this."

TR thought for a moment, then looked out at the gathering celebrating his graduation.

"Well, I suppose you're right. That sounds OK. But when we do get in the war, I want to serve my country."

"I'm sure you will, TR. When the time is right."

TR stood, followed by his Dad, who reached up to put his arm around TR's shoulders.

"I'm glad we talked. Now why don't we get back to enjoying this party."

CHAPTER SIXTEEN
Springfield Illinois

Inside the SoHo nightclub, all the patrons had left except for Mo and Max, still sitting at the piano bar as they talked to Janey. Waiters were busy setting tables for the next day as the bartender washed glasses and cleaned up the bar. The entrance door to the street was propped open, and the smoky air was beginning to clear from the room.

"Well, you fellas are the last ones here tonight. Thanks for coming in. It's been fun talking to you. And Max, you are quite the singer!"

"Thanks Janey."

Mo stood from his stool at the piano. "Janey, can we walk you out to your car?"

"Thank you, Mo, but my big brother is picking me up. When he gets here he'll come in to walk me out."

"Oh, OK."

Mustering up his courage, Mo blurted out his question.

"Janey, would you go out with me sometime? That is, unless you already have a boyfriend or something."

"Wow, Mo. You're a fast mover."

"Janey, I don't mean to be. It's just that in two weeks I head to South Carolina for six months of training."

"Oh. Well, in that case...my nights off are Tuesday and Wednesday."

Not letting two seconds go by, Mo jumped on the opening.

"Great! I can pick you up at six this Tuesday if you give me your address."

Janey smiled at Mo, who had a grin from ear to ear. She reached into her purse, took out a piece of paper and pen, and wrote down her address. As she handed it to Mo, the door from the street revealed a huge man. Carl Ryan, Janey's brother, stood six foot four and was built like a lumberjack. He came straight over to the piano.

"Janey, all set to go Honey?"

"Just about, Carl. Let me gather up my music. Carl, this is Mo and Max Gordon. We had so much fun at the piano tonight. Mo, Max, this is my brother Carl."

Max got up off his stool to stand next to Mo. Carl towered over the twins, who were both almost six feet tall themselves, but were dwarfed by this giant man. Carl extended his hand as he shook both men's hands.

"Howdy men. My little sister's pretty good, isn't she?"

Max answered first. "Boy is she ever."

"Janey knows every song" said Mo.

Janey looked at Carl as she talked to him.

"Mo is getting shipped out to South Carolina in two weeks but he asked me to go out before he leaves."

Carl now sized up Mo in a different light, and addressed him sternly.

"You just met Janey tonight here at the piano bar and you think that uniform's gonna let you make time with my little sister?"

Janey scolded her older brother.

"Come on, Carl. Don't be like that. I'm a good judge of character. I know Mo's a good person."

Mo stood up as straight as possible and looked Carl right in the eye, even though Carl towered over him.

"Carl, I guarantee you that I will treat Janey with all respect."

"Well you'd better. This girl deserves all respect." As Carl finished speaking, Janey handed Carl the pile of music from the piano, then reached down behind the piano bench to pick up two crutches that were on the floor. She put them out in front of the bench, swung around and pulled herself up to a standing position. Mo and Max saw for the first time that Janey had only one leg. Mo looked visibly shaken, which was no surprise to Janey. Max seemed dumbfounded and couldn't stop looking at her one leg touching the floor.

Observing the twins surprise and seeming inability to voice their feelings, Janey broke the awkward silence.

"You two look like you've seen a ghost. What's the matter, haven't you ever seen a one-legged piano player before?"

Then, looking at Mo, Janey continued.

"Mo, I won't hold you to taking me out on a date."

Finally, regaining some composure and regrouping, Mo stammered.

"No..it's just...I know lots of one-legged piano players...it's just...I never met one as amazing as you."

Carl, who had observed all of this with a stern look, couldn't stop from smiling at this statement before he chimed in.

"This guy says he knows lots of one-legged piano players? Better watch out for this one Janey."

Janey flashed a shining smile from her drop-dead gorgeous face.

"OK Mo. Then I'll look for you at six on Tuesday." Feeling more comfortable, Mo answered.

"How about we go to the Orpheum downtown for a movie, then grab a burger and shake after, OK?"

"That sounds fun. See you then."

Janey used her crutches like a pro to go out as Carl walked with her to the door. Mo and Max stayed next to the piano. Janey turned and waved to the guys and Mo and Max waved back before she disappeared into the night.

"Mo, I couldn't believe it when I saw she only had one leg. I just didn't know what to say."

"Max, I only know one thing right now. That is one strong, beautiful girl. She has real guts."

Narration

Certain individuals have surrendered to the evil. Souls beyond redemption. Their depravity has no limits. Human nature so corrupted that it is given over to acts which are unexplainable.

Messengers of the Devil, giving but a glimpse of the demonic powers that exist.

CHAPTER SEVENTEEN

Dachau Germany

In a crowded women's barracks, the prisoner's faces wore blank stares and hopeless looks. One small table toward the end of the building had four women praying together. Others moved about trying to buoy spirits and offer spiritual encouragement. With the bitter cold outside, some huddled together trying to stay warm. Others sat on their wooden bunks, simply waiting for a chance to escape from their harsh reality into slumber before beginning another day of living hell. Seeing their friends, family, even strangers beaten or shot on a daily basis was taking its toll. As horrible as the barracks were, the nights were a welcome respite from the cruelty and intimidation of the Nazis. Suddenly, the door to the building was pushed open before two German soldiers with machine guns entered followed by the officer who shot the woman in the face on the first day that prisoners arrived, Lt. Klein.

Already the prisoners knew Klein to be the most horrible and feared soldier in the camp, and he always had these same two German soldiers with him.

Klein was an ugly German, short with a completely bald white head. His uniform looked sloppier than other Germans with his fat belly that hung out over his belt. His nose flattened against his face with nostrils that faced straight ahead, making him look like a pig. When he opened his mouth, he revealed missing teeth, with those he did have being crooked and yellow.

As the two henchmen with Klein stood near the door with their weapons at the ready, Klein slowly moved among the women in the barracks, looking them over as he walked.

Stopping in front of one woman with her arm around her daughter sitting on a bunk, he studied them. With an evil smile, he pointed to the girl, who appeared only thirteen or fourteen years of age.

"We need kitchen help for our commandant. You will do. You come with us."

The other women close by did nothing, helpless to intervene, but the mother, terrified, pleaded to Klein.

"My daughter is much too young. She knows nothing of working in the kitchen. I am a good cook and I will work very hard. Take me."

Klein's evil smile quickly disappeared as he gave the mother a menacing look. "No. You work with the others in the factory. This is a privilege for her. The work is easy. Now be quiet and let go of her. I have no time for this."

Klein reached to his holster and pulled out his Luger pistol, aiming it directly at the mother's face.

The woman released the girl. The small girl got up and kissed her mother's cheek before walking toward the door where the other two Germans waited. Klein followed her to the door.

As she was being led out, the girl turned and looked at her mother, completely silent, but with tears streaming down her cheeks.

As the Germans and the girl exited, shutting the door behind them, the mother wailed, inconsolable in her grief. Another woman came to her side, and put her arms around her as the mother sobbed.

As the girl was taken through the gate by the German soldiers, one of the guards at the gate smiled knowingly and remarked to Lt. Klein.

"Another kitchen worker, Lt. Klein?"

Looking back with a devilish look, Klein answered.

"I have to teach them how to do everything."

The two soldiers always with Klein laughed as they climbed into the front seat of a waiting car with an open top. Klein ordered the girl to get in the back seat, then sat next to her.

She was crying, and kept her eyes from any of the soldiers. The car drove along the road, moving past the nicer villas and restaurant where the officers resided. Reaching the outskirts of buildings, the car came to a stop in front of the last building before a clearing next to a forested area.

The two henchmen got out and walked over to the front of a wood framed building and set their machine guns against the wall before they sat in two chairs, one on each side of the door.

Klein got out and barked at the cowering girl.

"Get out. We are here. Inside!"

Klein opened the door and yelled at her again.

The girl obeyed and walked into a dimly lit room, followed by Klein, who shut the door behind him. The two watching soldiers looked at one another, each giving the other a hideous snide smirk.

Inside, the room was furnished with only a chair against one wall and a bed against the other.

The little girl looked around, then back at Klein with absolute fear in her eyes. Klein looked over his prey, admiring the helpless child standing in front of him. Then in a low voice, he began to confirm her worst fears.

"If you behave, I won't have to hurt you. Do you understand?"

Seemingly numb and in another world, the girl nodded.

"Good. You're a smart little girl. First, you take off your clothes, but very slowly."

CHAPTER EIGHTEEN

Springfield Illinois

Edward Vernon's Ford pulled up to the curb and stopped in front of the address Janey Ryan gave Mo at the SoHo. Mo opened the driver's side door and got out, checking out the front of the home. A smaller one-story white house with wood siding. There was a porch with only two steps.

Although this was a much smaller home than the Gordon house, the Ryan family lived in a much nicer neighborhood. Mo noticed an automobile in almost every driveway.

Wearing his uniform, Mo checked his reflection in the window of the driver's door, brushed his brown curly hair back with his hands and straightened his uniform before heading toward the door of the house. Before he could get to the third knock on the screen door, the entry door on the inside opened. Through the screen Mo saw an older dignified looking woman. "You must be Mo."

Pushing open the screen, she continued. "Come in. I'm Janey's mom, Fern Ryan."

"It's a pleasure to meet you, Missus Ryan."

"You sure look nice in your uniform Mo."

"Thank you, Ma'am. I'm shipping out in two weeks for training and it won't be long before I'm fighting Hitler."

Oh, I hope that's not necessary Mo. I think once this

little war they're fighting over in Europe ends, they won't bother us over here."

"Well Ma'am, all the officers in training think otherwise. Our military is gearing up for full-scale war. Even my twin brother Max is getting ready for a war. He's going to law school soon, but he's gonna be in ROTC so when he gets out he'll be a second lieutenant."

"Well, enough talk about war. Come in and sit down. Janey will be here in a minute. She knows you're here."

Mo walked into the living room and sat in the first chair he came to. A tall radio stood next to one wall and an upright piano was up against another. Pictures were on all walls, mostly photos of what looked to be family members. He noticed one picture of Janey and Carl sitting next to each other on the piano bench that sat on top of the piano. Janey's mom sat in another chair close to Mo.

"You have a very nice house here, Missus Ryan."

"Thank you, Mo. We've lived here on South College for almost thirty-five years now. My late husband's family lived here. When we got married we moved in with them and never left. We couldn't afford to buy our own place."

"That's nice you were able to stay."

"What did you do before you joined the army, Mo?"

"I was training at the Sangamo Electric Plant to be a tool and die maker."

"Well that sounds like a good job. That plant has been in Springfield a long time."

"Yes Ma'am. But what I really would like to do is work for a newspaper. I like to write. I could be a journalist."

Just then, Janey came into the entry using her crutches, and looked very pretty. Seeing Janey, Mo sprang out of his chair.

"Hi Janey. You look great tonight."

"Thanks Mo. You're looking pretty handsome yourself in that uniform."

Watching the two interact, a smile came over Fern's face. "Janey tells me you're going downtown to the Orpheum."

"Yes Ma'am. We're going to see that new movie out, 'The Wizard of Oz'."

"Oh, that's nice. Janey, you'll have to tell me all about it tomorrow. I've heard the new little actress Judy Garland is very good in it."

"I'll fill you in, for sure, Mom."

"I think I'm all set, Mo. Shall we go?"

Fern rose from her chair and went to the door as Mo followed. Mo opened the door, holding it for Janey. Janey kissed her mom on the cheek.

"Bye, Bye Mom."

"Bye Honey. Nice meeting you Mo."

"Likewise, Missus Ryan. I hope to see you again soon."

Later, as Mo and Janey sat in the theatre, the lights dimmed and the previews and shorts began. A World News film clip came on the screen with a blaring headline "Europe at War". The announcer described the German blitzkrieg invasion of Poland, with grainy films showing German tanks triumphantly rolling through the city streets. He went on about the British and French immediately declaring war on Germany. Nazi soldiers appeared on screen doing their goosestep march in Warsaw as Adolph Hitler watched from a platform, his arm extended to the troops filing by in his Heil salute. Janey looked over at Mo, whose eyes were riveted on the screen as he watched intently.

After the movie, as the crowd exited the Orpheum flooding onto the street, one man jumped ahead to hold open the door for Mo and Janey.

"Let me get the door for you and your date, soldier."

Mo and Janey both smiled at him and Mo nodded.

"Thank you."

"No problem. And good luck to you, young man."

"Thanks again."

As Mo and Janey got to Edward's car, parked only a couple of spaces away from the front of the theatre, Mo opened the passenger door for Janey. She held the crutches in her left hand and held the door with her right as she eased herself into the seat, swinging her leg into the car. Mo took her crutches, put them in the back seat and hustled around to the driver's side, getting in.

"I guess people are usually nice to you Janey, when they see your crutches?"

"I think he was more holding it as a favor for you tonight Mo, seeing your uniform."

"Oh, I don't know. Anyway, how about we go grab that burger, some fries and a shake? I'm starving."

"OK. Where are we going?"

"I already decided. My favorite place, Maid-Rite. Best burgers in town. We can just drive through, eat in the car and talk. I thought that would be easy for you."

"I love Maid-Rite. Let's go."

As Mo and Janey sat in the car after driving through at Maid-Rite, Janey rummaged through the sack getting their food out. "Here's your burger...your fries...and your chocolate shake."

"Thanks. Boy this smells good!"

As Janey reached in to get her food, she started conversation. "Mo, things are scary over in Europe. The German army looks so powerful. I hope we don't end up fighting because of what's going on over there."

"We're going to. There's nothing else we can do. Hitler is a power-hungry maniac."

"Maybe the British and French can win the war."

"Not without us. The officers in basic were telling all of us recruits. Everybody let Hitler get too strong. They told us we should have helped to stop Hitler back in thirty-five. After the last war, the treaty said they couldn't build an army, but Hitler did anyway."

Janey stopped talking and sipped on her drink. "Oh."

Taking a bite of his burger and a big drink from his shake, Mo's look changed from serious to a smile. "Hey, let's not talk about what's going on over there. I want to find out more about you."

"What do you want to know?"

"Well, I've met Carl and your mom. How about your dad or any other brothers or sisters?"

"Poppa was killed in a car accident when I was five, but I can still remember him. I can still remember his smell. He used to put me on his lap all the time. It was hardest on Carl I think. Mom says Dad and Carl did everything together. And I have two older sisters, Susan and Judy. They're both married and out of the house."

"I'm sorry about your Dad. My dad was killed when Max and I were seven."

"He was killed? So you didn't have any dad either?"

"There's a boarder at our house named Eddie Vernon. He moved into the house a few years before our dad died. Mom and Pop needed extra money so they rented out two rooms. Eddie is the greatest guy on earth. He's been watching out for me and Max ever since."

"He's been there that long?"

"Yeah. He's my sister Cecilia's boyfriend. They're in

love, but they're not married, even though Max and me want them to."

"What happened to your dad, Mo?"

Looking straight ahead, then back at Janey, Mo finally answered. "It's a long story. I'll tell you someday, OK?"

"Oh. OK. Someday then."

Mo then continued talking, anxious to change the subject. "Janey, you don't even look old enough to be working at the SoHo. How long have you worked there?"

"Well, I am old enough Mo. I'm twenty. Actually, Carl was the piano player at the SoHo, but he's going to be moving to Chicago soon. He told them I played so they let me fill in for a couple of nights until they found another piano player. On the first night I was there the owner came over and hired me full time on the spot."

"You're telling me Carl plays the piano too? His fingers look too fat to fit on the keys. I can't picture Carl playing the piano."

"Mama made sure all of us could learn an instrument. Carl's a fantastic piano player and singer. He's also quite an amateur boxer."

"Now that I can believe. I wouldn't want to climb into the ring with that guy. He doesn't look like he could get hurt."

"He never has been. He's been beat by decision a couple of times by quicker boxers, but never knocked down."

Mo looked back out the window and a few moments of silence passed before Mo asked the question that was really on his mind. "Janey, it's a hard question. I was wondering...did something happen or did you always have just one leg?"

"I was wondering when you'd get around to that question, Mo. I was born perfectly normal, two good legs, just like most people. When I was a little girl, I was a tomboy. I wore my hair short. I was the fastest runner in the neighborhood, and I mean even faster than all the boys. When I started high school, I loved to dance, and was in all the plays and productions we put on. It wasn't until after I graduated that I lost my leg."

"What happened?"

"The summer after high school, my leg started hurting really bad. When it got worse, the doctors discovered I had bone cancer. They thought I was going to die, but I had a small chance if they took my leg above the knee. Three surgeries later, and I'm still here."

"Wow, I'm sorry Janey."

"Don't feel sorry for me Mo. I'm making do. I have my music, my piano. I've accepted this as my cross to bear. I think me losing my leg was harder on my mom and Carl than for me. I could see the sadness in their eyes. I had to be strong for them, especially my mom."

Mo stopped eating and stared out the windshield again when Janey started talking once more.

"It was Carl who sat with me in the hospital every time I went in for surgery. He never left my side. He was there more than Mama. He told me that life is like boxing. If you don't learn to roll with the punches, you'll get knocked out. He also taught me that if you get knocked down, get right back up again."

"I'm beginning to like your big brother more and more. You know, I think he and I are going to be good friends for a long time."

Janey looked at Mo and smiled, then took another sip of her drink while keeping her eyes on his.

"Janey, I'd like you to come and meet my family before

I go. I want everybody to get to know you, not just Max. Would you do that?"

"Sure Mo. I'd love to meet them."

"OK then."

CHAPTER NINETEEN

Dachau Germany

The full moon lit the night sky. Only a few dim lights could be seen around the barracks buildings as Aaron stepped out the door of their room. The perimeter fence was the only thing well-lit which allowed guards in the towers and those patrolling a clear view should anyone be foolish enough to attempt escape. This would be a bad night to try, with the illumination of the moon adding to the guards' vision.

Weeks before, one man tried to go over the fence, getting as far as the barbed wire at the top before he was spotted. He was machine gunned and his body was allowed to hang for days tangled in the wire. The Nazis made sure that everyone was witness as to what would happen to those who dared such a thing. On this night guards ignored Aaron as he stood in front of his building. They all knew the commandant had decreed that Aaron and his family were free to move about and had no curfew.

Aaron looked at the moon, staring for a few minutes. Outside the gates a patrol of four Nazis, three with machine guns ready and one holding the leash of an enormous German Shepherd that tugged at his restrainer as they walked, joked and laughed among themselves.

As he looked toward the direction of the commandant's villa, Aaron could see the sky brighter from nightlife going on and faintly heard music. A few moments passed before he walked back through the door into their building.

Abraham sat at the wooden table in the middle of the room, drinking water from a tin cup with a small round handle. A small candle in the center of the table was the only light. Golde laid on her back on one of the beds, her eyes open as she stared upwards. Aaron came over to the table and sat across from Abraham.

"Father, I don't know if I can do this any longer. This Nazi uses us. I don't want to be a Nazi tool. I would rather die than work for him."

Abraham looked at his son. His face showed no sign of fear, hatred or fatigue. A calm and serene look was in his eyes as he spoke.

"Aaron, we were not chosen for this by the Germans. Hashem has chosen this for us. We do not work for the Commandant for our own good. We do it for others. We stay in this room and we work for him so we get food and medicine for those in the barracks. We can save lives. It is a blessing that has been given us, not a burden."

From the bunk she was on, Golde spoke. "You know your Father is right, Aaron. Listen to him. You do nothing for Nazis. You do it for our people."

"Some in the barracks think we have turned against them by cooperating with the Germans and staying here."

Abraham picked up his cup as he studied his son, took a drink and set it on the table.

"Do not concern yourself with what others think. Only you know your own heart, they do not. Do the right thing. That is all that matters."

Frustrated, Aaron stood up and paced across the room.

"I know you are right. It's just..I hate the Nazis so much."

"Aaron, no matter what others do to you, make no room in your heart for hate. Better to pray for them."

"Father, why do they hate us so much? Why do they hate the Jews?"

"There are many reasons for hate. Those that hate had to learn to hate. Someone taught them to hate. It is sad for the world, because hate causes so much pain and suffering. But remember, my son, if it was not hate for the Jews, they would find something else to hate."

Narration

True love and family loyalty. Things that have sustained humankind through the toughest of times. They are beautiful things to behold.

CHAPTER TWENTY

Springfield Illinois

Mo pulled Edward's Ford up in front of Janey's house and hopped out, dressed in civilian clothes. He went to the door and knocked, and when it opened, Carl's hulking figure took up what appeared to be the entire doorway. Mo looked up at Carl, not really expecting him to be the person to answer the door. Carl was quite a different person to deal with than Janey's mother.

"Hi Carl. Just coming to pick up Janey."

"I know that Mo. Janey'll be here in a couple of minutes."

Without letting Mo enter, Carl came out onto the porch, shutting the door behind him.

"I hear you're taking Janey to meet your family before you ship out. You looking for a pen pal or what? You just want to tell your buddies you got a pretty girl back home? I want to know what your intentions are for my little sister that you just met."

Mo looked at Carl with a determined look, but also an appreciation for the protective attitude Carl had for Janey.

"Carl. I'm gonna tell you the truth. When Max and I went into the SoHo, the minute I laid eyes on Janey I knew she was the girl I wanted to marry. I told Max that night she was the one. Nothing has changed for me since that night."

"Mo, that girl's been through Hell and back the last few

years. I don't want her hurt any more. She looked death in the eye and stared it down. She's stronger than hell, but I worry about her when it comes to a man."

"Carl, the last thing I would ever do is hurt Janey. I love her. I want to be the guy who stands by her the rest of our lives. I'm gonna take care of her like no one else ever would."

As Mo finished saying this, the door opened with Janey standing behind the screen.

"Hi Mo. Are you being nice to Mo, Carl?"

"Yes Ma'am. Just shootin' the breeze 'til you got here."

"Yeah Janey. Carl and I are getting along just fine."

"Good. Well, I'm ready."

Carl opened the door for Janey and he bent down so she could give him a kiss.

"Bye Carl."

"See you later Honey."

"See you later Mo."

"Count on it, Carl. Take it easy."

CHAPTER TWENTY-ONE

Gloucester Harbor Massachusetts

Senator Royce and his grown son TR sat in large comfortable wicker chairs in the shade afforded by the porch. The Senator was smoking one of his fat, expensive cigars. Both men wore short sleeve white shirts and white slacks. The day was clear with not a cloud in the sky. The brilliant blue water in the harbor reflected the sun overhead, and light breezes created what looked like thousands of shimmering diamonds on its surface. Pleasure craft moved about leisurely in the safety of the harbor.

"TR, I never get tired of this place. Such a respite from Washington."

"Not quite the same atmosphere as the Capitol, huh Dad?"

"Hardly, son. And the atmosphere in Washington is getting uglier by the day."

"About the war in Europe?"

"Exactly. You've got a small group of us who know we're in for it unless we get involved, and those who just want to ignore it and go on their merry way."

"But attitudes are changing, aren't they?"

"Not quickly enough, TR. There's still a big majority who can't forget what it was like during the last war."

"You can't really blame them for that, Dad. A lot of

good Americans died in the last war, and now just a few years later we have another one."

"Sometimes you need to fight, TR. This is one of those times. I'm not a warmonger. I'd be the last person to want to be in a war we shouldn't be in."

"I know that, Dad."

"This is different. America is in real jeopardy. If England falls, we're next."

A black butler dressed in an impeccable suit came out onto the porch. He was an older man with white hair, tall and slender. He carried two large glasses of lemonade on a tray, setting one down for each man.

"I took it upon myself to squeeze some lemons, Senator. You two looked like you could both use a nice cold drink. It's warm out here."

The Senator reached over and took a glass, holding it up. "Thank you, Willis. You've done it again my good man. This looks very refreshing." TR took his glass and gulped a couple of long drinks.

"It's perfect, Willis. Thanks."

Willis nodded and smiled, then walked back to the door and turned.

"I'll let you two gentlemen get back to your conversation then."

TR took another drink. "Willis is always right on the money."

"That he is, TR. We're lucky to have Willis in the family. Where were we? Talking about all the infighting in Washington, that's right."

"Dad, you've been talking about bickering in Washington for years now."

"It's different now. We are at a critical juncture. France is a lost cause. The British can hold on for a while without us, but I don't know how long. Hitler plans on bombing them into submission."

"So what's going to happen?"

"I don't know, TR. I'm working with some other Senators and Congressmen. The President knows who's on his side. We're all going to the White House soon for a big sit down with FDR."

"You get along good with the President, don't you?"

"He's an amazing man. One of the most remarkable men of our time, TR."

Both men paused, taking a drink of their lemonade. The Senator re-lit his cigar before he continued. "TR. If you want to stay in the loop, Congressman Tucker asked if you'd like to work as an intern during summer between semesters at law school. He always asks about you and I've been keeping him up to speed. He likes you."

"I've always liked the Congressman, Dad. I know you two think along the same lines on a lot of things."

"His father was my best ally. He's following in his Dad's path. He's a smart one."

"You know, that sounds good. I'd like the chance to come to Washington to work."

That brought a smile to the Senator's face, as he leaned back in his chair and took another long puff on his cigar.

"Good. I'll arrange it. I'm going back to Washington in three days. Why don't we go together and you can start right in?"

"OK. We're on."

CHAPTER TWENTY-TWO

Springfield Illinois

As Mo and Janey drove across town for dinner at the Gordon's, they enjoyed conversation.

"It sure is nice of Mr. Vernon to let you use his car."

"Eddie's the best. I don't usually get to drive it, but he figured since I'm gonna be going away, he could let me use it just these few times. And he wants to meet you. I didn't even ask him to use the car, he just offered. And you better call him Eddie, not Mr. Vernon. He'll want that."

"OK. Will Max be there?"

"No, Max had to go to Chicago to register for some classes. He's not getting back until tomorrow."

"Will all of your sisters be there?"

"All except for Della."

"Why won't she be there?"

"Della was always jealous of Eddie liking Cecilia. She always wanted to be with him. Last year she snuck into his room at night and Eddie kicked her out. Woke up the whole house with all the ruckus. Next day, Della jumped on a bus and went to Chicago. She finally called a few weeks later and said she was married to some fella in the Navy. She's still up there."

"I'm sorry to hear that Mo."

"Don't worry too much Janey. We just hope Della's happy and it works out for her."

Then, cracking a little smile, Mo looked at Janey.

"Besides, we're having a big dinner tonight, and when it came time for the dishes, Della always needed to go to the bathroom right then. And she always seemed to finish just about the time the dishes were done. But we still love her. Well, here we are, the Gordon home."

Mo wheeled into the driveway and came to a stop. He jumped out quickly, going to Janey's door to help her out. The front door to the house opened, and all of the family except for Mo's mom came spilling out, down the stairs and over to the car.

"Hi you guys, this is Janey. Janey, these are my sisters Cecilia, Olga and Anne. And this is Eddie Vernon."

"Hi everyone. I didn't know I was going to get such a big reception."

All the girls took turns giving Janey a hug. Edward came over and gave her a gentle handshake while bowing slightly.

Cecilia put her arm around Janey's shoulders.

"We're so happy you came tonight, Janey. Mo's told us all about you. You're all he can talk about."

"C'mon Cecilia, you're spillin' the beans on me here."

The girls all laughed as Cecilia continued.

"Let's go inside. Momma's waiting to meet you."

Carefully taking the steps one at a time, Janey got to the top with little trouble.

When introductions were complete, the group visited in the living room, with Janey telling everyone about her family and her work. Edward left the room briefly, only to come back in with a decanter and glasses.

"What say we have a small drink before dinner? Would you care for one, Janey?"

"I'd love an aperitif. How nice."

Mo looked over at Janey with a quizzical look.

"What is that? Aperitif?"

"Why, Mo, it's a cocktail that people have before dinner."

"You're not even twenty-one yet, and you know that word?"

"I do work at a piano bar, Mo. My crowd has an aperitif or two before dinner, and then a few more drinks after!"

Everyone had a laugh hearing Janey describe the piano bar clientele.

Later, as Janey, Mo, Mary and Edward sat around the huge dark wooden dining room table talking, the three sisters busied themselves putting large bowls of food on the table. The formal dining area was ornate, with crown moulding at the top of a tall ceiling. A large china hutch covered most of one wall. The room sat just off the entry vestibule, and there was a passageway under the stairs, which led back into the living room. A third door toward the back of the house was open to the kitchen, a room big enough to hold another table in the center only slightly smaller than the one in the dining room. Finally, the three sisters sat with the others.

Mary sat at one end of the table, with Edward on the opposite end. Janey and Mo were on one side to Mary's left, with the sisters on her right, Cecilia being closest to Edward on the end.

Mary reached out to her left and right, and Janey realized everyone was moving to hold hands at the table. She joined hands with Mary and Mo. Mary then looked to the opposite end at Edward.

"Edward, would you say Grace this evening?"

"Yes Ma'am."

Bowing his head, Edward began.

"Bless us O Lord, and these thy gifts which we are about to receive from thy bounty, through Christ our Lord."

Everyone at the table, including Janey, ended the prayer in unison. "Amen."

Looking at the food, Janey looked at the sisters who just finished putting it all on the table.

"Everything looks scrumptious. Thank you."

Cecilia motioned to her left. "Anne has been in the kitchen all day. Since Mo told us you were coming she's been planning this meal."

Anne, a very sweet looking young woman, attractive, but not in Cecilia's category, smiled at Janey.

"If my little brother Mo thinks enough of a girl to bring her here, I know I better prepare something nice", as she smiled at Mo.

Mo tasted a bite of food, then looked at Anne. "You outdid yourself tonight Annie. This is great!"

"Thank you Mosie."

Hearing 'Mosie' for the first time, Janey turned to Mo, who felt he must elaborate a bit.

"To my sisters, since we were little guys, it's been Maxie and Mosie."

"Well I think it's cute. Can I ever use it?"

"Maybe someday."

From the far end of the table, Edward jumped into the conversation. "Janey, when the boys went to the SoHo, little did we realize he'd meet a girl like you playing the piano. Is that what you want to do, be a professional for your career?"

"Yes Eddie. And Mo told me to be sure to call you Eddie. Someday I dream of going to New York or Hollywood to play and sing."

Mo looked at Janey now.

"You do? I didn't know that."

"Well I do. I can't run. I can't dance. But I can sing and play the piano. I enjoy people and love to entertain them and make them happy. Imagine Carnegie Hall."

Looking over at Janey, Mary addressed Mo. "Mo, this girl has some big dreams. From what I see, I don't think there's anyone or anything that can hold her back."

Mo looked to his right at Janey.

"I don't think so either, Ma."

Edward, from the other end of the table, cut in.

"When you're playing at Carnegie Hall, Ceil and I will drive to New York to see you. I've always wanted to go to New York. Right Ceil?"

"Yes Eddie. That would be fun."

Mo looked back at Janey, then down toward Edward. "If that ever happens, Eddie, you and Cecilia will probably be visiting me there too then." Eddie looked over at Cecilia.

"Oh Boy."

Later that evening after Mo had driven Janey home, he walked Janey to her door.

"Thanks for coming to meet my family, Janey."

"I had a great time Mo. They are all so sweet. I can see why you are who you are after meeting Eddie and everybody."

"So maybe Max and I can see you at the SoHo before I leave. We could just stop in quick the night before I go."

"I'd like that Mo."

"OK then. Goodnight."

"Goodnight, Mo."

Mo hesitated, then started to walk slowly away, when Janey stopped him.

"Mo, aren't you going to kiss me?"

Turning around, Mo walked back over to Janey. "I'd like to."

"Then do it."

"OK."

Mo tenderly put his hand on Janey's shoulder as he leaned in to give her a kiss.

Janey looked up into Mo's eyes after the kiss. "That was nice."

"Yeah, it was."

Mo pulled open the screen door and tried the front door, which had been left unlocked.

He opened the inside door as Janey stepped inside.

"Goodnight Mo."

"Goodnight Janey."

CHAPTER TWENTY-THREE

Dachau Germany

Aaron was outside his building with his shirt off, leaned over a wooden bucket as he splashed his face with water. He tried to keep the water from landing on the powdery dirt below his feet should it then become muddy. He wiped his face with his garment, then put on the same soiled and tattered shirt he had worn for weeks.

Opening the door to their room, he went in, retrieved the violin case and bow, and addressed his parents.

"I'm going now to meet the children of the Commandant. Their lessons begin today."

Golde looked over at her son standing near the door. "Aaron. Those children may not know hate yet. Do not give them any reason to learn it from you."

"Yes mother."

As Aaron went over to the gates leading out of the compound, holding his case and bow, one of the guards manning the tower yelled to the two guards outside the gate.

"Our Jew musician arrives. Let him pass. The Commandant expects him."

As they opened the gates, one of the guards chided Aaron.

"Come through Jew boy. Be careful to go straight where you need to go and straight back. You do not have the right to wander about on this side of the fences. If you are found in the wrong area you may get shot."

Aaron did not bother to give the soldier eye contact. He ignored his taunts, as he walked on the road toward the Commandant's villa.

When he reached the part of the road where it changed from dirt to cobblestone, Aaron saw a patrol of six soldiers marching toward him, all with machine guns. Aaron moved to one side of the road as they got close. They had no interest in him, only glancing his way as they passed. He then realized they had been instructed to ignore this Jew.

At the rear entrance, Aaron found no guards. The screen door was closed, with the inside door open. Aaron knocked on the outer door and waited until a man wearing the uniform of a cook peered out of the kitchen into the hall. He motioned for Aaron to come through.

As Aaron entered, the Commandant came into the hallway.

"Aaron, good, come with me. I will introduce you to my children, your new pupils." The men moved down the hall, through the kitchen, and into the front parlor of the villa, when Aaron saw a young boy and a younger girl sitting on the couch.

Aaron quickly surveyed his surroundings. He had never been in a room as beautiful as this. A large window looked out onto the street, stately draperies framing the window. A rug covered most of the shining wood floor, wide plank with intricate patterns. Original oils from great masters hung on the walls. A beautiful ebony grand piano stood in one corner and the furniture appeared plush, comfortable and new. One entire wall was adorned with medals, ribbons and pictures of the Commandant in his uniform. One of the largest pictures showed a group of officers flanking Adolph Hitler, who was standing in the center of the officers. The Commandant was at the far end of the line. Two long sabre swords crossed above the pictures.

Mouldings covered the ceiling and the doorways into the adjacent rooms. The entry door toward the street was heavy dark wood with raised panelling.

"Aaron, this is Erich and Greta. Children, this is Aaron. He plays a beautiful violin and has offered to share some knowledge with you. He can teach you both how to play this most wonderful of instruments."

The children, a boy of about twelve and his sister, perhaps a year or two less in age, both studied Aaron for a few moments before Erich spoke up.

"Why are your clothes so dirty?"

The Commandant answered quickly before Aaron had any chance to respond.

"Aaron has been doing some special work for me, and I did not give him enough time to bathe and put on fresh clothes." The Commandant looked over at Aaron.

"Aaron, I apologize. From now on I will make sure you and your family have enough time to bathe and have clean clothes at all times. Of course, you will be a much better teacher if you arrive freshened up. I will see to it."

"Thank you, sir. But I do have two questions today."

"What are they, Aaron?"

"Perhaps after the lesson, not in front of the children?"

"Very well, we shall talk after."

The Commandant turned to leave the room, but not before looking back at Erich and Greta.

"I expect you both to listen and treat Aaron with respect."

Both in unison responded.

"Yes Father."

After the lesson, Aaron and the Commandant stepped

out onto the road behind the villa, when the Commandant spoke first.

"Aaron, what do you think of the children? Can you teach them?"

"They are both very bright. I find them receptive. I think you have nice children. I got along well with them."

"Very good. And did you like the front parlor as a place to teach your lessons?"

"I have never been in such a room before. I will look forward to spending time there teaching."

"Wonderful. For future lessons I will be sure to have refreshments brought in at the end. Now, you said you have two questions?"

"Yes. Father and I want to help as many as we can in the barracks, but the amount of food and medicine is inadequate. We would like double of what you furnish."

Looking serious, the Commandant stared down the road into the distance for a moment before he turned back to Aaron.

"Aaron, even I cannot supply everything you ask for. I have superiors who would not like to find me granting favors to those in the camps. If word gets to the wrong people, it would not go well for my family or me. You can help some, but not all. I can do no more."

Aaron looked at the Commandant, not sure if he understood or believed him on this point.

"You have a second question?"

"When we were brought here, families were separated. The very old, very young and infirm were forced back onto the trucks and driven away. Where were they taken?"

"Aaron, this is a work camp. Those that were of no use to us here were taken to a different camp where they are being well taken care of. They were not strong enough to withstand the conditions of this camp. Our work here is hard, and we must be stern."

"So they are being treated more gently than those in this camp?"

"Yes. When the war has ended and Germany is victorious, families will be reunited and sent home. Everything can return to normal."

"Very well. I will return tomorrow for another lesson. Please have the children practice what we went over for no more than one hour, unless they ask to do more. Otherwise, they will grow to hate the instrument. They must love it to play it well."

"Yes, I want them to love the music. Aaron, from the moment you arrived and spoke up for your parents, even after seeing a woman shot, you have shown courage. You have much wisdom for a young man. It is admirable. Tomorrow then."

As Aaron turned to walk back down the road, after taking a couple of steps, the Commandant called out one more time.

"Aaron, from now on, your father and you shall enter from the front door of my villa."

"Yes Sir."

Narration

Not all heroes are created in battle, by saving lives or other glorious endeavours. Heroism can manifest itself in many different ways. Life has a way of sometimes being unfair. When individuals are dealt a bad hand, disadvantaged through no fault of their own, there are two ways they can react. Some lament a bad situation, feel sorry for themselves, and go through life dragging down everyone else around them. Then there are those who answer the challenges with courage, forging ahead with purpose and will, victorious in their response. Those are the people who create light. They show the way. Examples for all.

CHAPTER TWENTY-FOUR
Springfield Illinois

The SoHo was crowded as the three men walked through the door. As Mo, Max and Edward came in, Janey saw them instantly. She smiled and waved with one hand while playing the piano with the other, not missing a word as she sang. The stools around the piano were occupied, so they made their way to the end of the bar, finding three empty stools. The bartender, seeing the men approach, made a beeline for the three.

"Hello again fellas. Brought an old guy with you tonight, huh?"

Mo, dressed in his uniform, answered. "Yes sir. Eddie was nice enough to be our chauffer tonight."

"OK then. In that case Eddie, you get one drink on the house along with these other two." Then to Mo, the bartender continued.

"You're Mo. Janey's told us all about you. You're the one she's sweet on. My name's Artilio."

"Nice to meet you, Artilio. She told everyone that?"

"That she did. Listen, let me get you guys your drinks, then I'm going to tell you a little story about her."

After taking their order and delivering the drinks, the bartender put both of his ham hock forearms on the bar in front of Mo before starting his story.

"That's a special little gal over there Mo."

"You can say that again. I know that for sure."

"Well I never seen a more gutsy girl. She took over for her brother Carl here."

"I know."

"I'll never forget the first night she came in here. The place was packed, and noisier than hell. All of a sudden, the doorman opened the door and in hopped this gorgeous girl on crutches with one leg. She just stood there at the top step, looking the place over. I'm telling you, place went silent. Everybody, and I mean everybody, stopped talking and turned and stared at this girl. Coulda heard a pin drop. I didn't know what to think. She looked over at me behind the bar and gave me the damndest smile. Then she used her crutches to go over to the piano, all by herself. Nobody was sitting around the piano. Everybody in this place was still quiet, just watching her. She sat down at the damn piano bench, put up some sheets of music and looked around at the whole place. Then she smiled and said 'Hi everyone, my name's Janey Ryan and I'm here to entertain you tonight'. The girl started playing and singing, voice like an angel. I'm telling you, she's owned the place since that first song, and there's never an empty stool at that piano bar. That's who the hell's sweet on you Mo, so don't screw it up!"

The three men looked over at Janey, who gave them all a big smile from across the room.

Eddie then spoke to the bartender. "I've known this young man for most of his life. I think he knows what he's got."

"You bet I do Eddie. Thanks for that story Artilio."

Mo extended his hand to the bartender and the two men had a hearty handshake.

As the three talked and enjoyed their drinks, Janey finished a song and made an announcement.

"I'm going to take a ten-minute break. There's a soldier over at the bar who I need to say goodbye to. He'll be shipping out tomorrow morning for South Carolina for training to serve our country in the military."

As the three men got up to walk over to the piano, one man at a table stood up and began to clap. Following his lead, all the patrons stood and applauded Mo as he made his way through the crowd, his face turning red as he smiled and nodded, shaking men's hands as they extended them when he went by.

Mo reached Janey, still sitting on her bench.

"Janey, you didn't really have to do such a big announcement."

"Why not Mo? You deserve it. I know you're going to make us all proud."

"Well, thanks."

"Thanks for bringing the fellas down tonight, Eddie. That is so nice of you."

"Happy to do it for the men and you too Janey. And it's nice to see you again."

"Max, you're leaving town for law school soon too, aren't you?"

"Yeah Janey. The old house is gonna be pretty empty."

"Well I'm going to miss you both and I'm sure everybody else will too."

"Janey, we won't stay. I have to get up early tomorrow. I just wanted to see you again once more before I left."

"Well, you're going to get to see me one more time. Carl said he'll bring me to the bus station to see you off in the morning."

"Really? That'd be great! I'm getting a real send-off, men."

Eddie smiled.

"And by the prettiest girl in town."

Janey smiled at Eddie's statement.

"OK then Janey. See you tomorrow."

"OK. See you."

The three men walked to the door, Mo shaking more hands as people wished him good luck. When they reached the door, Janey threw them a kiss.

CHAPTER TWENTY-FIVE

Dachau Germany

The group of prisoners returning from working at the munitions factory outside the compound marched in a long line two by two. Guards were on each side at the front and rear of the column.

Almost a quarter mile from the gates, two prisoners toward the back suddenly lunged at one guard, stabbing him with a makeshift knife they managed to smuggle out of the factory. Two others tried to take away the machine gun from a second guard, and a struggle ensued.

As the stabbed guard fell to the ground, guards from the other side of the column scrambled around the back of the line. One prisoner attempted to pick up the machine gun from the fallen guard but was not fast enough, getting machine-gunned to the ground before he controlled the weapon. A second prisoner with him suffered the same fate. The guard who struggled with prisoners had his weapon fire, hitting four or five workers in line before he broke away. Wheeling around, he shot one of his attackers and rammed the other in the head with the butt of his machine gun, the prisoner smacking face down in the dirt. The prisoner was bloodied, but still alive.

The guard started to turn his weapon on the man down when one of the other guards yelled at him.

"Don't shoot. That is too easy. He hangs!"

The guard, uniform torn, face bloody, looked over at the guard who yelled, then back at the man writhing on the ground, and nodded.

The guard pointed to the fallen prisoner as he yelled at two of the Jews in line.

"Pick him up. Carry him back to camp!"

The two did as they were told.

As he knelt next to his stabbed fellow guard, one of the Nazis pushed a cloth against his stomach.

"Hold this against the wound. We'll send a vehicle to get you. One of us will stay here with you until it gets back."

The stabbed guard, holding his belly, nodded.

The guard yelled another order to the prisoners.

"Alright! Move quickly or be shot!" As the line moved toward camp, prisoners accidently shot during the fighting begged to be helped. The guards ignored the pleas, and screamed at the others.

"Leave them! Now move!"

When the line was no longer in sight of where the prisoners tried to revolt, the sound of machine gun fire from behind was heard.

The column marched through the gates upon reaching the compound, and after a vehicle sped back down the road toward the stabbed guard, Lt. Klein appeared with his two bodyguards.

"This is the prisoner who lived?"

"Yes Sir."

"Bring the other prisoners. They will watch. I want them to know what happens to anyone who tries such a stupid thing!"

The column of prisoners was forced to line up near one of the raised platforms with the posts and beams. The prisoner still alive from the escape attempt was dumped on the platform, where he tried to rise to his hands and knees, still groggy from being butted with the machine gun. His face was covered in blood. A soldier appeared with a thick rope, bent down and wrapped it around the prisoner's neck, tying a crude knot that squeezed the prisoner's neck. With a shorter rope he tied the man's hands behind his back, then stood and kicked the prisoner in the ribcage. Two other soldiers came over, threw the end of the rope over the top of the beam, and pulled hard on the rope, yanking the prisoner into an upright position by his neck, then lifted him a foot off the platform. As the prisoners lined up watched with sad and horrified looks, the Germans laughed and yelled insults at the man jerking on the rope. His legs kicked wildly as his eyes began to bulge out. Lt. Klein and the two soldiers with him seemed to enjoy the scene more than anyone else, as Klein turned to the prisoners, his face beet red, veins showing in his fat neck.

"Trying to escape will end with this...or worse!"

After a few more moments, the man's futile attempts to live were over. His kicking and movement stopped. His body hung limp.

Klein yelled once again at the prisoners who still watched the grisly scene.

"His kicking has stopped. I have the power to make this man move again!"

Klein grabbed a machine gun from one of the two soldiers with him and proceeded to riddle the dangling body with bullets, shredding the corpse. As the mutilated man's nearly unidentifiable human body swung, Klein turned to the lines of prisoners, a crazed look in his eyes.

"There, do you all see? I made him move again!"

CHAPTER TWENTY-SIX
Springfield Illinois

A Greyhound bus sat next to the curb as people boarded. The driver stood next to the door selling and checking tickets.

Mo, Max, Eddie and Cecilia were near the front of the bus, Mo in full army uniform, a large stuffed duffel bag sitting next to him on the sidewalk.

"Eddie, thanks for driving me down."

"Of course I was going to get you down here Mo."

"It just means a lot to me that the three of you are here."

Cecilia, tears in her eyes, reached up and hugged Mo as he put his arms around her. "Mo, we love you honey. You take good care of yourself." Mo hugged Cecilia even tighter.

"You're the best big sister any guy could have Cecilia. Don't you worry. Before you know it, I'll be back home."

Cecilia let go of her baby brother, now a grown man who towered over her, and moved over next to Edward, who put his arm around her.

Mo then shook Max's hand.

"Max, you get through your law schooling. We need a good lawyer in the family. You're the first in the family with a college degree and now here you are going to be a lawyer. You make us proud."

"Hell Mo. You don't know how proud I am of you, here in your uniform, going off for training. Don't worry about me, you just make sure you stay in one piece."

The two brothers gave each other a hug. Then Mo looked Eddie in the eye. Both men were having a hard time controlling their emotions, and Eddie was losing the battle, his eyes beginning to water up.

"Eddie, I don't really have the words."

Cecilia let go of Edward as the men gave each other a long hug.

Edward's voice was cracking, and he had a hard time getting his words out.

"Mo, maybe they'll let you come home before they send you somewhere, but if they don't, you listen to your brother. Get back here in one piece. No matter what happens, you get back here to us."

"You can count on it, Eddie."

All passengers had now boarded the bus, and the group was left by themselves on the sidewalk. The driver sat in his seat checking off paperwork as he prepared to depart.

Mo looked down the street nervously, expectantly.

"Janey said Carl was going to bring her down to say goodbye."

Eddie looked up and down the street, as did Max and Cecilia, before saying anything.

"Well, I hope that girl gets here real quick because the bus is ready to go."

The bus driver looked through the open door at the group below.

"You comin' or not, soldier? I got a schedule to keep."

The driver cranked the starter, and the engine fired up.

Mo had a distraught look on his face.

"I guess they couldn't make it. I gotta go everybody."

Mo shook both men's hands one more time and gave Cecilia a kiss, then turned and went up the steps into the bus, lugging his heavy duffel bag. The door shut and the bus started to slowly move away when suddenly a car screeched in front, blocking the bus.

The bus driver hit the brakes, making a jarring stop.

"What the.."

Mo was still standing next to the driver when he saw the car.

"That's my girl's brother. She was coming to say goodbye to me, but she's late."

"Well, he's gonna have to move. I'd like to stay soldier, but I got a lot of people who need to stay on a schedule."

Carl jumped quickly out of the driver's side and sprinted around to the passenger door to open it. Janey swung herself out of the car, and as Carl handed her a crutch, she pulled herself out of the car to a standing position. As this very pretty girl with one leg looked up at the bus, Max, Eddie and Cecilia rushed over to the car.

The driver, looking at the scene in front of him, could only mutter.

"Sweet Jesus..."

From the back part of the bus, a man's voice boomed forward.

"For the love of Christ. Let the soldier go say goodbye to his girlfriend. We got a few minutes."

A chorus of voices all called out in agreement from behind the driver.

"OK soldier, looks like you're in luck. Everybody wants you to say goodbye. Make it a good one, but be quick, OK?"

Mo turned around to the others on the bus with a big smile.

"Thanks everybody!"

As the door opened, Mo raced down the steps and ran over to where Janey and the others were standing.

"Hi Janey. I'm glad you made it!"

"I'm going to miss you Mo."

"I'll write you."

"I'll write back."

"OK."

Mo then stood there in a moment of awkward silence, until Carl piped up. "Dammit Mo. You'd better give my little sister a goodbye kiss, buddy. I almost killed us getting here."

Mo smiled at Carl. "Thanks Carl."

Mo put his arms around Janey and gave her a long kiss. Janey still had one arm around Mo's waist when she looked up at him. "You behave yourself, soldier."

"Yes Ma'am. You know I will."

Mo then turned to the others. "Max, Eddie, Cecilia..bye one more time."

Mo gave Cecilia one more quick kiss, then extended his hand to Carl, who gave Mo a good handshake. "You take care of yourself Mo. And good luck."

"Thanks Carl." Mo climbed back onto the waiting bus while Janey stood with Mo's family and Carl moved his car out of the bus's path. Mo took a seat next to a window and waved to the group as the bus pulled away.

CHAPTER TWENTY-SEVEN
Washington DC

A group of men stood in the hallway just outside of the conference room at the White House, speaking in hushed tones to each other. Senator Russell Royce and Congressman William Tucker as well as other various Senators and members of Congress, all close allies of the President, waited. This was an invitation only meeting.

A spokesman for the President cracked open one of the two massive doors and whispered to one of the Secret Service men standing alongside two uniformed soldiers. The man just spoken to then nodded to the soldiers, who pulled both doors open toward the hallway, allowing the men to move inside.

Sitting at the center of a long wooden table was President Franklin Delano Roosevelt.

Roosevelt was flanked on one side by Harry Hopkins, his closest advisor, and on the other side by Cordell Hull, the Secretary of State. Other seated cabinet members stretched out on each side of those men.

There were chairs all around the table and chairs lining all of the walls of the room.

Roosevelt had a big smile on his face, and smoked a cigarette in a long holder. His face looked full and healthy behind his round, rimless glasses.

Before everyone had a chance to clear the hall, the President spoke up in a robust voice. "Welcome to all of you and thank you for coming. I think we have plenty of chairs for everyone. Just grab a spot wherever you can."

Immediately across the table opposite the President a chair was left open by all until Senator Royce walked in the room. The other politicians understood that spot was reserved for the Senator. He moved to the spot and seated himself as FDR gave him a direct nod and smile.

"Good to see you Russ."

"It's good to see you too, Mr. President. You're looking well."

"I'm feeling good!"

The President sat for a moment and waited for everyone to get situated, then leaned over and whispered something to his Secretary of State. He surveyed the room, which was now absolutely silent, before he began to address the group.

"You have all been briefed on our meeting today. Now allow me to elucidate. The Nazis want Europe and Africa. The Japanese want the Pacific. And Russia will try to grab whatever is left." The President paused to let these words sink in before he continued.

"When that gets done they'll be looking at us. Yet we still have Senators and Congressmen who prefer to stick their heads in the sand like ostriches."

President Roosevelt stopped and turned toward his Secretary of State. "Frankly, I'm at a loss as to how we can convince the public that we need to get involved. If we could convince them, the politicians would follow suit."

The Secretary of State looked at the President, obviously wanting to offer something to the conversation, but making sure not to cut in on the President before he spoke. "Mr. President, the polls indicate the majority of Americans don't want any involvement. They feel we never should have been in the last war and we lost a lot of good men for nothing."

With a look of resignation and frustration, the President fixed his gaze straight across the table at Senator Royce.

"I know the history, dammit. People want us to mind our own business, focus on domestic issues and strengthen our homeland defenses. They're content to let the Europeans keep their wars over there and let us hide behind our oceans. Listen, I'm looking for some fresh suggestions here!"

Roosevelt paused to look around the room, then addressed Senator Royce. "Russ, what's the pulse in the Senate? Are we getting any support there?"

"Mr. President, I've been trying. It's like running into a brick wall. There are just too many people who believe the only reason we get in wars is greed. They're convinced companies that build our war machines are merchants of death and they're willing to kill our boys for profit."

"Russ, unfortunately, oftentimes there's truth to that. But everyone in this room knows it's different this time. If we don't stop that fanatical Hitler and get in soon it's going to get very bad for us."

President Roosevelt appealed then to Congressman Tucker.

"Congressman Tucker, do you have any good news to share with us about the House?"

"I'm afraid even less support than in the Senate, Mr. President. My colleagues, more localized in their districts, are even more afraid to buck public opinion. Most know deep down we should be getting in this war, but politics is keeping them from stepping up. The people just have no taste for this war right now."

As he listened to this, the President sat, all eyes in the room on him, before he spoke.

"Hell, we have that damn Lindbergh out there telling everybody the Luftwaffe can't be beat. Then we've got others who are afraid as hell of the Nazi armies. We're running out of options."

Again, the Secretary of State spoke up.

"Mr. President, our isolationists come from all walks of life. Most are truly driven by moral commitment. Then, when you add big business critics, German Americans, Communists and the Anti-Semites, our support base is almost non-existent to become involved in the war as an active participant."

Roosevelt looked around the room with an impish grin. "And let's not forget those people who simply hate my guts!"

As the President smiled at his own statement, there were muted laughs among the crowd.

The President continued. "It's just that these closed-minded morons don't understand that Hitler and his allies represent a threat which will bring on a fundamental change to our Western Civilization. Russ, before we break this up, do you have anything to add?"

"Yes, Mr. President, I do. As we move forward, and mobilize where we can, a day will come when we are forced into the war. The isolationists can delay involvement, but they won't keep us out forever. I just hope America doesn't face an all-powerful Germany and an emboldened Japan on two fronts with no allies left."

"Russ, Heaven help us all if we wait that long."

The faces of the men in the room were serious and solemn as that sobering statement settled in, spoken by the President of the United States, the most powerful man in the world.

Then the President continued. "Gentlemen, keep up the good fight. I know we shall come out the other side on this one a better and stronger nation, but there will be dark days ahead before we do. I appreciate the hard work you do. My door is always open to the men in this room whenever you might have a suggestion. Thank you all for being here today."

Looking straight across the table, the President addressed Senator Royce directly, the cue for the room to vacate.

"Russ, would you mind sticking around for a couple of minutes? I'd like to talk to you." Senator Royce looked surprised and flattered.

"Yes sir, Mr. President. Of course."

The President turned to whisper once again to his Secretary of State as the room cleared, finally leaving only the President, Harry Hopkins and Cordell Hull in the room with the Senator.

All the men still sat in their chairs.

"Russ, I have a little fishing vacation coming up around the end of July. We'll be on the floating White House. I'd love it if you can break away and tag along."

Senator Royce knew the President well in the professional sense, and both men realized that the Senator was one of the President's staunchest supporters. The Senator even felt he had a genuine friendship with Franklin Roosevelt. But that did not diminish the delight Senator Royce felt in being asked to join the President.

"Mr. President, I would be honored. Thank you. Of course I will come."

"Great. And, will you ask young Congressman Tucker if he can make it too? I know you two get along. We might have some good discussions."

"Absolutely Mr. President. He'll be ecstatic to hear he is invited."

"Great Russ. Staff will be in touch with details as we get closer."

Getting up from his chair, Senator Royce started to backpedal to the door.

"Thank you, Mr. President. Take care."

"You too, Russ." Waiting outside in the hallway, Congressman Tucker raised his eyelids at Senator Royce as he walked out of the room.

"Wow. Singled out by the President in front of everyone to stay and speak in confidence. In these crucial times."

The men started down the hall together. The Senator looked straight ahead as he talked. "Our President may be physically infirm, but I've never known a man to work harder or care more for our country and every American. He is the most powerful man in the world, yet he knows that true power is not in controlling people, but in serving them."

He then turned to the Congressman. "I don't know if it's business or pleasure, but it seems there's going to be a little fishing vacation on the USS Potomac in July."

"And the President asked you to come along?"

"That he did young man, but there's more to it. He invited you too."

The Congressman stopped dead in his tracks and looked at the Senator in amazement.

"I can't believe it. I'm going fishing on the floating White House with President Franklin Delano Roosevelt?"

"Better practice up on your casting, William. You won't want to look like a novice. That is, if it's fishing we end up doing."

CHAPTER TWENTY-EIGHT
Dachau Germany

Abraham and Leo, a prison supervisor, albeit he himself a prisoner, walked through a barracks. The prisoners they viewed were gaunt and weakened, their bald heads looking more like skulls with skin. Sunken eyes followed the two men as they moved through. The look of hopelessness, sadness and fear was pervasive.

"Leo, tell me who among these men exhibit heroism. Who are the ones that struggle to sustain not only their own life, but others as well? Genuine concern for humanity and moral values must not perish."

"Abraham, we do have those men among us. I know them. I know the noble ones. I also know those who do not treat their brothers well."

"Tell no one but me. The good men must not die needlessly. We will need leaders, men of goodness, when this ends."

"But when will this end, Abraham? When will the Nazis ever let us go? Their evil and cruelty have no limits."

"Germany is at war. Wars do not last forever. One day this war, like all others before it, shall end. Pray that Hitler and his Nazis are defeated, and we are liberated by his conquerors. Until then, the righteous need to be kept strong."

"Stay strong, Abraham? We have slop for food. We have no medicine. The guards whip us, beat us and torture us every day."

"Leo, I am only able to help certain kapos like yourself. You, I know to be a good man. But not all kapos are so. Some are harsh, caring only for themselves. I can supply a few prisoners better food and medicine, but only a select few. They must be worthy. This is the reason my son and I help the Commandant. It is the deal we have struck with him."

"Abraham, you were not a rich man before coming to this camp, but now you are a great man."

"No Leo. I am a common man who wants to do right, like you."

Leo looked at Abraham.

"There are others who report to the Nazis for favors for themselves. They have turned on their own people. You are nothing like them. I know that."

"Leo, it takes courage to survive here. Anyone who turns on his brother to save himself has no courage. And, they are shortsighted fools, because the Nazis will only end up doing evil to them eventually."

As the men moved toward the door to the barracks, Leo looked up once more at the tall, thin man walking with him.

"Abraham, do you think we will ever get out of here? Will we ever go home?"

"I do not know. But deliverance shall come either while we live, or in the hereafter. Remember to stay strong, pray for that day to come, and never give up hope."

The men kissed each other on the cheek before Abraham left the barracks.

CHAPTER TWENTY-NINE

Springfield Illinois

Janey lounged in a chair in the corner of her living room, alone. She had her lap and leg covered by a blanket as she read a book by the light of a lamp on a side table. The family's new Zenith floor model console radio was tuned to the afternoon symphony music show, with one of Janey's favorites playing, Rachmaninoff's Piano Concerto Number Two.

Her mom, Fern, walked into the room with an envelope in her hand.

"Janey, a letter from South Carolina just arrived. Looks like Mo is true to his word. Here's your first letter from that nice young man."

Janey immediately set her book on the table and turned down the radio, as she took the envelope from her mother. "Thanks Mama. Oh, I can't wait to hear what Mo's written."

Janey's mother made no attempt to move and remained in front of her daughter.

"Well, Mo said he wants to write for a newspaper when he gets back, so he must be some kind of writer."

"I'll read it to you if you want, mama."

"Oh that would be nice. I really like Mo."

Janey's mother quickly sat down in another chair, anxious to hear what the letter held.

As she finished opening the envelope and pulling out the letter, Janey looked back up at her mom.

"OK, here goes."

Dear Janey,

I hope everything is good back home. I started missing you the minute the bus pulled away. Every day the realization hits that my life has changed so much, so quickly.

Only a couple of years ago I was playing on my high school football team, and hanging out with Max and friends. Funny, but life seemed so complicated then. I was planning my future to be working at Sangamo, learning to be a tool and die maker like Eddie. It's obvious I didn't really know what complicated was back then.

I find myself in a barracks with lots of other guys on a base with thousands more.

I'm preparing to fight in a war that seems more certain every day we'll be getting in.

Anyway, the big news is that I won't be in Charleston too much longer. I'm in a new detachment and we're headed up to Canada in two weeks.

My commanding officer came to me and said they were looking for some volunteers with intelligence, good health and a serious disposition, and he thought I fit the bill.

That made me feel pretty good. He went on to say it was special combat training to learn demolition, hand to hand combat and guerilla tactics. I volunteered.

Then he asked me if I was willing to die for my country. I told him I was willing to die, but I didn't much plan on it.

That answer must have been adequate. He said I was in. After Canada, we're coming back to South Carolina before shipping out to God knows where.

They've told the troops they're going to do their darndest to get us all home for Christmas before we ship out. I sure hope so.

I think about you every day. I hope you wait for me. I'm coming home for good someday. I promise. Take care you brave girl.

Love, Mo

Janey had tears in her eyes as she kissed the letter, leaned back in her chair and held the letter to her chest.

CHAPTER THIRTY

Washington DC

Senator Royce and Congressman Tucker waited outside of the White House on a crushingly hot early August afternoon. There was a line of cars and the Secret Service was present in force, as they would be when the President was on the move.

Congressman Tucker took his handkerchief from his pocket and wiped sweat from his forehead and neck.

"I hope they don't misplace my trunk. I'd hate to be dining with the President on the Potomac if my clothes don't make the trip."

"Not a chance of that, young man. Not to worry", answered the Senator. "Here I am, sixty-eight years old, and I feel like a kid again, waiting for the President to go on a fishing trip. Not only that, but we're part of the Presidential motorcade to the submarine base at New London."

"It is exciting Senator. My wife is extremely jealous. How about yours?"

He looked at his younger friend with an impish smile.

"Livid."

Both men laughed.

At that moment, the doors of the White House opened, and the President was wheeled out in a wheelchair. No press members were allowed here, and the cars and Secret Service effectively shielded the President from long-range onlookers.

The President looked sharp dressed in a grey suit and tie, with his signature cigarette holder between his teeth as he smoked a cigarette.

"Russ, William! The USS Potomac awaits us. So glad you could both make it!"

Both men smiled broadly as Senator Royce answered. "Wouldn't miss it, Mr. President. We're honored."

"Well listen, Gentlemen. We've got a lot to discuss, and believe me when I tell you that we'll have an eventful and unforgettable trip. We do have one small glitch which has come up just in the last day or so. Seems we had a rather unfortunate overlap of Washington guests so I've invited Crown Princess Martha of Norway to enjoy the cruise for the first couple of days. It will look good for the press, and give us some good photo opportunities. Her group is meeting us at the Potomac. Of course, while she's with us I'll need to give her my undivided attention. Hope you fellas will forgive me on this one. Of course, everyone will dine together, but it will sure limit our conversation, if you know what I mean."

The Senator, unflappable, smiled at his Commander in Chief.

"I'm sure we'll have ample time for some excellent fishing and dialogue, Mr. President."

"I knew you'd be OK, Russ. You're a good man! OK, then, on to New London to board our ship."

The Secret Service wheeled the President to his car where he was transferred to the back seat. The Senator and Congressman walked to the rear, three vehicles behind the President's, and stepped in as the back doors were held open by two young soldiers.

CHAPTER THIRTY-ONE

At Sea on the USS Potomac

Senator Royce and Congressman Tucker faced one another in wooden deck chairs. A small table with a chess board filled the space between them.

"Senator, we've been nothing but window dressing for the President so far. I'm wondering if he only brought us along so he'd be saved from the burden of entertaining Crown Princess Martha during dinner."

"Well William, I'm not sure. I think we might get a better idea of why we're here now that the Crown Princess has departed with her entourage."

"I hope so. One can only play so much chess, or eat largemouth bass."

The Senator looked at the young man with a smile. "I do imagine you're getting bored beating me at chess. I've never been more thoroughly trounced by anyone as you have these last couple of days. However, the bass are excellent when the President's chef prepares them, and they do put up a good fight when we hook one of those fat buggars!"

The two men got back to their game of chess when a ship's steward approached.

"Excuse me gentlemen. The President has freshened up and changed into more comfortable attire. They're bringing him topside and he has requested you to join him."

Both men rose immediately.

"Please follow me."

As the President spied the men when they arrived on the upper deck, he greeted them robustly, once again, speaking while he clenched his cigarette holder between his teeth.

"Come on over fellas and sit yourselves down. Now that the Royalty has gone, we can relax a bit. I haven't had a moment to drop a line in the water yet, what with giving the Princess tips while she snagged the fattest bass of the trip. And I saw you pull in a big one yesterday Russ."

"It was a fatty, Mr. President."

The President reached down to open a cigar box on the table, exposing some thick, long cigars.

"Russ, I know you enjoy a good cigar now and then. William, how about you? Cuban Camachos." Both men reached into the box and took a cigar. Immediately a steward appeared with a silver tray. He politely took each man's cigar, expertly cut the ends and produced a silver Ronson lighter to torch each man's cigar. When the cigars were going strong, he smiled and departed.

The President's face, friendly, now took on a serious look.

"I hope you both won't think I've kidnapped you against your will when I tell you this."

Both men wondered what the President of the United States was prepared to divulge.

"I wasn't able to tell you the real reason for our voyage before we left. Top Secret. Classified stuff, you know. But now that we're secure and at sea with our visitors gone, I can let you in on what's going on."

The President leaned forward a bit in his chair and the two men with him instinctively leaned in closer, even though no one was around to eavesdrop.

"Tomorrow morning at zero five hundred hours, we

transfer to the heavy cruiser USS Augusta waiting for us in Vineyard Sound."

The President took a long drag on his cigarette.

"We're heading full steam for Placentia Bay Newfoundland. We'll be having a rendezvous with the Prime Minister of England himself, Winston Churchill. That's why so hush hush. He's aboard the British Battleship HMS Prince of Wales, and if the Nazis got wind of his crossing, every U boat in the North Atlantic would be hunting him. It's dangerous for him to be making the trip. Frankly, the man has balls of steel if you ask me. I do, however, have a few boxes of these Cuban Camachos for the old boy. They're his favorite." The President stopped speaking, waiting for the reaction from his two guests, and the Senator recognized the opening to speak.

"Mr. President, far from feeling kidnapped, I feel honored that you would include us on this mission."

The Congressman concurred, nodding his head.

"Thank you. I knew you'd understand. This is an important meeting, and I do think it doubly important that Churchill sees my two strongest allies from Congress with me. Men, you are now a part of history."

CHAPTER THIRTY-TWO

At Sea on the USS Augusta

The USS Augusta sliced through the water on its way back to Vineyard Sound to reunite the President and his party with the USS Potomac after the top-secret meeting between the heads of state of England and the United States was completed.

The President, Senator Royce and Congressman Tucker enjoyed one final meal together.

Until this evening, the Captain of the vessel and his highest-ranking officers had been invited to dine with the President, Senator and Congressman. Dinner conversation had been dominated by the Navy men, as they eagerly regaled the President and two members of Congress with naval stories.

On this night, however, it was just the three men alone, and the conversation centered on policy, the situation in Europe and the extent of America's involvement and future commitments to the war which now raged around the globe. The men enjoyed what FDR called his 'favorite hour of the day', as the President himself took special pride in mixing martinis for his two guests before dinner was brought in.

The menu consisted of Caesar Salad, thick cut Filet Mignon Steaks, Asparagus tips with Hollandaise sauce and fried potato thins, all followed by a slice of three-layer chocolate cake and steaming hot coffee.

As the men ate dessert, the President opined with his guests.

"Much was accomplished in the last few days men. I think the United States got what we needed from our Joint Declaration."

"I agree Mr. President," intoned Senator Royce. "And Congressman Tucker and I both agree that your negotiations with the Prime Minister tilted greatly in favor of America."

"You're both right on that point, Russ. You might say the Brits are hanging on by their fingernails. Churchill is a bit short on bargaining chips."

The Congressman then offered his take.

"Churchill would have liked to have returned to his conservative party with more of a win, Mr. President."

"That he would, William. The old boy is under tremendous pressure. Those Brits do not want to abandon their Imperial preferences on trade. They fear this war will be the beginning of the decolonization of their subjects worldwide, but it surely will be. However, they need us, and they need us badly."

"Mr. President, we pushed through the Lend Lease Act back in March to give them material support, but as you are all too aware, we still have too many isolationists back home who don't want to send our men into war," added the Senator.

"That's the problem Russ. Churchill told me when we were alone the real reason he made the trip was 'to get the Americans into the war'. I told him in confidence that I and my allies are committed to do just that, but he'd better keep it under his bowler. It will only hurt the cause if it gets out that I want us in now. I can't afford to lose the trust of the people."

The men sat in silence, eating their cake. A steward

knocked on the door before he entered carrying a tray with three coffee cups. He replaced each man's drink with a fresh cup of coffee, then immediately left the room. When the man was gone the President spoke.

"Well, all in all, even though his options were limited, Churchill was smart to accept my vision for a postwar world once this war ends. The only hope for prosperity is a world where free trade, self-determination of government, disarmament and collective security exist."

As he looked at the President, Senator Royce emphatically made a statement.

"And that, Mr.President, is why you are the leader of the strongest and most civilized nation on earth."

CHAPTER THIRTY-THREE
Dachau Germany

Klein pulled on his pants, his fat pasty white belly hanging over his belt line. He sat in the chair to put on his boots, and looked over at the small girl huddled on the floor in the corner, as she attempted to cover herself with a coarse blanket. She looked blankly at the wall through eyes bruised from physical abuse. Her cheeks were puffy with an open cut across one. Her face streaked from dirt and tears.

As Klein stood up, he grabbed his wrinkled shirt, put it on and tucked it in, continuing to look like his usual sloppy self. Finally, he put on his holster with his Luger pistol.

"You are through here. My men will take you to the kitchens to work now."

Klein left through the door where his two usual henchmen waited. "She's yours now. I want her out of here by the end of the day. I never want to see her again. Clean the room when you are done. I expect it clean when I use it."

One of the two gave the heil salute.

"Yes Lt. Klein. Thank you. We shall take care of everything."

As Klein walked away, the two Nazis smiled, wicked intent in their eyes. They had been waiting for this moment. They opened the door to the room and went in. The girl had not moved since Klein left. Now she turned and looked up with terrified eyes, trembling as the two men entered.

The Nazi who spoke to Klein turned to the other soldier.

"I wish Klein did not beat them so badly. By the time we get them they don't look good."

The second Nazi stared back down at the girl.

"I don't care about that. You were first last time. I get her first this time."

"Go ahead. But don't take too long. I'm ready for my turn."

Both soldiers set their machine guns against the wall. One took off his helmet, boots, shirt and unbuckled his belt, took down his trousers, all while he eyed his victim. The second man sat in the chair, eager to watch.

After the second soldier had finished ravaging the little Jewish girl, he stood and dressed.

The girl curled up on the bed naked, sobbing, her brutalized face turned away from them, when one of the soldiers yelled at her. "Get dressed. We're done with you. Put your clothes on and be quick or get beaten! We need to take some pictures before you go to the kitchens to work."

The girl, like a zombie with no feelings, moved to cover herself with crumpled and dirty clothes heaped in a corner.

The two men led the small child out of the room into the open, then walked her over to a building close by and took her inside.

They proceeded to stand the girl in front of one wall and yelled another command in her face.

"Stand here. Do not move. Do not turn around. We are going to get the camera to take your picture."

Both men went through a door into an adjoining room, the girl left standing in front of the wall. Inside the dimly lit room the two Nazis had entered, they walked over to one wall adjacent to the room they just left. One of the men pulled out his Luger pistol, as the other silently pulled back a short curtain exposing a hole in the wall directly behind the girl's head. The soldier with the pistol raised his gun to the hole and fired.

Narration

Sometimes humans become too comfortable. They ignore the problems of their fellow men and women when they need to act. It can be selfish, cowardly and shortsighted. What man sows, he shall reap. There are times when an entire society falls into this trap. It has been the downfall of many nations and empires throughout history.

Eventually, nature will force action. Events inevitably occur which thrust humans into crisis.

This was one of those times for America.

CHAPTER THIRTY-FOUR

Washington DC December 8, 1941 Joint Session of Congress

The chamber was full to overflowing. People stood wherever they could find a spot. The level of noise was deafening as everyone awaited the President's arrival to begin his address to the Joint Session of Congress.

Senator Russell Royce and Congressman William Tucker sat side by side, looking around at the clamor.

"Well, William, the isolationists can finally sit down and shut up. What we couldn't convince the nation to do in six years the Japs did all by themselves on one Sunday morning."

"Even Lindy's on board now," answered the Congressman.

"He'd sure as hell better be. Otherwise he may as well fly his butt over to Germany!"

Out of the tunnel leading into the chamber came the Sergeant at Arms as he yelled in a loud voice. "Senators and Representatives, I have the distinguished honor of presenting the President of the United States."

The President appeared, walking with a cane, holding onto the strong arm of his son, a United States Marine. The entire chamber rose as one, giving the President a thunderous ovation as he walked. The Congressman turned to the Senator as the President laboriously made his way to the podium.

"No way today that our President would let himself be

wheeled in. He's wearing his leg braces, persevering through the pain."

The Senator watched the President as he ascended the stairs one by one.

"Thank God that America has this leader for this day."

The President, with a solemn face, looked out over the assembly before him, then, with a determined voice, began his speech.

"Mr. Vice President, and Mr. Speaker, and members of the Senate and House of Representatives. Yesterday, December 7, 1941...a date which will live in infamy...the United States of America was suddenly and deliberately attacked by naval and air forces of the Empire of Japan.

The United States was at peace with that Nation and at the solicitation of Japan, was still in conversation with its government and its Emperor looking toward the maintenance of peace in the Pacific. Indeed, one hour after Japanese air squadrons had commenced bombing in the American island of Oahu..."

Interior of Army Barracks Charleston South Carolina

A cluster of about thirty men crowded around a radio receiver listening to President Roosevelt address the nation. Mo was close in the front row, attentive as the speech continued.

"...Oahu, the Japanese ambassador to the United States and his colleagues delivered to our Secretary of State a formal reply to a recent American message. And while this reply stated that it seemed useless to continue the existing diplomatic negotiations, it contained no threat or hint of war or of armed attack.

It will be recorded that the distance of Hawaii from Japan makes it obvious that the attack was deliberately planned many days or even weeks ago. During the..."

Springfield Illinois Inside the Ryan Residence

Janey sat on the couch next to her mom, Fern. Her sisters and their husbands were in chairs while Carl stood, as the President's voice came over the large console radio.

"...During the intervening time the Japanese government has deliberately sought to deceive the United States by false statements and expressions of hope for continued peace. The attack yesterday on the Hawaiian Islands has caused severe damage to American Naval and military forces. I regret to tell you that many American lives have been lost.

In addition, American ships have been reported torpedoed on the high seas between San Francisco and Honolulu. Yesterday the Japanese government also launched..."

Springfield Illinois Inside Gordon Residence

Eddie, Cecilia and Mary, like the rest of America, listened to the broadcast.

"...also launched an attack against Malaya. Last night Japanese forces attacked Hong Kong.

Last night Japanese forces attacked Guam.

Last night Japanese forces attacked the Philippine Islands.

Last night the Japanese attacked Wake Island.

And this morning Japanese attacked Midway Island.

Japan has, therefore, undertaken a surprise offensive extending throughout the Pacific area.

The facts of yesterday and today speak for themselves. The people of the United States have already formed their opinions and well understand..."

Cambridge Massachusetts Inside Fraternity House

TR sat with a group of fraternity brothers, and listened to the large radio on one wall.

"...understand the implications to the very life and safety of our nation. As Commander in Chief of the Army and Navy I have directed that all measures be taken for our defense. But always will our whole nation remember the character of the onslaught against us.

No matter how long it may take us to overcome this premeditated invasion, the American people in their righteous might will win through to absolute victory. I believe that I interpret the will of Congress and of the people when I assert that we will not only defend ourselves to the uttermost but will make it very certain that this form of treachery shall never endanger us again..."

Interior of Army Barracks Charleston South Carolina

Mo was still listening with rapt attention to America's Commander in Chief.

"...endanger us again. Hostilities exist. There is no blinking at the fact that our people, our territory and our interests are in grave danger. With confidence in our armed forces..."

Mo got up from his chair and made his way through the soldiers crowding around the radio to go out the barracks door. Not a soul was visible outside, the road in front of the barracks empty. As he stood by himself, he took out a cigarette, lit up and took a big puff as he stared ahead at nothing in particular.

Washington DC Joint Session of Congress

Senator Royce and Congressman Tucker, like every other person in the chamber, continued to give their undivided attention to the President as he neared the conclusion of his address.

"...with confidence in our armed forces, with the unbounding determination of our people, we will gain the inevitable triumph, so help us God. I ask that Congress declare that since the unprovoked and dastardly attack by Japan on Sunday, December 7, 1941, a state of war has existed between the United States and the Japanese Empire."

Outside the chamber, after the President of the United States had finished his address to the people of America and the entire world, Senator Royce and Congressman Tucker walked together down the long steps of the Capitol Building.

"William, we have just witnessed one of the most significant speeches in our nation's history. America is at war. God help us."

CHAPTER THIRTY-FIVE

Springfield Illinois

Janey was seated in front of a mirror at a small vanity in her bedroom as she applied her makeup, getting ready to go to work at the SoHo supper club downtown when Fern's voice could be heard from another room.

"Janey, you just received another letter from Mo. Do you have time to read it before you have to go?"

Fern walked into the room and handed the envelope to Janey, who stopped everything to tear it open.

"I have time." Fern seated herself on another chair, waiting for Janey to read the letter out loud to her.

Janey looked at her mom with a big smile.

"I think you wait for Mo's letters with more anticipation than I do, mom."

"It is fun to get these letters. I love it when you read them to me."

"OK. Here goes."

My Dear Janey,

Well, all hell has busted loose now. The activity here at the base has really ramped up since the Japs attacked us. New recruits are arriving faster than they can process them, and every man here wants to kick the Japs' behinds.

Now that we know how tricky those little devils are, we're training even harder than before.

I only have a few minutes, but I wanted to get this in today's mail. This damned war has already hit close to home for me. I lost some friends a couple of days ago. The detachment I was with before I got pulled out for special duty and assigned to Canada was aboard a troop ship headed to Honolulu in the middle of the Pacific. Jap Subs torpedoed the boat. The hit killed or maimed almost all of the men in my old group. The torpedo hit right on the side of the ship where they were all sleeping.

The ship limped into Honolulu without sinking, but the loss of so many men I became friends with hurts to my core.

There were just so many good men on that ship. It's just a hell of a way to have this war start is all.

Mostly I want to tell you they're letting us come home for Christmas. Then, by the time I get back here we'll have our orders to ship out somewhere. I let Eddie and Cecilia know. They have a big Christmas Eve dinner planned.

I'd like you to be there. Think about it.

I'll come and see you when I get home.

Love, Mo

"Mama, can I go to Mo's Christmas Eve? I know we usually have everyone here."

"Of course. I'll make sure everyone comes on Christmas day instead. I'll fix a big Christmas meal and you bring Mo here to see us."

"Thanks Mama. I love you."

"Now hurry, Mr. Kruse from next door will be here any minute to pick you up."

"OK."

Janey got back to putting on her makeup, a big smile on her face.

CHAPTER THIRTY-SIX

Springfield Illinois Christmas Eve 1941

The oversized dining table at the Gordons' was decorated with Christmas and patriotic decorations. A giant golden-brown turkey, partially sliced, occupied the center of the table with bowls of traditional dishes all around. Christmas carols could be heard playing softly from the radio in the living room.

The Gordon family was seated, along with Janey Ryan. Mary Gordon and Edward were at their usual spots on each end, and everyone held hands while Edward said the blessing.

Although Mary was noticeably growing older, she still very much possessed all of her mental faculties, and remained the strong matriarch of the family as she looked around the table at her family before speaking. "This is such a celebration for us to be together for Christmas Eve. We are truly blessed. And Janey, we're all glad you can be here."

"Thank you, Mrs. Gordon. I wouldn't miss it."

Janey looked at Mo as she reached out and put her hand on Mo's hand resting on the table.

"I'm just glad they let Mo come home for the Holidays."

Mo looked at his mother, then at Janey.

"They made it a point to let all the guys go home this Christmas."

An awkward moment of silence came over the table as

everyone knew what Mo was saying. Many men all over America who were enjoying Christmas with their families would never celebrate with them again after this year. Finally, Eddie lifted his glass high in the air at the end of the table.

"Well, we're all here tonight. And when this damned war ends and we win, I know we'll be celebrating again and for many years to come. I'd like to make a toast to the two greatest young men I've ever known, Max and Mo!"

Everyone held up a glass when Max looked down the table at Eddie.

"I'll drink to that Eddie!"

Everyone laughed, then touched their glass with those closest to them. The tension broken, everyone started passing the food around the table.

Cecilia started conversation when she asked Mo a question. "Mosie, after you go back down to South Carolina, where are you going? To Europe to fight Germany?"

"I don't think so, sis. Word is we're on a troop train to the west coast. After that it's anybody's guess. But they did say we were headed to the other side of the globe. I'm thinking I'll be Jap hunting."

Max jumped into the conversation.

"After what those bastards did to us at Pearl, I hope you get a bunch, Mo."

Sensing the direction of the conversation not fitting Christmas Eve dinner, Mary stepped in.

"That kind of language shouldn't be at our Christmas Eve table. Can't we talk about other subjects at this beautiful table on this holy day?"

Max looked a bit sheepish as he answered his mother.

"I'm sorry Ma. You're right. Mo's gonna be fine whatever happens."

"You bet I am Max."

Mo continued.

"Family. I want to apologize. I didn't get anyone a gift this year. I haven't had a minute."

"You just sitting there is our gift, Mo", answered Edward.

The table heartily concurred as silence came over the table as everyone started enjoying their sumptuous Christmas feast. When dinner had ended, the family moved into the living room and exchanged gifts around the Christmas tree. After all the gifts had been opened, everyone sat and enjoyed each other's company, continuing the celebration.

When the evening came to a close, Mo and Janey headed out to Edward's auto, Edward and Cecilia walking them out. At the door to the car, Cecilia gave Janey a big hug. Then Edward gave Janey a hug, as Janey gave Edward a kiss on his cheek.

"Eddie, it's really nice of you to let Mo pick me up in your car. You know, one day I'm going to drive a car by myself. I know it."

"I'm sure you will little lady. I don't doubt that."

Then Eddie looked over at Mo before looking back at Janey.

"Besides, I'm going to be looking to get a new model pretty soon and when I do, this car is Mo's when he gets back."

Surprised by this offer, Mo shook his head.

"Eddie, you don't have to do that."

"Sorry son. It's a done deal. Case closed. Now, you two go on and enjoy the rest of your evening. Bye Janey."

"Bye Eddie. Bye Cecilia."

When Mo and Janey were back on the porch at Janey's house, they stood, facing each other and held hands. "Mo, I don't know how long it will be before we see each other again, but no matter how long it takes, I'll be here waiting for you."

As he wrapped his arms around Janey, Mo answered.

"That makes me feel good to hear you say that Janey. That you'll wait for me. I won't let you down."

"You know, the first night I saw that handsome soldier come through the door at the SoHo my heart jumped. I'm so glad you came over to the piano that night."

"How could I not? I was a moth and you were the light."

"Well, wherever you go and whatever it is you do on the other side of the globe, you just get back here."

"Yes Ma'am."

Then Mo gave Janey a kiss to remember. A kiss to last a long time.

CHAPTER THIRTY-SEVEN

Boston Massachusetts Christmas Eve 1941

Inside the estate of Senator Russell Royce, the resplendent living room bedecked with Christmas decorations was filled with guests. A mountainous tree fit easily in the room. White gloved servants were all about, serving Champagne and finger foods from silver trays. A piano player at a grand piano played softly as a group of four performers sang Christmas carols. A gathering of guests stood around the piano, some choosing to join in the singing.

TR and his father were with Congressman Tucker next to the grand stone fireplace with a large carved wooden mantle. A crackling fire provided warmth and ambiance in a room that belied the frigid weather which had enveloped New England outside. The men all held a glass of champagne as the Senator spoke. "William, I know it's only been a few weeks since we were pulled into the war, but it seems slow to get mobilized."

"The pace will pick up. Every base in America is bulging with recruits. They're training them as fast as possible. Right after the holidays we have troops shipping out from both coasts."

At this statement, waiting for a perfect time, TR cut into the conversation.

"Dad, Congressman Tucker. I'm thinking about

enlisting right after Christmas and finishing law school later when I get back from fighting."

Both men looked surprised at TR's announcement. After a few seconds, the Senator appealed to TR's common sense.

"TR, I'm proud of you for your sentiment, but this is going to be a long war. Not months, but years! You should stay in school and graduate. Finish your training."

"Your Dad is right, TR. You'll do your part. America and our military will be better served if you complete school and go in as an officer. We need leaders not only during the war, but after it's over."

"I just don't want the war to end before I have a chance to get in."

The Senator was quick to answer his son.

"Trust me TR. You're a patriot, and it's noble and brave to want to jump in now. But even after you graduate, there will be ample time to defend your country. Your deferment will keep you in school until you graduate and you need to use it."

TR studied both men. The Congressman was nodding his head in agreement with everything the Senator had said. "Alright Sir. I'll finish up. But when I graduate, I'm going right into the army."

"TR, I want you to serve your country. We both do. You are being very wise and level headed to listen to us."

Putting his hand on TR's shoulder the Senator continued.

"I'm proud of the man you've become."

CHAPTER THIRTY-EIGHT

Dachau Germany Christmas Eve 1941

Abraham, Golde and Aaron were at the table in the middle of the room. A candle was lit in the center as they ate.

"Father, the others in the camp cannot give thanks, and because of the Nazis, this is the best we can do."

"The others who are worthy give thanks in their hearts. Many keep our faith alive in the camps. They teach those they can. That gives them strength. We have not been abandoned. It is said this storm may batter us. The water may be violent on top of the sea, but if we live in deep waters, it is peaceful and still."

Golde reached out and took each man's hand. "Even as we are here, imprisoned, I feel blessings. I am so proud of my husband, and my son. In the worst of times, Abraham, you are a most courageous man, never thinking of yourself first. Your righteousness and holiness have never been greater in my eyes than I see tonight. And Aaron, you show us that no matter what happens to us in the future, we know our son follows in his father's footsteps. We could never ask for more than this from a son."

As he looked at his mother's calm and beautiful face, even after the hardships of these previous years, Aaron gave her a look of love.

"Mother, thank you. I will always love both of you. The Nazis can never take that from us."

Abraham nodded. Then, to both his wife and son.

"The Germans control our physical bodies. They do not control our minds, our hearts, or our souls. We are the masters of our own salvation."

Aaron got up from the table.

"I must go now. The Commandant expects me at his villa tonight to play for his guests."

Aaron bent down and kissed his mother on her cheek before leaving the room.

CHAPTER THIRTY-NINE

Dachau Germany Christmas Eve 1941

Inside a barracks filled with women, a group around a table held hands praying. Others were in bunks, some awake, others sleeping, when the door opened to reveal Klein and his two henchmen. Coming in out of the snowfall outside, Klein began his stroll through the barracks, eyeing the women.

"Your barracks is lucky. It has been chosen to supply our next kitchen worker. The work is easy. The rewards are great."

The women throughout had heard the stories of girls being taken by Klein. None had ever been seen again. Klein noticed a girl clutched by her mother, trying to keep her daughter out of Klein's sight. Klein pointed to the young girl.

"You there. You come with us."

The girl looked at the ugly Nazi standing in front of her and begged.

"I want to stay with my mother. Please don't take me."

"Silence! You have no choice. You have been chosen."

Then a pretty girl, but with deadened eyes, perhaps slightly older, stepped forward.

"My parents are dead. My brothers and sisters are gone. I'm the only one left. Let me go with you. I know what you want. Leave her."

Klein stopped and looked her over, his eyes open wide at her statement.

"Yes, you will do nicely. Come with us."

The girl left with the soldiers into the frigid night, not turning to look back.

CHAPTER FORTY

Five German officers and their wives were in the living area of the Commandant's villa. Holiday decorations filled the room, and a large tree sat in front of the window, a Swastika at the top.

Servers with trays served food and champagne. The wives filled the couch while the Commandant stood with a group of officers talking and laughing. Finally, the Commandant addressed the women as well as the officers standing with him.

"This is truly a wonderful holiday evening. We celebrate Odin and the winter solstice, which our Great Fuhrer allows us to enjoy. Before dinner, I have a special treat. I have found a young Jew boy who is very gifted playing the violin. He will perform for us. Then, after dinner, I invite you all into my study, where I have put together a wonderful art arrangement for your viewing." The officers all moved to chairs, which had been placed around the room, as a tall, handsome young man entered the room carrying a violin and bow.

Aaron was dressed nicely with new shoes, pressed pants and white long-sleeved shirt. His black hair was short, combed neatly. He did not resemble the appearance of the other Jews in the camp. The Commandant placed a chair in the center of the room for Aaron.

"Aaron, I trust you have selected some beautiful works for us this evening."

Aaron nodded.

"Yes Sir. I'm sure your guests will enjoy them."

"Excellent! Ladies and Gentlemen, I present Aaron Gittelsohn."

The Commandant moved to a chair, looking around at his guests and smiling broadly. Aaron began to play.

CHAPTER FORTY-ONE
Springfield Illinois Summer 1942

Carl and Janey sat side by side on the piano bench playing a lively duet as their mom Fern listened. As they played in perfect sync, Janey sang. When they finished, Janey put her arms around Carl, hugging him.

"Oh, how I've missed these duets, Carl. We used to do this all the time when you were at home."

"Me too, sis. That's why I ran down this weekend from Chicago. I've been missing you both. But it's going great up in Chicago, and they pay really well at the big hotels up there. Piano bars are all over the place. I want you and Ma to come up sometime soon."

"Well we would if the SoHo will give Janey some vacation time. They work her tail off down there", said Fern.

Looking back at Janey, Carl started talking again. "Ma says the bartender Artilio picks you up now and brings you home. Is that right?"

"Yes. I love Artilio. He's such a nice man. They pay him an extra hour a day just to make sure I stay. I don't drive, you know."

"You must be making them a ton of money down there for Dom Muzio to pay Artilio. He's a tight son of a gun."

"Well, Mr. Muzio treats me very nice, Carl. And he just gave me a raise."

Carl got up off the bench and walked over to sit next to his mom.

"Chicago is full of the rich and famous now mom. Lots of people from California and New York are living in Chicago now. They're afraid of the Japs and Germans landing on our coasts."

"I can understand why Carl", said Fern as she continued.

"You never would want to be there and have bombs from ships start going off."

With a worried look, Janey asked her brother.

"Could that happen, Carl?"

"Who knows? Safer to be in Chicago I guess. But I'm sure we have lots of soldiers stationed on both coasts just in case. But, hey, I want to tell you both something. A guy from the biggest local radio station came in the other night, and after listening to me for a while said he was interested in me doing a fifteen minute show a couple of nights a week."

Janey's eyes lit up. "Oh my. Big brother might be a star someday. Take me with you when you become famous, will you?"

"Let's see if anything comes of it first, OK?"

Janey started to play another piece on the piano as Fern looked at Carl.

"Carl, would you be so kind as to see if our mail carrier has left us anything?"

"Sure mom."

Carl left the room as Janey stopped playing to talk to her mom.

"Wouldn't it be something, mama, if Carl was on the radio?"

"It sure would be, honey."

Coming back into the room, Carl had envelopes in his hands, thumbing through them.

"Not important, not important, hey, we got one here for Janey all the way from Hawaii! Looks like Mo's ship made it past the Jap subs."

"Oh Carl, give it to me!"

Carl walked over and handed it to Janey as he smiled at his mom, then went over and sat before he asked Janey.

"Well, are we going to hear you read it out loud, or is it too mushy?"

"Mo doesn't write mushy letters. Of course I'll read it to both of you. But if it does get mushy, I'll stop." Janey stared at the envelope for a minute, before saying out loud 'Honolulu Hawaii'. She opened the envelope, unfolded the letter and started reading it.

My Dearest Janey,

Well, we made it to Hawaii. We heard reports of subs on the way, but had no troubles. Looks like someone is watching over me so far.

When our ship entered the harbor at Pearl, it was a sad and somber sight. The wreckage has touched every man here deeply, and we know why we're here.

Troops are arriving on this tiny island by the tens of thousands, and they've built a massive tent city up next to Hickam Air Base. That's where my detachment is staying. I've met some great guys in my group, and I know we're going to become fast friends. Their names are Riley Meadows, Tex Bowlin and Duke Marlow.

Hickam was hit hard by the Japs. Buildings were riddled with bullet holes. Runways are being repaired. Everywhere you look is a reminder of what happened here December seventh of last year. With all we see every day, it's no wonder the level of cooperation and camaraderie among all the men.

I guess nobody could have seen this coming. Our

commanding officer said they were guessing the Japs might hit the Philippines, but never come this far. Admiral Kimmel and General Short here on the islands were more worried about sabotage from Japs that live here. There's lots of them here in Hawaii. A lot of fellas don't trust them, and you can understand why.

Lots of the men hate any Jap they see. I know not all are dangerous, but how do we know who we can trust? You've got to think lots of these people are still faithful to Japan. They might even have family still over there.

Anyway, we're going to be training here for a couple of months, maybe longer. They've been marching us hard, up and down mountains and through some thick Hawaiian jungle terrain with full gear and packs.

This will be my last letter for I don't know how long. We've been told no one will be allowed to write home about what we are undergoing or what kind of training after today. Everybody, and I mean everybody, is scribbling something to go back home. This is our last chance.

None of us knows where we're headed though. No matter where I end up, I'm going to make the best of it, and I'm going to stay alive for you. I think of you every day.

Please give my love to your wonderful Mom, and say hi to that big brother of yours, Carl, when you see him.

Bye for now.

Love, Mo

By the time Janey finished the letter, she had tears in her eyes. Carl got up and went over to Janey and sat back down next to her, putting his arm around her consolingly.

"I knew I liked that guy the first time I met him."

Janey wiped away her tears, and then gave Carl a smile upon hearing this.

"No you didn't Carl. I think you almost scared Mo away the first time you met."

"Nah. That guy can't be scared. He's the real deal."

Then Janey sat up straighter, a serious look on her face.

"Mama, Carl, when Mo gets back, I want two things. I want to be able to drive and I also want to be standing on two legs when he gets here. No crutches. I'm going to learn to walk on an artificial leg! Will you help me?"

Her mother smiled and answered.

"Of course we will Janey."

"Damn right we will baby sister", as Carl pulled Janey close to him.

Narration

Working side by side with others can create lasting friendships. Fighting side by side for a common cause forms a bond stronger than blood. Those with conviction and clarity will begin to put more value on those around them to a greater extent than their own wellbeing. A selflessness reveals itself which can be absent in more normal, easier times. Soldiers become brothers.

CHAPTER FORTY-TWO

India June 1943

One Thousand tents elevated on wood platforms in straight rows of fifty were being battered by the winds, torrential rains pelting the canvas. Tarps bowed with the weight of the water as it poured off the sides. Soldiers on guard duty wore ponchos and tried to stay dry as they sat in thatched topped towers on stilts, high above the muddy ground. A few vacant jeeps and assorted military supply and troop trucks were visible. Hundreds of mules in pens stood in mud under thatched overhangs, getting soaked from the rain blowing sideways. Inside one tent were four soldiers, Mo Gordon, Riley Meadows, Duke Marlow and Tex Bowlin. The sound of the wind and rain outside was deafening, as the sides of the tent billowed in and out. The inside of the tent somehow stayed dry. A lantern swung, suspended by a wire from the peak of the tent. Each man had a cot and a large duffel bag at the foot. Their Army issue weapons leaned together near the flap of the tent, tightly secured.

As he sat on his cot smoking a cigarette, Mo was not happy.

"It's been raining for three weeks straight. I hate this goddam place."

Riley looked at Mo. Riley was a mountain of a man, standing six foot three and weighing two hundred fifty pounds, all of it muscle. His white face with red freckles was topped by even redder hair cut into a tight crewcut, the same cut as all of these men. His face could have been better looking except for his pugilist beaten nose and cauliflower ears.

"Get used to it Gordon. It's just started. They say it's gonna rain until November, and it's only June. Does this every year here during monsoon season. Anyway, gives you plenty of time to write that book you're always workin' on."

"Not really a book Riley. I'm just writin' about my time in the army. But the six months I'm gonna be spending in this tent with you guys while it rains is gonna be the long boring part. If I was back in Springfield, it'd be perfect weather right now. June was always one of the best months."

Riley had a look of resignation on his face as he retorted.

"Well, you're in India now baby, and the Japs don't give a shit about the weather. They're just gonna try to kill us all."

From another cot, Duke Marlow cut in. Duke was the best-looking guy in the tent, even more handsome than Mo. Duke had Hollywood star good looks. His face was chiseled with a square jaw and perfect mouth. His eyes were deep blue, topped by a white blond crew cut.

"That's why they got us out there in the mud every day training in these damn monsoons. So we don't get killed."

"Yeah, it's sure they're getting us ready for marching where we might be moving through mud. Almost seems sometimes like the mud's gonna suck the boots right off your feet", said Mo.

Riley got back in the conversation.

"I don't mind the mud. It's those damn leeches I hate. Those little bastards get ahold of you and the only thing you can do is wait 'til you get back to the tent and burn 'em off with a cigarette. I got scars all over my arms and legs from them damn things."

"If that's what we gotta do to get ready for the Japs, so be it", said Duke. "Besides, the Japs ain't gonna believe it when Duke gets done with 'em. My daddy taught me to track in the forests when I was five. I've been huntin' since then, and I was the best damn shot in all'a Kentucky. They sure as hell ain't gonna kill old Duke."

"That's the spirit Duke", said Riley.

Duke started right back up.

"Well, that's what's gonna happen. I can't wait to go lookin' for Japs. I want to kick some ass for what they did at Pearl. An' I'm goin' home when this is over and I'm gonna be in one piece when I do!"

Mo looked over. "Duke, we all want to see you go home in one piece, because if we're around to see it that means we're goin' home too."

Tex Bowlin, who'd been sitting on his cot writing a letter to his girlfriend that would never be sent back home, looked up from his writing. Tex had the look of a typical cowboy. Standing about five foot ten, he was what you might call beefy. His face had full round cheeks and a thick neck, brown eyes and brown hair. When he walked, he looked like a bow-legged rodeo rider getting ready to take down a steer in the ring. But even with his bow-legged walk, Tex had proven himself the fastest runner in the entire detachment during training. Just as Tex started to talk an extreme gust shook the entire tent.

"Jesus, sometimes that wind blows so damn hard I'm sure this son of a bitch tent's gonna get torn right off the base."

"Hell, it's probably the rain holding the tent down", answered Duke. "We used to have damn hard rain in Kentucky, but compared to this, we were havin' sprinkles."

Tex went right back at Duke.

"Duke, you and me'll have to shoot and track sometime. I'll show you how it's done. I been doin' that down in Texas since I can remember. I doubt a Kentucky boy can out-track or out-shoot a Texan."

"You're on Tex. Anytime."

As these men started to get a little fiery with each other, Riley jumped in. "Settle down you two. You'll have plenty of time to hunt pretty soon. An' it'll be for the enemy. We're all on the same side here, but we ain't goin' anywhere 'til these damn monsoons stop. Get used to the fact we're gonna be sick of lookin' at each other by the time they do."

Duke and Tex stopped and looked at Riley, when Tex couldn't help himself from needling Riley.

"Aw, c'mon Riley. Who'd ever get sick of lookin' at your cute face?"

Riley shot a glare at Tex, then lightened up and smiled.

"I am kinda cute, ain't I?"

At that, all the men had a good laugh.

CHAPTER FORTY-THREE

Springfield Illinois June 1943

Max and Edward sat on the front porch of the Gordon house on a spectacular summer evening. Both men held a bottle of beer, Max in full military uniform.

"Max, it's impressive young man, to finish law school in just under two years. No one does that. I'm proud of you."

"Thanks Eddie. I doubled up on almost everything and studied until I dropped every night. I wanted to finish and get into this war, so I ramped it up, and now we're starting to win."

"As far as I'm concerned, Max, the longer you're in the States training, the better chance this war ends and we keep you here."

"Eddie, last we heard Mo was training in Hawaii, and now we don't know where he is. I want to do my part. I'm not afraid. Mo's never been afraid."

"You'll do your part Max. It's just that with Mo way over there someplace and you in the army now..."

"Don't worry Eddie. Nothing's gonna happen to the Gordon twins."

"I know that, I do. So, now that you're officially in, what's next?"

"First stop is Fort Riley Kansas, Eddie. Military Police Training. You get assignments like that when you have a degree beyond college. You know, special duty."

"Ceil and I drove by Fort Riley a couple of years ago on a vacation."

"After I finish training there, we're headed up to Fort Custer in Battle Creek. I'll be going in for Officer's Candidate School."

"You're gonna ace that Max. You've always been a natural born leader. Our army is lucky when it gets guys like you."

"We'll see. I've heard it's tougher than hell."

Eddie reached over and slapped Max on the knee.

"Well in that case it'll weed out the others, and you'll still be there, becoming an officer in the United States Army. College graduate, Law School graduate, and now you're going to be an officer. You sure have made your Ma proud, young man. Hell, you make us all proud."

Max looked down, his face getting red.

"Thanks Eddie." Looking out over the front lawn, and the walkway he and Mo used to race up after getting home from school, Max paused.

"Eddie, remember when Mo and I were little? You used to take us to your farm outside Havana almost every weekend. And I loved it when the corn was getting ready to harvest."

"That I do Max. You fellas loved running through the corn when it was ten, twelve feet high. You were a couple'a scamps I tell ya."

"And then, Eddie, we'd walk through the forested area to get to the other fields where the wheat and soy beans were growing."

"Farm's doin' OK this year too, Max."

"Seems like we just kinda stopped goin' up there, Eddie."

"Max, fact is, you and Mo as you got older just had bigger fish to fry. High School, friends, girls. Farm can't compete with those things when a young man's comin' into his own."

"Well, when Mo and I both come back when this war is over, promise me just the three of us make a trip up to the farm, OK?"

"You got it Max."

As the men both took a drink out of their long neck beers, Cecilia opened the door and poked out her head.

"OK, you two. Dinner's on the table. Come in and wash up."

Edward answered Ceil obediently.

"Yes Ceil."

CHAPTER FORTY-FOUR

Dachau Germany June 1943

Early morning and the sun was rising as a long line of trucks waited on the road in front of the camp. Dozens of soldiers with machine guns were deployed outside the front gate, which was open. Other guards inside the compound yelled and prodded at prisoners as they filed out of barracks. An officer at the gate barked orders at the soldiers.

"Hurry, get these trucks loaded. One truck must move every thirty minutes exactly!"

Prisoners cried and pleaded, asking where they were being taken, only to have guards push and kick them when they spoke. The officer at the gate yelled at the prisoners when they dared open their mouths.

"You are all transferring to another camp. Nothing more. We need your space for Russian prisoners from the Eastern Front." As a truck filled, it slowly pulled away, making its way down a dirt road away from the camp. Each truck was followed by two vehicles carrying Nazi soldiers with machine guns. The officer barked again.

"Keep those prisoners loading. We have a schedule to keep. Hurry! One truck every thirty minutes!"

When the first truck had driven almost an hour, it came to a jarring stop. The soldiers pulled back the tarp and ordered the prisoners out. Lt. Klein, waiting for the trucks to arrive, screamed at the prisoners as they unloaded.

"You all go to another camp where you will work in the fields harvesting. We need to film all of you for our Fuhrer to see. We will send pictures of our workers to the Americans so they see how good we treat you."

Fifty yards from the road, three large bulldozers were parked next to a large pit dug into the ground about one hundred meters long, fifty meters wide and ten meters deep. Huge mounds of dirt were piled in the field next to the hole. The entire surrounding area was forest, except for this large clearing. A photographer with a movie camera on a tripod stood in the field with a camera aimed toward the pit.

Lt.Klein walked out next to the photographer, yelling.

"Hurry, get them out. We want them to look like they are ready to work in the fields for our cameraman!" The soldiers herded the prisoners out and led them to the edges of the pit, lining them up, then spread out on each side of the photographer.

"Now turn this way for the camera!"

Sad and defeated eyes stared as the cameraman started filming.

"Now turn away, look toward the east!"

As the line turned away, the soldiers raised their weapons and began firing, killing the prisoners and knocking them down into the pit. When the machine guns subsided, one bulldozer cleared the bodies that didn't roll into the pit during the shooting as well as the bodies still alive and moving, as the other two pushed a layer of dirt over the bodies.

Klein yelled again.

"Hurry. Hurry. Another truck will be here soon."

The empty truck turned around to return to the camp, disappearing down the road. Soon, the next truck rolled into the clearing and stopped. As the prisoners lined up with

Klein's same commands, the first pictures were taken. When Klein ordered them to turn around, one man looked down into the pit and saw a leg sticking out of the dirt. He started screaming then bolted toward the forest. A Nazi guard gunned him down as he ran while the other soldiers began spraying the second group. When the guns stopped, the bulldozers went to work again.

Animated, with hideous glee on his face, Klein exhorted the Nazis once more.

"Good work. Now hurry. We are falling behind schedule. It is a busy day! We have many more Jews to kill!"

CHAPTER FORTY-FIVE
Springfield Illinois

Five people were having dinner at the Gordon house. Mary Gordon, Edward, Cecilia, Max, and his new girlfriend Ellie Daniels. Ellie was a pretty girl with blond hair and blue eyes. Her skin was tanned and her face covered with freckles. She looked young. Younger than Max by far.

"So anyway, a few of us guys were in Junction City playing some pool when Ellie and a couple of her girlfriends came in. That's where we met."

Ellie, not shy, chimed right in.

"As soon as we walked in, I told my girls I had dibs on Max."

Then, looking over at Max, she continued.

"He was so handsome in his uniform." Edward eyeballed the two, then asked Ellie a question.

"So Ellie, you live right in Junction City then?"

"Oh no. I live on a farm about ten miles outside of Junction City. My family has over one thousand acres with the Smoky Hill River runnin' right through it. Five hundred head of the best Black Angus beef you ever saw."

"Ellie's farm has been in her family for about seventy-five years now, right Ellie?"

"Yes Max. You know that."

"I was just telling Eddie."

Then turning toward Edward and Cecilia, Ellie continued.

"I can do everything as good as all the hands that work on the farm. I can ride. I can kill, pluck and cook a chicken. Shoot a gun. Slop a pig. Heck, I can even butcher a steer."

"That is impressive, Ellie", answered Edward.

Mary Gordon listened to the conversation quietly until now, when she asked Ellie another question.

"Ellie, are you in college or going to school?"

"Oh no Ma'am. I just graduated High School last year. I don't see no reason to do more schoolin'. My family's rich."

Mary looked at Max, raising her eyebrows.

"I see." Max nervously looked away from his mother's gaze.

Cecilia got up from the table, and picked up her plate and Edward's.

"Well, I'm going to clear these dinner dishes so I can serve our dessert. I baked a nice apple pie for us."

Ellie jumped up out of her chair, grabbed her plate and Max's.

"Let me help, Cecilia." Then she looked at Max, smiling. "I'm also good in the kitchen."

When the two had cleared the table and it was Mary, Max and Edward in the room, Edward quietly addressed Max.

"Max, that little gal is only eighteen? I know her family may be well off, but do you think this relationship can go somewhere? I'm not sayin' it can't. I'm just wondering what you're thinking here."

Mary also asked. "Yes, Max, I'm interested also."

"Well, Ellie's cute and all, but I don't see myself ever getting serious with her. She's not really my type, you know, for a long-term relationship."

"That's the way it seems to me too, Max, although a

man can never be sure how another man feels when it comes to women. Max, you're going to be gone for some time soon. Battle Creek, then somewhere else, maybe overseas or wherever they send you. Wouldn't be fair for you to make this nice little lady to pine for you while you're gone if nothing is going to happen."

"No. I suppose it wouldn't."

"I'm glad you agree. Don't make her write, get her hopes up, then break her heart."

"I won't Eddie."

"I know you wouldn't want to do that, Max. You be sure to be honest with her when you put her on the train back to Kansas, even if it hurts her a little now. She'll get over it quick."

"Yes sir, I will."

Mary Gordon looked down at the end of the table at Edward with a knowing and thankful look.

Cecilia and Ellie came back into the room carrying plates and the apple pie.

"I hope you're ready for some apple pie" said Cecilia. Glad to change the subject, Max smiled. "Always ready for your apple pie, Ceil."

CHAPTER FORTY-SIX

Dachau Germany

Abraham and Aaron were outside of a barracks building talking to Leo, the elder Kapo. Leo looked thinner, his face with a look of despair.

"Abraham, Aaron. We work hard to keep our names. To the Nazis we are a number they put on our bodies. We live in filth. The healthier and stronger among us are starting to get sick. Tattered and oily clothes cling to our bodies. Our sense of smell is so muted that normally putrid odors no longer matter. We wake to only another day of living hell. We never know if any day shall be our last, and some days we wish it would be."

Abraham looked at his good friend with an earnest and urgent look. "Leo, you must stay strong. People look to your strength. All we can do is live every day like it is our last. And we must treat others like it is the last time we will see them."

"Abraham, they took many truckloads of people away. Where did they go? What did the Nazis do to them? I'm afraid for those they took."

Aaron looked at Leo.

"I will try to find out. When I get the chance to ask the Commandant, maybe he will tell me."

"Aaron, don't believe a word the Nazis tell you", answered Leo, before he went on.

"They get more brutal every day. A work crew was being brought back in yesterday. Klein ordered the merchants Goldmann, Artur and Erwin Kahn and the lawyer Benario out of line. Without a word, the two Nazi guards with Klein shot them all in the head. Klein yelled only that they were 'hostile elements' and had received their 'due punishment'."

Abraham and Aaron, having already witnessed so much death and suffering, could only react with subdued resignation, as Abraham addressed Leo.

"Klein takes great joy in inflicting pain and causing death. None are as evil. His day will come. Then that day will become the darkness of the eternal night."

CHAPTER FORTY-SEVEN
"Letter to Janey"

My Dearest Janey,

I'm writing this letter in my journal knowing you may never see it. I don't even know what we're going to do or where we're going, but I'll keep on writing them.

I will tell you that while we were in Quebec and in Hawaii, and where I am now, they have some really tough, seasoned fighters training us. I mean, these are really some bad boys. We're still getting ready, and soon we're going to get into the thick of something big. I'm looking at it as my once in a lifetime opportunity to do something meaningful.

That being said, I mean just once. Don't know if I could do this more than one time. But a lot of what I've learned I'll be able to pass on to any sons or daughters in the future, because they're skills every person could use.

Not all of them for sure, but some. I'm proud to be in this army and I'm proud to be able to know these men. The will and sheer determination of every man here is awesome to see, while humbling at the same time.

Every guy here wants to get back home alive and in one piece, and every guy knows that not all of us will. But nowhere do I see fear on anyone's face. I only see fierce resolve to do the right thing. I honestly think every man here cares more for the guys on his left and his right than for himself. And that's why we're going to win this war.

I see you now in my mind. Your beautiful smile. I still feel your kiss. I don't feel alone. I know you're with me every step I take.

Love, Mo

CHAPTER FORTY-EIGHT

Washington DC

Senator Royce was behind his desk in his office inside the Capitol Building by himself when TR came to the open door, dressed in his army uniform. Looking up from the papers he was reading, the Senator saw his son.

"TR, come on in. Boy, you look great in that uniform young man. I'm just finishing up here."

"Thanks Dad."

TR sat in a chair across the desk. "Your mom and I are taking you to the best steak house in Washington tonight before you head back to Battle Creek. I hope you're hungry."

"Nothing wrong with my appetite, Dad."

"Yes, I guess I know that. I've watched you put it away for years now. The government's going to be saving me some money while they feed you."

TR smiled at his Dad's statement.

"Yeah, the food's not as good on the base as it is back home, but they give us plenty. We do eat a lot better when we get off the base."

"I'm glad you're having the opportunity to meet some other young men at officer's training."

"Yes I am sir. So far my best friend is a fella just graduated from Law School at Loyola. His name's Max Gordon."

"Excellent. Where's Max from?"

"He grew up in Springfield Illinois. He has a twin brother named Mo who's also in the army. He's somewhere in the Pacific, but Max doesn't know where."

"So Max comes from the land of Lincoln. Good. Well I hope he makes the cut at OCS."

"Oh, he will. Everybody knows that. He's the sharpest guy there. I just hope I do."

"Look at you! How could you not? I'm not the least bit worried about that."

"You're not pulling any strings for me I hope."

"I wouldn't do that TR. I know I don't need to. Everything you've ever done, you've done on your own."

"I don't want to get special treatment because I'm a Senator's son."

"TR, if anything, I'd think those officers might even be tougher on you. Do you think you've received any preferential treatment so far?"

"No, I don't think so."

"There you have it. No one can be a better judge of that than you are."

Standing up, the Senator left his work on the desk.

"This work will still be here waiting for me when I get back tomorrow. Let's go pick up the family. I'm getting hungry myself."

"OK, but I'm warning you, Dad. I'm ordering the biggest, thickest steak they have in the place."

"That's what I like to hear!"

CHAPTER FORTY-NINE

Springfield Illinois

Edward was in an easy chair in the Gordon's living room, holding a letter in his hands. Mary Gordon sat in her usual spot as Cecilia came into the room to sit on the couch near Edward.

"OK, Eddie. I'm ready now. Go ahead and read Maxie's letter."

Edward put on his glasses, pulled the letter out of the envelope and unfolded it, then cleared his throat before starting.

Hi everybody back home,

Here's the latest from Fort Custer up here in Battle Creek. Although I'm only a few hundred miles from Springfield, it may as well be thousands. It's all business up here at Officer's Candidate School. Probably only a third of us will become officers. The others will wash out. Our training is intense. The whole purpose here is to test our leadership qualities, at the same time seeing how we can follow orders. I'm working my you know what off. I want to be in that top third.

When we got off the train from Chicago, our ride up here was a canvas covered army truck. Thirty of us crammed into a dark hold. We called it our 'GI Taxi.'

Momma would be proud of how good I've learned to make my own bunk. If the Sergeant can't bounce a fifty cent piece off of it, we get a demerit. We call them 'gigs'. Get three gigs and you're assigned to barracks over the weekend and given jobs to do. My bunk, footlocker and area around my bunk are spotless. I don't want to spend any weekends at this place.

One week I got two gigs. One was for a dust ball under my bunk, and the other was because the half dollar didn't bounce right. When I say that these fellas up here mean business, I'm not kidding.

But the big news is that since I've been up here, I've struck up quite a friendship. We really hit it off. My buddy's name is TR Royce. He's from the East Coast. TR works harder than anybody else here, besides me, and he's a real stand-up guy. I'm sure he'll make it through to the end.

The people here in Battle Creek treat us like kings. When we go off base, they pay for our checks and buy us drinks.

I'm realizing there's an awful lot of good people in the United States, and this war seems to be bringing out the best in most of them. I'll keep you posted on my next move, and how I fare in my training. Nose to the grindstone.

I think of all of you all the time, and I pray for Mo.

I love you all.

Max

Edward finished reading the letter. Cecilia and Mary could see that Edward was tearing up at the end. Cecilia got up and moved over to the arm of Edward's chair and put her arm around his shoulder.

"Eddie, Maxie sounds like he's doing just fine. Don't worry about those boys. They're coming back home to us. I just know it."

Mary looked at Edward with a very reassuring look.

"You've done all you could for our boys, Edward. They are in God's hands now. He'll watch over them."

CHAPTER FIFTY

Burma February 1944

A line of soldiers stretched almost three quarters of a mile, marching on a low mountainside dirt path approximately twenty feet wide. The mountain rose steeply on the left of the path, rocky and with very little vegetation. Below the men on the right side started the tree line, thickening into deep jungle further down the side of the mountain. Far to the bottom, moving swiftly, was the Irrawaddy River.

Every soldier of the two-thousand-man troop wore a full pack to go with his weapons. Groups of one hundred men marched two by two, separated by breaks of about fifty yards. Bringing up the rear of the march were several hundred pack mules fully loaded with supplies and heavy weapons.

The sun blazed down with oppressive heat in a cloudless sky, as a junior officer walked next to another officer toward the front of the column.

"The men look a little ragged sir."

The officer turned to a soldier with a radio gear backpack next to him.

"We'll break for ten. Let 'em know."

"Yes sir." Into his mouthpiece, he alerted those behind. "Check down ten."

The troops began to get the word, and down the line soldiers popped off their packs and set them down next to their weapons. Their shirts were soaked with sweat as they sat on their packs or an available rock. The men took out canteens and drank, with many going into the tree line to relieve themselves.

The commanding officer, standing and drinking from his canteen, scanned the area, studying ahead and down into the jungle below.

"Anything back from recon patrol?"

"Yes sir. Everything's clear next five thousand meters. They're sittin' tight."

"Good. We just crossed into Burma a few days ago. I'd sure as hell like to get in a little further before we run across any Japs."

Mo, Tex, Riley and Duke were all sitting on a rock outcropping toward the front of the line as the troops rested. "Does anybody know where we're goin' or how far?" Tex asked no one in particular.

Riley looked over.

"Hell no. Don't even know if the head man up there knows. Doesn't seem like they're gonna tell anybody. 'Cuz what happens if Japs get a hold on any of us? They'd torture the hell out of us. But if you don't know anything, you can't tell 'em anything."

"I already told you guys Japs ain't takin' me alive", snarled Duke. "If I go, I'm takin' a bunch of those bastards with me."

Mo, sitting on the rock smoking a short government issue cigarette, just looked over at Duke smiling.

"You'll get your chance pretty soon Duke. We've been marching six days now and haven't seen hide nor hair of those damn little rascals. I'm gettin' so I kind of expect 'em around every bend now. They're out there somewhere."

Riley jumped in.

"I sure wish I could tell everybody back home what we're doin'. They wouldn't believe where the hell we are. We just keep getting deeper and deeper into this damn jungle. I'd like to write my folks a letter."

"I sure as hell don't see any post offices around, so that ain't gonna happen Riley," answered Tex. "I thought I lived out in the boonies back in Texas. Hell, this place makes where I come from look like a big city."

Mo mustered a laugh. "You got that one right Tex. I was just thinking the same thing. Makes Springfield look like New York City. At least I think it does, since I've never been to New York City. But anyway, how could anybody live in this Godforsaken place?"

An officer walked down the road as he rousted the troops.

"Load up men. Moving in two minutes."

Narration

Evil doers, when they pass from this world, will see Paradise, but only for the most fleeting of moments. They will catch sight of what they could have inherited. Realization of their squandered opportunity will be their last instant. But the pure of heart will not only see Paradise, they will partake of the banquet. Angels are created anew on a constant basis.

CHAPTER FIFTY-ONE

A hundred or so people stood outside St. Joseph's Church as Mary Gordon's casket was carried down the steps by six men. The first on each side of the casket were Edward Vernon and Max, in full uniform. They moved to the back of the waiting hearse, carefully sliding the casket into place before the driver closed the back door.

All of Mary's girls were there, including Della with her husband. Every neighbor from Black Avenue was there. Mary was much loved. Janey Ryan stood with the group, using her crutches. Edward and Max walked back over to Cecilia and the other girls, all of whom were crying. "I asked the driver to wait for a bit before starting the procession to the cemetery, Ceil," said Edward. "It will give us a chance to thank some of the neighbors who won't be going."

Edward then turned to the sisters.

"You girls be strong for your mom. Go around and talk to these people and thank them for coming. They've all known you since you were born."

All the girls except Cecilia moved out among the mourners, hugging and thanking those who came to pay their respects, leaving Cecilia, Edward, Janey and Max.

"I feel so sad I couldn't be here for Momma when she passed away," said Max.

Cecilia reached over and put her arm around Max.

"Maxie, one of the last things Momma heard was that you had become an officer. She was so proud of you, getting ready to go to Washington and serve your country."

"That's right Max," added Edward.

Max continued as tears welled in his eyes.

"Mo doesn't even know Momma's gone. There's no way to even let him know."

"It's a blessing he doesn't, Max. And you need to go and be the best soldier you can be and not think about it too much," said Edward.

"Eddie's right, Max. It's hard enough on you, but at least you get to be here with the family. Mo would be devastated, being so alone wherever he is. It's better Mo doesn't know," said Janey. "Your mom was such a beautiful person. I loved her."

"She loved you too, Janey," said Cecilia. Max looked over at the hearse bearing his Mother's casket.

"Momma really was a great woman, a strong woman."

"Yes she was Maxie," answered Cecilia. "And we have a lot to be thankful for. Momma got to pass away while she was sitting in her favorite chair. When Eddie went in and found Momma, he called me into the front room. Momma had the most peaceful look on her face, and she was holding her rosary in her hands. She had been praying to the Blessed Mother and reciting the rosary every day for both of you boys since you left."

"Janey, thank you for singing 'The Lord's Prayer' during the service," said Max. "It was just what Momma would have wanted. You did a wonderful job."

"It was beautiful, Janey, thank you," offered Eddie.

"Mary touched my heart, Eddie. It was my honor to sing for her."

Edward looked over in the direction of the hearse.

"Well, I think we're about ready to go. The driver is giving me the signal for the procession to start."

Max looked at Eddie.

"OK, Eddie. Let's go lay Momma to rest."

CHAPTER FIFTY-TWO

Library of Congress Building Washington DC

Inside a cavernous room with row upon row of shelves filled with books, and almost thirty tables running between them, Max Gordon and TR Royce were hard at work as they sat at side-by-side tables. Books were piled high on each man's table as they wrote on pads of paper.

Without warning, TR slammed his pencil down on the table.

"Max, we've been working on this clerical crap for two months now. This is not what I signed up for!"

Stopping, Max put down his pencil and looked over at his friend.

"I know exactly where you're coming from, TR. I signed up to fight Nazis, not work on a new Army Manual."

"If we're here much longer, I'm going to call my father." Max's eyes arched as he heard his friend's statement.

"Your family has a phone? They turned ours off in Springfield a couple of months after Pearl Harbor. And if you could call, what would your dad do, write his congressman for you?"

"Max, my dad is Senator Russell Royce from Massachusetts. Our phone works. And I'd also like to know if he has anything to do with us being here."

Max looked over with an astonished look on his face.

"No way. All this time we've been palling around and you didn't tell me that?"

"Max, we've become good friends. I need to know who my friends are before they know who my dad is. You know what I mean?"

"Yeah, I guess I can understand that."

"Do you want to know what the TR stands for?"

"What?"

"Theodore Roosevelt Royce. My dad thought Teddy Roosevelt was our greatest President. He did, until FDR became our President. Now he has a new favorite."

"Yeah, Teddy was a good one alright. The great trust buster who worked more for the common man than the robber barons."

Sitting back in his chair, Max mused.

"Wow, I'm buddies with a Senator's son. A guy from the north side of Springfield hobnobbing with Washington DC royalty. That is really something."

"Let's just keep this between the two of us, OK Max?"

Max made like a zipper across his mouth with his hand. "My lips are sealed, Theodore."

"Don't start getting funny now Max. It's TR!"

"Okay. Okay."

CHAPTER FIFTY-THREE
Letter to Janey

My Dearest Janey,

The days are long here. I'm on the other side of the world marching through Burma, and nobody knows we're here except some of the bigwigs in the army and Washington, I guess.

We've stopped for the night, just had rations, and it's still light enough to write. My buddies think I'm keeping a journal of our march, and I guess they're pretty much correct. Someday, these letters will tell a story.

So far though, the story isn't interesting, unless endless marching deeper and deeper into the jungle can keep your attention. Instead, what keeps me going are two things. The men who serve with me, and thoughts of home.

Here I am sitting on a hollowed out log in dense jungle, and I'm going to write about home. I have so many memories of Springfield and every person back there. They all seem so good to me now, even when I think back to when Max and I were little guys and we were in the middle of the depression.

Eddie would take us downtown on most Saturday mornings for breakfast at Strong's Cafe. We could go through the line as many times as we wanted. We used to eat 'til our stomachs hurt. They had the best hot cinnamon rolls you ever tasted.

I even remember when we would walk down the street after breakfast. I can still see the looks on people's faces. People were hurting, but so many held their heads high. The men would wear long sleeves with neckties, coats and hats, even if it was ninety degrees. Their clothes might have been tattered, but they were clean and pressed.

I remember when Max and I would wait for Eddie and Cecilia outside the fences at the Sangamo Electric plant. At four o'clock the whistle would blow. You could hear it all over the neighborhood. The workers would start flooding out of the doors of the factory, then finally we'd see Eddie and Cecilia come out and we'd all walk home together.

I remember when momma would ask me to go into the basement to put coal in the furnace. It's the only place I've ever been afraid of. It was always dark down there, and I was always sure something was down there waiting for me.

I remember Eddie feeding the birds in the winter. He'd shovel our long walkway from the house to the alley. The birds would be lined up on the wires on both sides of the yard. Eddie would start putting seed on the walkway and birds would swoop down to eat from both sides before the first seed could hit the walkway. By the time Eddie would come inside the house, the entire walk was covered with Edward's feathered friends.

I remember Eddie more than anything. He always called himself just a common man, but he's the most uncommon man I know. The kind of guy that bought food for neighbors when they had no money. He was always ready to take care of somebody else.

I remember going up to the farm with Max when Eddie would take us with him. We'd look at the corn and wheat, and run in the forested area looking for frogs and snakes. A lot of the times up at the farm, Eddie, Max and I would go into Havana for a big catfish dinner. Nothing better than Sangamon River catfish!

Sometimes Eddie's friend 'Cholly' would come with us

during mushroom season. We'd go through the forest on Eddie's farm 'shroomin'. 'Cholly' always knew the good mushrooms from the bad ones. I want to do all those things again, or do them with my kids someday. I don't know what tomorrow will bring, but thinking of sharing new memories with you is something I know will happen.

Getting too dark to write, and we march at dawn.
Time to put away this letter.
Love, Mo

CHAPTER FIFTY-FOUR

Dachau Germany

Abraham was writing at the table in the center of the room, laboring over a small book. Golde kept busy sewing on a machine off to the side which had been brought in so tailoring could be done for the Commandant's uniforms. One of his jackets was in front of her as she worked. The door opened, and Aaron entered, as Abraham looked up from his writing.

"How did the children's lessons go today?"

"They are both musical, Father. And they are good students. I find them to be good children."

"That is good then."

"Father, I don't think the Commandant is an evil man."

"It is not always necessary for a man to be evil yet take part in evil things. I do not condemn him for what he does. It is not our place to condemn. I think he tries to keep his family alive. Perhaps if it were just him alone, his choices would be different."

"Father, since the Commandant has furnished you with writing materials, you work so hard to document life in the camps. Why? No one will ever see them."

"They may never be seen. But if they can be preserved, I want to give testimony to what our people endure. History should know of the humanity and moral values so many of our people have shown. It should also document the degree of cruelty that depraved humans are capable. These are things which should survive long after we are gone."

"I think we will all die at the hands of the Nazis," answered Aaron.

Golde looked up from her work at Aaron.

"Aaron. We all die sooner or later. The good and the bad will die. There is only one who knows when that day will be, and it shall not happen until the appointed time. You are young and strong. You must never give up hope. Promise me, your Mother."

Walking over, Aaron leaned down and kissed his Mother tenderly on her cheek, then answered. "For you, then, Mother. I will never give up."

CHAPTER FIFTY-FIVE

Washington DC

TR and Max were working at their desks when their commanding officer, Major Thomas Brandwyn walked into the large hall. Both men jumped to their feet and saluted, standing at attention. The Major saluted back as he as he observed the stacks of books on each man's desk.

"At ease gentlemen. I have news for the two of you. New orders have been issued, and they take effect immediately. Next week, you board the converted ocean liner 'Ile De France', to cross the Atlantic. She's fast enough to avoid the U-boats, so you won't be in a convoy. Your crossing will take ten days. Here's the good news men. Until then, you've been granted liberty through the weekend here in Washington."

TR was first to respond. "Finally! That is great news Sir! Thank you, Sir!"

"Yes Sir," said Max. "It's been a pleasure working for you here, but we both want to get in this war."

The Major looked at Max with a grin on his face.

"Max, I know damn well that you've hated every minute here working on the manual. But I must say that despite not wanting to be here, you've both done a hell of a job."

"Thank you, Sir. But I do mean it when I say it was a pleasure to get to know you."

"Well, I've tried to do my best while I'm stuck here too,

Max. Perhaps you two lads can keep in touch after this damn war is over. I'd like nothing better than to see where both of you end up. No limits on the two of you, I'm sure."

"Thank you, Sir," answered TR. "Do you know where we're going?"

"Yes. Upon arrival in London, you will both work out of the British Military College at Sandhurst. You will be learning German, French, social customs, school systems, public health and agriculture. As we push the Germans back, your jobs will be to make sure the systems of local government begin functioning again."

Max looked over at TR with a puzzled look on his face.

"Then we won't be up fighting the war?"

"Max, you will certainly find it dangerous enough. The Germans bomb London daily. Do your jobs well and you will save lives. What you will be doing is as important as firing a gun for your country. That's all men. Thank you for your work here. And good luck to both of you." The Major shook each man's hand, then turned and left the large hall. Max looked at TR, disgruntled.

"I want to fire a gun for my country."

"I know Max, but what the hell. At least we're getting out of Washington and to where some of the action is. Major says they bomb daily. We're not getting any of that over here. Might get exciting."

"Yeah, we're heading to a place where we could get blown up. What could be more exciting than that?"

CHAPTER FIFTY-SIX

New York Harbor

A thick mist fell under a grey sky. The 'Ile De France' sat at rest at the dock as soldiers streamed up the gangplank. Families all around, huddled under umbrellas, were saying their goodbyes to soldiers. Senator Royce's entire family surrounded TR as he prepared to board the liner to go to London.

The Senator put his hand on TR's shoulder and looked him in the eye as he spoke.

"TR, take care of yourself over there. Use common sense and keep me posted."

"Yes Sir. And I'll write as regular as I can."

TR gave his sisters and Mother hugs and kisses, then turned back toward his Father. "Dad, don't you pull strings to keep me safe. Stay out of the way, OK?"

"Absolutely, TR. Your commanding officers will be telling you where to go and when. It won't be me. I have no influence with the military."

"OK, then."

TR shook his Father's hand, grabbed his bulging duffel and tossed it easily over his shoulder before saluting to his family, a big smile on his face.

"Okay then, folks. Don't worry about me. I'm heading over to kick some Kraut ass."

At that remark, TR's sisters giggled and laughed, their big brother using language they had never heard from him.

As TR walked briskly up the gangplank, he stopped to turn around to wave at the family.

The Senator moved over next to his wife and put his arm around her waist as they watched TR disappear into the throngs of servicemen on the ship's deck. TR's mother turned to her husband with a worried look.

"Russell. There are so many men getting on that ship who will never come back. Is there anything you can do to help keep TR safe?"

The Senator looked over at his wife with a reassuring look.

"Already taken care of my dear. Don't you worry."

CHAPTER FIFTY-SEVEN

Dachau Germany

Aaron was in the living room of the Commandant's villa with his two pupils, Erich and Greta. Erich played one selection of music well as his sister watched, as Aaron listened intently. The Commandant was out of sight in the hallway, but listened to the lesson as it proceeded. When Erich finished, he waited for Aaron's appraisal.

"Erich, that was excellent! You and Greta are natural musicians. If you continue as you are doing, you could someday play first violin in a major symphony orchestra."

"I would like that," answered Erich. "Aaron, you are the best violin player in the world! Will you play first violin in the symphony someday?"

Aaron looked at both of the children for a moment before he answered. "One day I may get the chance to play the violin for people to hear. One day I may play with a symphony."

Erich then went on with his questions.

"Aaron, I would like to play in Berlin for our great Fuhrer. Do you think I will play for him someday if I practice very hard?"

Hesitating once more before he answered, Aaron finally did.

"No doubt you will play in front of many powerful and famous people, too many to even list."

This answer satisfied Erich, when his sister asked Aaron a question.

"Aaron, you live inside the fences, don't you?"

"Yes, with my Mother and Father."

"What is it like on the other side of the fences, and why do you have to stay there?"

Aaron thought for a moment before he answered.

"While Germany is at war, they must keep some people separated. It is for the security of the people."

"The guards in the towers are protecting the people inside the fences?"

"They watch over us."

Erich then spoke.

"Our Father commands all of the guards."

"Yes he does Erich."

"So he takes care of you while he commands them as they watch over you."

"Yes. And your Father gives assistance to some who live behind the fences. He gives food and medicine."

"Then our Father is a very good man to help them, is he not?"

"When your Father helps, he is a good man, yes."

When Aaron had finished this statement, the Commandant walked quickly into the room, as though he were coming from another part of the villa.

"Children, lessons are over for today. How did they do today, Aaron?"

"They play beautifully. They are gifted."

"Wonderful! Now Aaron, let me walk you out into the street."

As the two men approached the road in front of the house, the Commandant stopped Aaron, putting his hand on his shoulder.

"Aaron, I could not help but overhear some questions from my children and the answers you gave. Thank you."

"Commandant. You have two fine children. They will never learn of suffering or hatred from me."

"Once again, Aaron, thank you."

Aaron nodded, then turned and walked down the road to return to life behind the fences.

CHAPTER FIFTY-EIGHT

Hundreds of uniformed men filled a voluminous auditorium. The architecture was very intricate with carvings of Gothic creatures under the wooden balconies which ringed the entire building.

The concrete floors were old and worn smooth from centuries of use, but spotlessly clean. The tall ceilings appeared as ornate as the balconies, with heavy solid wood beams and carved corbels. There was, however, somewhat of an acrid moldy smell which permeated the great hall.

Every man sat in an individual seat with a clipboard on his lap for note taking. TR and Max were in the center toward the front of the room paying close attention to the man in front on the stage, as were the other men in attendance. The speaker, an older man, wore a uniform with a chest full of ribbons and medals. His face was thin with a neatly trimmed white mustache, and he wore frameless glasses with round lenses.

"We've been covering a lot of territory in a short amount of time, and you all seem to be sticking with me quite well. Excellent! It does seem so much easier being an instructor when the students' very lives depend on grasping the subject. So.."

The speaker's voice trailed off as he turned and walked

the length of the stage, looking out at the men. Then, he turned again and paced completely down to the opposite end, not saying a word. Finally, moving to the center, he faced the assembly.

"I have one final point to impress upon all of you today, of utmost importance. You must be smart in how you write home to your sweethearts, or your mommies."

A laugh erupted from the men.

"Yes, that may seem funny, but listen up, men! Never give location. Do not discuss numbers of troops. No one need know your mission, training details or assignments. We do not want to help the enemy should your letters fall into the wrong hands. This is serious business, Gentlemen. We are at war with a ruthless enemy. Your lives and many other lives are at stake. Remember that! Alright then, that's it for today. I thank you for your attention. You are dismissed."

CHAPTER FIFTY-NINE

Boston Massachusetts

Senator Royce was with the family at the dining table having lunch when their butler Willis came into the room.

"Senator, looks like a letter from TR from London."

Willis walked over to the Senator and handed him the envelope.

"Thank you, Willis. I've been wondering when the young man would take the time to drop us a line."

The Senator's wife put down her silverware and sat up, waiting to hear the news from Europe. "Russell, why don't you read the letter to all of us right now?"

"Of course I will."

Willis had not moved since handing the Senator the envelope.

"Willis, sit yourself right down at the table! I know you're as interested as the rest of us to hear this."

Willis hurried to an empty chair, and as he sat, he smiled at the Senator and the family.

"Thank you, Senator."

The Senator's wife looked over at Willis.

"You had an important part in raising TR, Willis. We know how much you love him."

"Yes Ma'am. Thank you."

The Senator opened the envelope and studied its contents before he began to read.

Dear Mom, Dad, my beautiful sisters and Willis,

The Senator stopped and looked down the table at Willis, who was beaming after hearing his name.

I'm speaking passable French and German now, and learning that customs in Europe can be much different than ours. After being here only a short time, however, I also realize different nations and people have more similarities than differences.

Max Gordon and I are still moving through the Army together. Our orders have been lock-step. I've found out Max is a Catholic, as I suspected when he told me he graduated from Loyola. But that doesn't prevent us from getting along great. If Max is any barometer, there's not much difference between Catholics and Protestants.

We're not on the front lines, but there's no doubt we are in a war zone. Air raids from the Germans are every night, lasting about thirty or forty minutes. You have to be somewhat stupid to stay out and watch the show, as occasionally people are hit with shrapnel if a bomb happens to go off near where they are. I have to admit that Max and I are guilty of being stupid once in a while, but it is quite the show to see.

You are able to follow the paths of the bombers by watching anti-aircraft fire. Giant lights search the sky, and when they locate a plane, cross beams keep it in view for the ground gunners.

When a bomber gets hit, you watch it as it falls from the sky. The scenes are spectacular, certainly more memorable than any Fourth of July.

Hundreds of volunteers risk their lives to get people off the streets, and many die or are injured every night. When the raid ends, other volunteers have the damage cleared in the morning and things get boarded up. Some days, you would hardly know there was a bombing the night before. The English suffer much

and complain little. I for one am proud to have them as allies.
I think of you all, and hope everyone is well.
I miss you and love you. Take care.
TR

CHAPTER SIXTY

Dachau Germany

Aaron was finishing the children's music lesson when the Commandant came in the room.

"Children, your dinner is ready. Go in and sit with your Mother at the table after you wash up. I will be in shortly. I want to talk to Aaron."

"Yes Father," both children answered as they got up to leave the room. When they reached the hallway, they both turned around.

"Goodbye Aaron."

"Goodbye Erich. Goodbye Greta."

"Aaron, let me walk you out to the street."

When the men reached the roadway out front of the villa, they stopped. "Aaron, I've been called to Berlin and will be taking the family with me. The Fuhrer has called a meeting with all the heads of the labor camps. We will be gone three or four weeks, so there will be no lessons during this time. I have left orders for my men. Things will continue uninterrupted for your family and those you choose to help while I am gone."

"Thank you, Sir. Have the children practice while you are away."

"They will. I appreciate all you do for them Aaron. They like you very much."

"I like the children. I like teaching them."

"Very well then. I will see you when we return."

Aaron walked down the road as the Commandant watched him until he disappeared from view.

CHAPTER SIXTY-ONE

Burma

Riley, Tex and Duke were lying on their bedding relaxing. Mo wrote in his journal while there was still light to see. Men stretched out along the road in both directions for a quarter mile.

Guards patrolled on the roadway, strolling among the men sprawled out.

Duke got up on one elbow and looked around at the others in the group.

"Seems like we been marching forever now, and haven't seen one Jap. I'm losin' track of the damn days."

Riley, lying on his back looking up at the sky, answered. "Yeah, Duke, I know what you mean. An' while we're marching in the jungles, I feel like someone's watching us the whole time, but nothin' happens."

Mo looked up from his writing.

"We're bein' watched alright, but it ain't the Japs. The natives know we're here but they're invisible. They're steerin' clear of us. They don't know if we're the good guys or the bad guys."

"We're the good guys," said Tex. "This whole damn war is about good against evil. We're the good and the Japs are the evil."

Still leaning on his elbow, Duke answered.

"Damn right Tex. And that's why we're gonna kick their asses and win this war. The good guys always win in the movies and we're gonna make sure it's just like the ending in the movies."

"Yeah, only this time it's real bullets."

Putting away his notebook, Mo looked at the others.

"You know guys, life has some crazy twists. I was just thinking about a buddy I have from Springfield. I remember back when I was a little guy and got into trouble for fighting with the neighborhood bully, Tommy Kelso. Later in high school, we became good friends, played on the same football team. You never know what's going to happen. We ended up enlisting in the army on the same day. I don't know where Tommy is now, what with our men scattered all over the world. I was just sitting here and it hit me as kinda crazy."

Then, getting back to the conversation everyone was talking about, Mo added. "I got a feeling we're gonna get plenty of action pretty soon fellas. I think all hell's getting ready to break loose."

"Well I'm ready!" exclaimed Duke.

"Me too," added Tex.

Looking at the other men with a big grin, Riley boomed. "Me three!"

"I guess that makes four of us then," said Mo.

Narration

There come times in all human lives when choices are made.

Roads laid out, with different directions offered. Some decisions are easily made, others difficult. These paths will determine, one after the other, an ultimate destination.

CHAPTER SIXTY-TWO

Burma

Dim light just began to illuminate the eastern sky. The coolness of the air belied the oppressive heat of the coming day's march. A sentry moved along the road rousting sleeping GIs. As he moved down the road, he repeated the same line with gusto.

"Time to move ladies. Sunrise. Shit, eat and roll in twenty. Let's go."

Riley pulled himself up to a seated position and looked at the rest of the men still horizontal.

"Well, we made it to another wretched day. Question is, do we make it to tomorrow?"

Tex stood, then ripped a growling fart.

"Jesus. You better check your britches with that one, Tex," said Riley.

"Nah, but I am gonna go take a King Kong dump," answered Tex.

"Please do," said Mo, as he stood and stretched his arms over his head.

All along the road, troops rustled, ate and fulfilled nature's call. On time, every man on the road was ready to move.

The men marched down the side of an open mountaintop, toward thick jungle below. As they marched, men exchanged small talk on occasion, but most marching was silent as the soldiers kept their eyes trained on what might be ahead or in the deep jungle to their right.

After two hours of marching, the commanding officer at the front stopped and issued an order to his radio operator.

"We stop here. Let the men eat something and relieve themselves. Get recon patrol on the radio in ten minutes. I want a report."

"Yes Sir."

The word traveled quickly and the soldiers stopped to unload packs and weapons.

Mo's group sat, breaking out rations.

"I'm sure as hell glad we stopped. My belly's been growling for a half hour," said Riley.

Tex, eating out of a can like he hadn't seen food in a week, concurred.

"Me too, Riley."

Duke finished off a can of k-rations, stood up, and let out some wind of his own.

"Duke, you're right next to me man!" exclaimed Mo. "Go take a shit, dude."

"I'm planning on it. Just gotta grab me some wipin' paper."

Duke headed over toward the jungle on the right side of the road, going far enough into the growth to be out of view, pulled down his pants and squatted. Close to the ground, Duke noticed movement off in the jungle away from the road. As he peered into the jungle, he saw a Japanese soldier stand and motion to other soldiers.

"Oh my God. Dammit!"

Duke stood up, trying to pull up his pants as he ran back to the others while holding onto his belt. As he hit the clearing, he yelled at the closest radioman and the others.

"Japs in the jungle about a hundred yards in!"

Everyone within earshot jumped to grab their weapons and helmets, while the radio operator yelled into his headset.

"Japs sighted in jungle one hundred yards east!"

Within seconds, the entire line of men was scrambling for weapons all along the road.

At the front of the column, the commander looked at his radioman.

"How'd they get by recon? Why didn't they warn us?"

The radio operator looked at the officer.

"Can't get recon on the radio, Sir."

"Dammit. We're sitting ducks on this road. Get everyone to the jungle. Set up a line and start moving in. If they see the enemy, shoot!"

The radio operator got on the radio. "All platoons move into the jungle. Hold your lines together. Advance toward the enemy and engage."

Duke grabbed his weapon and helmet to join the others.

"I still got poop all over my ass. These damn Japs!"

"This is it, boys." Mo said in a low voice to the men closest to him. "Let's give 'em Hell!"

The men ran into the first row of jungle trees, then started slowly advancing. They moved about twenty or thirty yards before heavy machine gun fire started blistering through the jungle, splintering the shafts of big trees and shredding the foliage.

The men hit the deck, trying to take cover behind anything they could, and started shooting back into the direction where the gunfire was coming at them. Mo and his group were flat on their backs behind the trunk of a fallen tree, which was getting blown apart by large caliber bullets.

A soldier out in the open nearby was hit and fell to the ground, unable to move. Mo left his weapon and crawled on his belly, then pulled the soldier back behind the log. Blood spurted from the soldier's shoulder. Mo reached into his pants, pulled out a big kerchief, wadded it up and crammed it into the hole in the man's shoulder.

"You'll be OK. Hold this in here. Push hard on it so you don't lose any more blood. Medics'll get you. Understand? Push hard! Stay alert!"

The soldier grimaced and nodded. Gunfire still exploded all around. Duke was lying on his back, holding his rifle up over the log, firing wildly toward the enemy position.

"None of our guys can move. We're pinned down. Can't even see the bastards! They've got some big caliber guns set up out there. We're getting ripped up!"

Mo was on his back, sweat streaming down his face.

"Guys, give me your grenades. Mo opened the bag hanging around his neck and yanked out the canteen, throwing it aside. Grabbing the grenades as the men gave them to him, he stuffed them into the bag, grabbed his bayonet and let go of his rifle.

"I'll be leavin' this baby here. Start firing like crazy. Try to give me cover. I'm gonna crawl up close and lob these babies."

Bullets were zinging overhead, and men were getting hit.

Riley looked at Mo with wide eyes.

"That's not a good idea Mo. You're gonna be killed!"

"And sitting here is a good idea? Just cover my ass and don't shoot me by mistake."

Mo stuck his bayonet between his teeth and started crawling flat like an insect, super-fast, and stayed as close to the foliage on the jungle floor as possible. Mo got about forty more yards out, bullets still whizzing over his head toward the men he had left behind, when he saw the first line of shooters. They stretched ahead along a line one hundred yards wide. Large caliber machine guns working non-stop behind sandbagged areas.

Mo rolled over, then looked up through the canopy of the jungle that loomed over him. He grabbed his canteen bag, now crammed with grenades, put it in front of him on his chest and opened the flap. He grabbed two grenades in his left hand, got poised and leapt to his feet, pulling both pins and rifling them through the trees straight at the closest machine gun position.

They were direct hits, each grenade sending Jap soldiers and big guns flying in the explosions.

Back at the American position, Duke screamed.

"Hold fire. That's Gordon!"

Jap positions on the flanks turned their attention toward Mo as he grabbed two more grenades, pulled the pins, and lobbed one to the right and one to the left. Each grenade found its mark, with Japanese guns on both sides getting blown away. Mo clutched the bayonet in his mouth as he ran straight at the Jap positions, closing to throw more grenades. He hit every target with precision.

Back at the American lines, big guns now silenced along this section, American soldiers jumped up and started sprinting toward the Jap positions.

Mo threw his last two grenades for strikes further down the line. Bullets were scorching by Mo, none hitting. Mo reached the first bunker as a Japanese soldier started to wheel around with his weapon. Mo flew through the air, tackled the Japanese soldier and stabbed him with his bayonet. He grabbed the dead soldier's weapon and started firing as Japanese soldiers were falling back in retreat. The firefight continued as other Americans reached Mo's position from where they were.

Duke yelled at Mo.

"Mo, you OK? You hit?" Mo yelled back.

"These sons of bitches are really bad shots!"

Duke only shook his head as he ran forward.

"Jesus, Gordon!"

As the Americans overran the Japanese along this stretch, they circled behind the other machine gun posts. Caught in a crossfire with the Americans now coming through the jungle, the Japanese were soon overwhelmed by the superior numbers of American soldiers. A complete victory was in hand.

CHAPTER SIXTY-THREE

Burma

Activity was thick on the road. Medics attended to wounded. A row of bodies lay in a line, jackets covering the heads and shoulders of the dead. Guards patrolled the edge of the jungle, on alert for any rogue Japanese who may have somehow eluded the Americans.

A soldier in full gear approached the commanding officer, a Captain, who stood with a group of officers under a tarp. The commanding officer stopped and addressed the soldier.

"What do you have to report young man? What's the damage?"

"Sir. All patrols have reported. There's no more enemy within two miles unless they're hiding in a log. We killed 'em all sir. The ones we didn't kill seemed to have killed themselves rather than be taken alive.

The Captain looked around at the other men. "These sons of bitches would rather die than be captured. Poor bastards have been brainwashed!"

The reporting soldier broke into reporting again.

"Sir?"

"Yes soldier?"

"Once we broke through their lines about five hundred yards back, our men circled around, hitting them from behind and on both flanks. And we recovered eight heavy machine guns that weren't damaged, with ammunition."

The Captain smiled and nodded approval at this news.

"It was damn nice of those Japs to get those guns this deep into the jungle for us. I'm sure we can put those into good use."

Looking back down the road toward the soldiers moving about, he continued.

"God knows this must be the best damn bunch of marksmen in the entire United States Army."

The reporting soldier still stood, not moving.

"Do you have something more to report soldier?"

"Not good news Sir. We have wounded and twenty-four died."

The Captain's face turned solemn. "Twenty-four damn good men. Brave men. Great men. I want a good spot found to bury these men. The Chaplain will conduct a service. And I want the tags from every soldier that died today."

"Yes Sir. We have five wounded who need to be flown back over the hump. Three others refuse to go back with only minor wounds. They want to go further in with the others."

"Get me twenty men to take the five wounded back to the clearing we passed two kilometers back. It's long enough for the piper cub to land. Let's get that plane there to rendezvous by the time our men arrive. When the wounded have been picked up, the others can double time it to catch us."

"Right away Sir. One final thing, Sir."

"What's that soldier?"

"It's traveling fast through the men. They tell me one soldier was responsible for us breaking their lines. First he went into the line of fire to pull a wounded soldier into cover. Then he went on a suicide mission throwing perfect grenade strikes at their machine gun positions. Thing is, Sir, he made it. Without getting killed. Didn't even get hit."

"One man? I want to meet that soldier. Find out where he is and take me to him."

"Yes Sir!"

CHAPTER SIXTY-FOUR

Burma

Mo, Tex, Riley and Duke relaxed with a group of soldiers, eating, smoking and talking among themselves. Riley attended to a deep cut on Mo's face and put on a butterfly bandage to close the wound. Mo had a cigarette dangling from his lips.

"You're gonna have a good lookin' scar on this cheek, Mo. You ain't as pretty as you were before."

"That's OK with me Riley. At least I'm here."

Suddenly, everyone jumped to their feet when they heard a command. "Ten Hut!"

The Captain, accompanied by four other lesser officers, walked into their midst.

The Captain stood and looked over the group of men, then spoke.

"I understand this group led the charge through the jungle today and overtook the Japanese machine gun positions. I want to congratulate you on your bravery."

Riley waited only an instant for his opening before blurting out.

"Sir!"

"Yes soldier?"

Riley pointed at Mo next to him, effusive as he gave his description of the battle.

"It was Gordon here, like a damn crazy man. Took all our grenades and went runnin' straight at the machine guns, throwing grenades and blowin' 'em all up. If he hadn't done what he did, we all woulda been wiped out."

Now all the officers looked over at Mo, his cheek puffy with a deep gash with tape on it.

The Captain walked over to Mo and extended his hand toward Mo. Mo reached out and shook the officer's hand as the Captain addressed him.

"It's an honor to shake your hand soldier. Men like you are the reason we're going to win this war."

"Thank you, Captain. Just did what I needed to do at the time. My boys were gettin' shelled pretty bad."

The Captain kept his gaze on Mo for a moment, scanned around at the other men and officers, then smiled back at Mo. "Still. A hell of a day, soldier."

The Captain saluted his troops.

"Alright men, carry on."

After the officers had left, Duke walked over to Mo to shake his hand.

"Mo, I didn't know you'd turn out to be the baddest ass I ever met, maybe even a little crazy. You saved our lives and you're a legitimate hero. I'm proud as hell to know you."

"Duke, every guy who followed me into that hell fire today is a hero. If we stick together, we're all gonna make it out of here."

CHAPTER SIXTY-FIVE

London England

TR and Max walked up steps of a centuries old brick building on a teeming military base. Jeeps and trucks moved about, with soldiers all around. The sky was grey with clouds obscuring any hint of sunlight above, and the streets proved a recent downpour.

Inside one windowless office with the door closed, Captain Irwin Thrushwell sat at a large and very worn wooden desk. He finished writing, set his pen down and opened the bottom drawer on the right side of the desk, reaching down to produce a pint of whiskey. He unscrewed the cap and gulped a big swig, finishing the bottle. When he heard a knock on the door, he hurriedly screwed the cap back on the bottle before dropping the empty into a trashcan behind his desk.

"What is it?"

The door opened to reveal a pretty young woman in civilian clothes. "Captain Thrushwell, two American soldiers would like a word."

"Send them in."

TR and Max walked in, stood at attention, and saluted. The Captain waved them off, motioning for them to sit down.

"So it's you two. Again. I should have known. Lieutenants Royce and Gordon."

TR and Max exchanged a glance as they moved to the chairs in front of the Captain's desk.

With an impatient and disgusted tone, the Captain scowled at the men.

"Alright, who's going to talk first?"

TR leaned forward in his chair.

"Captain, our training at Sandhurst has wrapped up as you know. There are quite a few of us who wonder. When we are moving?"

"When are you moving? Gentlemen, move where?"

Max listened as TR peered at the Captain sitting across the desk from him.

"Well, you know, the European mainland. To fight the Germans."

The Captain sat back in his chair, put his hands together in a prayer fashion and spread his fingers wide in a thoughtful pose. "Of course. The European mainland. Let me see. Why don't we just run a couple thousand of our brightest officers across the channel so they can get their asses blown off."

The Captain paused, TR and Max silent.

"Listen you two. When I know something, anything, you'll be the first two I tell. This is the third bloody time I've seen your faces, and it's not doing a damn bit of good. If you both find it absolutely impossible to enjoy yourselves while awaiting further orders, go sit on your barracks bags and smoke a cigarette. Then, when you finish that cigarette, light up another one. Et cetera. Et cetera. Et cetera."

TR and Max did not say a word in response.

The Captain looked back down at papers on his desk, and as he ignored the eyes of both men before him, he waved his hand.

"You are both dismissed."

The men saluted as they both stood in unison.

"Yes Sir."

As the men were leaving the room, the Captain hailed them one more time. They both turned anxiously.

"Close the door behind you!"

"Yes Sir." When the door had closed, Thrushwell opened the same drawer and pulled out a full unopened pint of Whiskey. Holding it out in front of him, he admired it for a second, smiled, twisted off the top and took a big chug.

CHAPTER SIXTY-SIX

London England

TR and Max emerged from the army building after their meeting with Thrushwell, descended the steps and stopped next to the busy street. TR turned toward Max.

"Captain reeked of booze, Max."

"Tell me about it. Guess that's why everybody calls him 'old lushwell', huh?"

Both laughed.

"Well, we have free time, Max. What do you want to do? Ride our bikes to Oxford?"

"Nah. Let's take old lushwell's advice and enjoy ourselves while we wait for orders. How about we go to the Savoy and have lunch? I've been wanting to see that place since we got here. We might want to check it out before the Germans find it with a bomb."

"OK, you're on Max. And I'm buying today."

"Wow, big spender. You know that no place can charge more than five shillings for a meal now, right?"

"Why do you think I offered?"

When the two men reached the Savoy, a short line stood just inside waiting to be seated by the Maître D'. While the men waited, they looked around at one of London's most famous spots. The tables had white linens with perfectly placed china and silverware. The diners numbered about half civilians and half military, and included many couples. Waiters were dressed fit to serve the Queen, all with white gloves. As Max surveyed the scene, he remarked to TR.

"You wouldn't know there was a war going on by the looks of this place."

"Yeah. The only giveaway is all the uniforms."

When the men reached the reception podium of the Maître D', he looked up at the two handsome young Americans and smiled.

"Welcome Gentlemen. If you'll follow me. Right this way."

He escorted them to a table in the center of the room and when they were both seated, handed each man an oversized leather-bound menu. "Your waiter will be with you momentarily Gentlemen. Enjoy your lunch."

As the Maître D' walked away, TR and Max opened their menus. After only seconds, Max looked at TR.

"I can see it's going to take me awhile to make up my mind."

TR laughed.

"Me too. Let's see, sausages with potatoes and brussels sprouts or beef with potatoes and brussels sprouts. It's going to be a tough decision."

An older waiter hurried over to the table, his order book out.

"Have you Gentlemen had sufficient time to peruse our selections?"

Max gave the waiter a knowing look.

"Quite enough. After much deliberation, I believe I'll try the sausages."

"Very good, sir."

He looked at TR. "And you sir?"

"I'll be going for the beef. Looks delicious."

The waiter gave both soldiers a smile.

"Wonderful. Both excellent choices. I'll put in your orders immediately," as he took the men's menus and left the table.

As they sat, TR started conversation. "Max, this seems kind of strange. There's a full-blown war going on all over the globe, and we're getting ready to have lunch at the Savoy."

"We're only following orders. That's what you do in the army."

"I guess. Max, would you really want to be on the front lines?"

"I don't know if I'd want to be there, but if those were my orders, I don't think I'd be afraid to be there. I mean, there are thousands of young officers here in London waiting for orders. Like lushwell said, 'two thousand of the brightest officers.' Every guy at Sandhurst just came out of an advanced degree program back in the states. Lawyers, Doctors, Professors. They want us to do different kinds of things in this war than carry a rifle and I'm beginning to get that."

"Yeah, Max, you're right. But there are a lot of officers on the front lines too."

"Most of those officers graduated from one of the military colleges. You know, they studied battle theory or some other war related class, TR. Or maybe they're career soldiers or cops back home. Anyway, they've been training us for what we're going to be doing so we'd better be ready to do the best job we can once we get the chance."

"Right again, Max. I'm glad we had this talk."

"Me too. It's been on my mind. I've been thinking a lot about what we're going to be doing. It's a worthy job."

The men sat in silence for a bit, when Max noticed something in a booth against the wall, then pointed as inconspicuously as possible. "TR, over in the corner booth. The guy with the British Officer's uniform with that pretty young girl. That's David Niven, the actor."

TR turned to look, not being inconspicuous at all.

"Wow, what an operator. Takes that beautiful girl to lunch at the Savoy and it's only costing him ten shillings."

"Some guys really know how to do it, don't they TR?"

"Yeah. Some guys have it made, alright."

CHAPTER SIXTY-SEVEN

Dachau Germany

Aaron opened the door to the Gittelsohn's room to see Abraham giving Golde a drink of water, Abraham propping up her back with his hand. Aaron hurried over to the side of the bunk, and knelt next to his mother.

Golde looked at Aaron, her eyes with purple circles around them. Her cheeks sunken, her skin an ashen color. Perspiration covered her forehead.

"I need to rest, Abraham. I'm weak and have chills. My body has pain."

Abraham gently lowered Golde, putting a cool cloth on her forehead, then turned to his son. "Your mother's skin feels warm. She has a low fever. We will use a damp cool cloth to wipe her forehead. It will help lower the fever. We must help Golde drink much water."

"I will stay with her Father. You go to the barracks."

"We will both stay. There is not much we gain at the barracks while the Commandant is away. Though he said everything would be taken care of when he was gone, his men refuse to do anything."

"I will tell the Commandant when he returns," said Aaron.

"Perhaps, but that helps no one now. We will watch

over your mother. If she does not lower her fever, you go get the German doctor. Maybe this will pass and she will feel better in a day or two."

CHAPTER SIXTY-EIGHT

Burma

Mo and the others were around a small fire, drinking coffee and talking as they prepared to bed down for the night. All the men smoked a cigarette.

Duke stood with his coffee in one hand and cigarette in the other.

"They found recon team in the jungle. Japs butchered them up good. They coulda just killed 'em, instead they tortured the hell out of 'em."

"They were trying to get any information they could out of them before they killed them, Duke," said Mo.

Riley looked over at Mo. "I just feel real sorry for them guys. I just can't figure out how the hell they let themselves get captured. Those guys were supposed to be the sneakiest we got."

"Tells you something about the Japs. They're trickier than we were giving them credit for," said Tex.

"Yeah, I guess. I just don't know what to make of it," answered Riley. "And now we're short of recon and scouts out front of us."

Silence came over the group, each man in thought.

His cigarette dangled from his lips when Mo suddenly stood, yanked the cigarette out of his mouth, and addressed his three friends.

"The four of us will volunteer."

"Volunteer for what Mo?" asked Duke.

"Hell, we'll volunteer to be the new recon unit."

Riley looked at Mo.

"C'mon Mo. We can't do that."

"Why the hell not, Duke? Tex and you both said you'd been hunting and tracking since you were whippersnappers, didn't you?"

Both men answered at the same time.

"Yeah, uh huh."

"OK then." Mo paced a few steps then turned around. "Only difference is, we won't be hunting animals. We'll be hunting Japs." Mo paused as the men let this concept sink in.

"Anyway, they should be a lot easier to track than animals. Humans are stupid. They don't rely on instinct. C'mon guys, somebody's got to do it. Why not us?"

Duke looked at Mo.

"Mo Gordon. After what the hell you did back on the trail, I'm thinkin' any damn idea you get is a good one. I'm in."

Tex and Riley nodded in agreement, as Tex spoke up.

"Me and Riley agree. We're in too."

"OK then. Tomorrow morning the four of us go see the Captain."

CHAPTER SIXTY-NINE
Burma

At the first signs of light on the horizon to the east, soldiers all along the road rustled. Mo, Riley, Duke and Tex were packed and ready. They moved to their platoon leader about fifty yards forward who was sitting on his helmet eating. Mo walked up to him, standing slightly out front of the others.

"Sir, may we have a word?"

"Gordon, you just saved everybody's ass. Of course you can. I feel like I should fucking genuflect to you."

The other men standing behind Mo all smiled as they glanced at each other. "Sergeant, we'd like to volunteer to be the new recon patrol."

The Sergeant paused, looking at the four men standing in front of him before he answered.

"So now you wanna be our scouts?"

"Yes Sir," answered Mo in earnest. "Duke and Tex have been hunting and tracking their whole lives. We can do it."

The Sergeant got an amused look on his face.

"Think you boys are looking for wild pigs out there in those jungles?"

From behind Mo, Riley answered in his booming voice.

"No Sarge. We'll be hunting Japs. But when we run across 'em, we'll treat 'em like wild pigs."

The Sergeant's amused look turned to a full-blown smile.

"You can go to the front and run it by them. It's OK with me, men. Good luck."

"Thank you Sarge," said Mo.

A few hundred meters further up, the four soldiers reached the lead group. As they walked into the midst of troops getting ready to move out, they came across one of the junior officers who was with the Captain when he came back to meet Mo and the others after the firefight from earlier.

The men saluted and Mo started speaking for the group. "Sir, our platoon Sergeant gave us permission to come forward. We'd like to speak to the Captain if we could."

"What about soldier?"

"We want to volunteer for recon duty, Sir."

The officer had a surprised look.

"We just had a trained recon team ambushed and killed, and now you four want to do it?"

"Yes Sir!"

The officer studied the four men.

"Come with me."

The group moved to a bivouac tarp with a radio set up and a small folding table. The Captain and some officers were gathered as he pointed to a map set out on the table. As the four men and the officer entered the area, the men all turned, recognizing the four soldiers from their earlier meeting. The officer who had led them to the tent and the four GIs all saluted.

"Sir, these men have requested to talk to you."

"Good morning soldiers. What can I do for you?"

Mo addressed the Captain in front of the other men.

"Sir, we would like to volunteer for recon patrol. My men are expert trackers and hunters."

The officer looked around at the men standing with him, then at the four GIs in front of him. "Men, I appreciate what you're doing here, but you don't know these jungles. We're about ready to move off the road. We suspect the Japs know we're on the move. We can't travel in the open and we have four translators who know this area. They'll be recon backup for now."

Then, as he thought for a second, the Captain continued.

"But, with losing one of our recon patrols, we are shorthanded. We're heading to a Kachin village. They hate the Japanese. When we hit their village, we'll be deep in the jungle. Then we're blazing another route. When we reach the Kachins, we'll see how much they'll help us, maybe give us more guides. No one knows these jungles like they do. This is their home turf. If we get more guides I'll take your offer under consideration. Fair enough, gentlemen?"

"Yes Sir, thank you Sir."

Narration

Faith, Hope and Love. These are built on a solid foundation.

They will not wither. They will not decay. They are everlasting.

Evil exists not forever. Constantly changing, never permanent. It is only transitory. Though at times it appears to have strength, it is only an illusion. In reality it is weak.

Fear and paranoia spring forth, but having no firm permanent foundation, evil will crumble into oblivion in the end.

CHAPTER SEVENTY

Berlin Germany

After a week in Berlin as they waited for Hitler to return from Wolf's Lair in Prussia, Commandant Hermann and the rest of the commanding officers from each of the other concentration camps were led deep into the bowels of Hitler's new place of residence, the Fuhrer Bunker. Four SS soldiers with submachine guns escorted them to a large room with only a long wooden table surrounded by simple wooden chairs. The room was otherwise empty.

Each officer had been relieved of his sidearm and holster, any briefcase or bag, and been thoroughly patted down and searched prior to being allowed to enter. When the men had been seated, the SS soldiers took up watch, two on each side of the door and two at the opposite end of the room.

The men, some of whom were acquainted, exchanged hushed small talk while they awaited Adolph Hitler. After ten minutes or so, the door opened as two more soldiers with machine guns entered, followed by Heinrich Himmler, head of the SS, Adolph Hitler by his side. Two more soldiers followed from behind. Himmler carried a large briefcase.

When Hitler entered, every officer jumped to his feet and gave the heil salute as they gave a hearty 'Heil Hitler!' Hitler and Himmler returned the heil to the officers, and walked to the center of the table where a larger chair was set for the Fuhrer, with another set aside for Himmler.

Himmler motioned for the officers to sit, leaving only the Fuhrer and the soldiers on guard standing.

Hitler looked around the room with a stern look of absolute authority, then spoke.

"The war is going well! We are winning in Russia! We are winning in England! We are winning in Africa! And we will soon drive the Americans back across the Atlantic!"

With little emotion, the officers applauded the Fuhrer's announcement. Hitler then continued his speech.

"Now, we must finish this business with the Jews! It is time to move forward with our master plan. It is time to implement the Final Solution to it's inevitable end! The Jews and all of our prisoners occupy my soldiers needlessly. I need soldiers on the battlefields, not guarding Jews!"

Hitler slammed his palms down on the table and his face turned red as he worked himself into a frenzy. "All of you will be given a packet here today by Herr Himmler. It will outline your newest orders. Each of you are to carry them out immediately upon your return to your camps! This is necessary for the good of Germany and the pure race! I expect reports back to me each month on your actions!"

Himmler rose from his chair which was next to Hitler and opened his briefcase, producing a pile of large envelopes, as Hitler continued.

"Himmler will give you orders after I have left the room. I expect loyalty and complete obedience from you!"

Hitler looked around at the men, then exhorted all of the officers.

"Do I have everyone's loyalty here?"

All of the officers nodded in unison throughout and yelled as they saluted. "Yes Fuhrer!"

Hitler became completely calm as a smile came to his face.

"Good. Good. I have the best military and officers in the world. That is why Germany shall prevail!"

Hitler turned and walked to the door, accompanied by his guards, then turned back to address the officers once more.

"As thanks to all of you great Officers, you are invited to stay in Berlin for another week before you return to your camps. Take your families to enjoy all that our wonderful city offers. The Fatherland forever! Heil!"

All of the officers stood and saluted with a boisterous yell 'Heil Hitler'. The Fuhrer left, then Himmler walked around, handing out each man's assigned orders.

CHAPTER SEVENTY-ONE
Washington DC

Senator Royce and Congressman Tucker walked down the hall in the White House toward the office of the President. Two burly Secret Service agents in suits with crew cuts stood on each side of the entrance. As the two politicians approached, one of the two Secret Service, showing no emotion, reached for the handle to the door.

"The President is expecting you, Gentlemen. I've been instructed to show you in when you arrive."

President Franklin Roosevelt sat behind his desk, smoking a cigarette in a short holder, and carried on a conversation with his closest advisor, Harry Hopkins. They stopped conversation when the Senator and Congressman came into the room. FDR smiled broadly at both men. "Russ, William, come on in! Good to see you both again. It's been too long. I apologize for not making myself available more often. Sit down."

The President motioned for the men to sit in two chairs just across from the desk.

"Thank you, Mr. President," said the Senator. "We know how busy you are. Certainly no apologies are in order."

"Yes Mr. President," intoned the young congressman. "It's always an honor to be invited to the White House."

"Well, it's long overdue to have my best allies in Congress in to visit, right Harry?"

Harry Hopkins, sitting off to the side, smiled and nodded.

"Yes Sir. Hi Russ, William."

Both men smiled and responded.

"Maybe you're wondering why I asked you both here today?"

The Senator quickly looked at the Congressman sitting next to him, then back at the President.

"We did try speculating on the way here, Mr. President. Neither of us could come up with a reason. But rest assured, Mr. President, whatever it is, we're at your service."

"And you both have been for years. We've worked well together and we're finally seeing some daylight in this war! We're getting good reports back daily. Our soldiers with our allies are pushing back on the Nazis and Japs. The Germans know they're losing now."

Pulling the cigarette stub from its holder and putting it in the bowl of a standing cigarette ashtray behind his desk, the President reached into a box on his desk, grabbed yet another cigarette, inserted it into the holder, then pulled the big lighter on his desk up to light it. He took a big puff before he leaned back in his chair and continued.

"How's your boy TR doing, Russ? I like that young man!"

"Thank you, Sir. He's in London. Just finished some lessons at a British War College over there. When we get a foothold on the European mainland, looks like that's where he'll be headed. At least that's what I'm told by people I know in Defense."

"I'm sure you're proud of him. When he gets back here after the war, you bring him to see me, you hear?"

"Yes Sir. TR will be very happy to see you again. It's been a few years. He's turned into a man."

"I'm sure he has. I think that young man is destined to follow his dad into politics. Maybe he'll be sitting behind this desk someday Russ."

The President paused for a moment before he went on.

"Actually, the reason I asked both of you here today is, hold onto your hats, to have lunch!"

The Senator and Congressman had surprised looks as the President continued. "The kitchen's bringing the four of us some big sandwiches, potato salad and then some ice cream. How's that sound?"

The Congressman now smiled.

"Fantastic, Mr. President. What a surprise!"

"Well, you're both good and loyal friends. The other day I put this on my calendar. Besides, we have to eat, right?"

The door opened, and staff rolled in a large tray of food.

"Right on schedule. Let's have a bite, then put our heads together on one little item I'd like some feedback. I trust both of you to give me straight and honest thoughts."

As he reached over to the tray, the President took hold of a monster size sandwich.

"I hope everybody's hungry. Dig in, men. I'm starved."

CHAPTER SEVENTY-TWO

Dachau Germany

Aaron and Abraham sat next to Golde's bunk. Golde was in agony as Abraham tried to have her drink water. Aaron wiped her head with a cloth repeatedly, dipping the cloth in a bowl and squeezing out the water each time.

"Mother's fever is raging, father. This is doing no good."

Abraham moved over to the side of the room and motioned for Aaron to walk to the other side of the room with him. Out of range of Golde hearing them, Abraham whispered.

"Your mother has the rash of Typhus. She can't drink. She is weak. We need strong medicine or we will lose her. Go see if the German doctor can come."

"Alright Father." Aaron quickly left the room while Abraham went back to try to comfort his wife as he applied a moist cloth to her forehead.

Aaron went to the gate, where the guards outside glared at him.

"I must go to the German village. The Commandant said I could go there if I needed to."

One guard scowled at Aaron. "You may not pass. The Commandant gave us no such order when he left."

"Yes he did. He told me he gave those orders."

"He told you that, Jew boy?"

Both guards laughed, mocking Aaron.

Aaron begged. "I need to go get the doctor. My Mother is very sick. She needs medicine."

The sentry looked at the other guard, then sneered.

"German doctors help no sick Jews."

"Please, the Commandant left orders."

"No. You will not come through the gates. Go back to your barracks. That is an order!"

"Not until I get the doctor. My Mother will die if she does not get medicine now."

One sentry began to raise his weapon toward Aaron when the second soldier spoke.

"Put your gun down. You can't shoot the music teacher, idiot."

The guard turned back to Aaron. "We do nothing for you. Now go back, or things will get ugly for you. Go now before something bad happens."

Aaron looked at the sentry, then at the one anxious to shoot him. He then turned away to return to his barracks.

Aaron opened the door to see Abraham weeping over his wife's lifeless body. Golde was on the bunk, her eyes closed, her suffering over. Aaron hurried over and leaned down close to Golde.

"Mother, Mother."

Abraham looked at his son, tears on his face.

"Golde has gone to her reward my son. She is now in Hashem's hands. She feels no more pain."

Aaron knelt next to his mother's body on one knee and kissed her forehead, crying.

Abraham sat silently as he put his hand on his son's shoulder.

CHAPTER SEVENTY-THREE

Dachau Germany

When the Commandant and his family arrived at the camp the morning following Golde's death, he gave orders to bring Aaron and Abraham to his villa.

When the men arrived, the Commandant walked into the parlor unaware of Golde's death.

"I trust everything went well in the weeks we were away?"

Aaron looked at the Commandant.

"My mother died yesterday. I tried to go to the doctor for medicine but the guards would not permit me to pass through the gates. They did nothing for us while you were gone."

The Commandant was stunned, then his face turned to the look of an enraged person. "I left different orders!"

The Commandant turned around, not facing the two men. After a few moments, he turned back and looked both men in their eyes.

"I am sorry for your mother, Aaron, and your wife, Abraham. Tell me which guards. They will be on their way to the Eastern front by nightfall!"

"That will not bring back my wife," answered Abraham.

"Still, they will go!"

The Commandant continued.

"I cannot bring her back, but I can arrange a correct and dignified burial. I will have her taken to Munich and buried properly, and we will erect an excellent stone for her grave. That I can do."

Abraham looked down at the floor. "Thank you."

"This will never happen again. I will make sure, when you want to see me, I will know about it. You will be allowed to see me anytime. You have my word on this."

CHAPTER SEVENTY-FOUR

Burma

Thick jungle on all sides surrounded a clearing over a mile square. A wide stream ran along one side of the clearing. Enormous bamboo pens were erected near the stream to house elephants.

The open plain was almost level. Clusters of thatched huts ringed the area. In the center of the clearing was another group of larger thatched huts, tarps extending out as sunshades. The day was typically hot and humid, as American soldiers, some nineteen hundred strong, milled about or washed up in the stream. The mules had been relieved of their burdens, and were tied up in the shade of the jungle near the water.

In the center, under one of the tarps connected to the largest hut, the American Captain and a group of officers, along with their interpreters, sat in a meeting with the Kachin tribal chieftains. The Captain looked at the chieftains while he talked. All the while, they carefully studied him with their eyes.

"I have given orders to my men. They are good men. My American soldiers will respect your village. They will respect your women. We will defend your village and its people against the Japanese if we need to. We ask for your friendship and cooperation."

After the interpreter finished, the chief elder spoke, with the interpreter relaying the message.

"He says Americans are not like Japanese. They burned and plundered other Kachin villages, and took their women."

"Tell him the Japanese attacked Americans for no reason and killed many thousands of our people. That is why we are at war with them now. We are a peaceful people and did not want a war. We only defend ourselves against their aggression."

"They want to help. They want the Japanese to leave this place."

"Tell him we will work together to make them leave, but there will be battles."

"He thanks the American soldiers. He says through their network, they know of no Japanese for at least fifty kilometers. Word travels quickly from village to village."

"Ask if we can stay here tonight, but we must be moving in the morning."

"You are their honored guests tonight. And he will furnish guides to lead you. He says paths will need to be widened to have this many men, mules and big guns go through. You will need to hack your way through the jungle."

"Then that's what we'll do. Thank him for our guides." The elders of the tribe all smiled, then the tribal chief spoke again.

"He says the big guns are too heavy for the mules where the soldiers will go. He is willing to trade elephants for mules."

"Tell him we are happy to trade the animals. And we have chocolate and cigarettes as gifts of thanks for the village."

This news made the elders even happier, then they all stood, with the Americans following suit immediately as the chief said one more thing.

"He says Americans are good and they are friends to the Kachins. They would like to entertain the troops with some ceremonial dances."

"Tell him the Americans are honored."

Later, as the hundreds of soldiers found a spot for the night, refreshed and relaxed, the villagers were in the center area as they played drums and did ceremonial dances in colorful costumes. The Captain and other officers sat with the tribal chieftains in places of honor while they enjoyed the celebration.

Mo, Tex, Duke and Riley sat together watching the dancers as their platoon Sergeant walked over with one of the interpreters and a small villager, who was no more than five feet tall.

Height put aside, this diminutive native was an incredible physical specimen. His brown skin was flawless. His facial features were handsome, and he had perfect white teeth. Shoulder length straight jet-black hair matched his eye color. His body was muscular with not a trace of fat. He wore no shirt, only two arm bands tight at the top of his biceps. His shorts were ragged at the bottom and he had no shoes or foot coverings. The four men looked the Kachin over as the Sergeant spoke. "Well, gents, looks like you got your wish. Captain just pulled you out of my platoon and put you on recon patrol. I hate to lose you guys, but congratulations, I guess."

The men, still sitting, looked at each other as Riley slapped Mo on the back.

"Damn, Mo. You did it again. I can't wait to see you walk on water!"

The Sergeant's face broke into a big grin when he heard this remark, then he continued.

"This interpreter will travel with you and this Kachin guide is yours."

The interpreter then addressed the men.

"My name is Thura. This is Cucarin. He is the best Kachin guide in the village. He knows this jungle well."

Hearing his name, this little bit of a person smiled broadly at these huge Americans and nodded.

Mo looked over at him with a smile on his face.

"Cucarin? I think we'll call you CooCoo. OK? CooCoo?"

Coo-Coo noddded enthusiastically, the smile on his face not leaving. Then, CooCoo sat down right in their midst, next to Riley, who would make up about four CooCoos.

Riley looked over at the little man sitting next to him.

"Make yourself right at home, CooCoo. Get a load of this guy."

Duke laughed.

"I like the little rascal."

Tex chimed in.

"Me too. This boy's got balls!"

Riley pulled out two cigarettes and candy bars, then gave them to Thura and CooCoo.

Duke leaned over to light their cigarettes. CooCoo had a big smile as he puffed, beaming at his new American friends.

Mo looked at the Sergeant, who had been watching all of this with amusement.

"Sarge, say hello to the new recon unit."

CHAPTER SEVENTY-FIVE

Oxford England

Max and TR landed in a small hotel room in Oxford. Crammed into the tiny space were a table with two chairs, a small chest between two beds, a radio set on top. A gas heater took up one corner, and one small window looked down on the road below. The room reflected the age of the building, the old 'Mitre Hotel', built seven hundred years before.

TR sat at the table writing a letter while Max was propped up on his bed, staring straight ahead when TR asked.

"Max, you haven't written a letter back home for weeks. How come?"

"I've been going to. I keep hoping I can tell the folks we're going to the mainland, where the action is. I just don't want to say I'm still in England doing nothing."

"It doesn't matter to your family where you are or what you're doing. They'd like to know you're alive, or at least were alive when you wrote the letter."

"Yeah. Maybe I'll write one tomorrow."

Max leaned over and started fiddling with the radio dials.

"Max, are you trying to tune in that little traitor lady, Axis Sally again?"

"Yeah. I'll find it. It's the only thing that comes in clear on this damn radio."

"I wonder what's the story with her, Max?"

"I don't know, but I'd like to wring her scrawny little neck. When the Americans get to Berlin, she'd better skedaddle."

Max found the channel he was looking for, and leaned back on his pillow to listen while TR continued writing.

Over the radio came an American woman's voice, very sultry and sexy.

"All you American soldiers should not be way over here. You should be home. To mount any attack against Germany is sure to get so many of you killed and maimed. Why? You've been sent to fight a war for crooked politicians in Washington. They're making money and you are dying. You are just being suckers and dying for a bad cause. Hitler has nothing against Americans. He likes Americans."

Max interjected quickly as he screamed at the radio.

"That's a crock of shit!"

The woman on the radio continued.

"I know what you boys really want. You're yearning plenty for someone, but I'm just wondering if she isn't running around with the 4Fs all the way back home." Max reached over and flipped off the radio.

"That's enough of her crap. Apparently Axis Sally doesn't remember Pearl Harbor! C'mon TR, let's get out of here and grab some dinner at that little pub down the road."

TR stopped writing and folded his letter, leaving it and the pen on the table.

"Sounds good, Max. Let's go."

Narration

The lives of the good are rewarded when they have walked the walk. Divinity awaits them. Much as when steel is hardened by tempering, life can do the same.

Those with unwavering faith will refuse to let trials and tribulations, no matter how unfair or severe, to undermine their core values. With deep seated knowledge that all things shall come to pass, hope is never lost.

CHAPTER SEVENTY-SIX

Dachau Germany

Aaron and Abraham sat at their table eating.

"Mother would still be alive if it weren't for the Nazis."

"Aaron, many people would be alive if not for the Nazis. Your mother is one of thousands, maybe tens of thousands."

"Do you think the Commandant really buried mother in Munich?"

"Yes. I want to believe it. Golde lived with dignity and she deserved to be laid to rest with dignity. He said he did, so I choose to believe him."

"Father, our people are worked to death. When they can no longer work, they disappear from the camps."

"That is why we work for the Commandant, Aaron. To feed as many as we can to keep them strong. To keep them alive. I do fear for those that disappear or are taken away in trucks."

"I think the Nazis take them away and kill them. What is the point? We are all going to die here."

"Aaron, remember your promise to Golde. You must never give up hope. If it is the will of Hashem for any of us to perish here, so be it. You must have courage and never lose hope."

Both men sat, eating slowly, nothing being said, when Aaron finally broke the silence.

"The Commandant told me that Americans now fight the Nazis."

"Then that is good. Perhaps the Americans will help to overtake this evil. We must pray the Americans are victorious against Hitler. If they defeat the German army, then you must keep yourself alive. Aaron, you could go to America. There can be opportunity for you there."

"Opportunity in America, Father? For a Jew?"

"Americans are not like the Nazis. Your uncle sent letters before we were brought to this place. We were going to go there to join him. In America, there are successful and famous Jews, and they are not hated. Not like here."

"But how will I ever get to America? The Nazis will never let us free from this camp."

"My son, no matter what men do, if it is Hashem's plan, it will happen. If he wills it, you will live. And your talent with the violin will open doors. You have a gift not many have with your music."

"Father, with all that you have seen, and after losing mother, I do not know how you keep believing."

"Aaron, trust in what I say. I believe in your future. I have seen it in my dreams and in my mind. You will use your gift for all, and bring beauty to the world. Promise me as you promised Golde. Promise me you will stay strong."

"Alright, Father. For you. And for mother."

CHAPTER SEVENTY-SEVEN
Boston Massachusetts

Boston was covered with a blanket of snow. A late April storm crashing down from Canada had dropped four inches of white powder overnight. After arriving from Washington after midnight, Senator Royce had risen before his family to walk in the fresh ground cover before the city had the chance to turn the glittering white flakes black with soot. The storm had moved through quickly, and the clear skies and early morning sun created a freshness and sparkle enjoyed by the Senator.

As he walked by himself, he listened to the sound of the snow beneath his feet.

He wore a felt gentleman's hat, a thick long brown coat and brown leather gloves, walking comfortably as his warm breath was revealed with every exhale in the cold morning air. The Senator neared a small family restaurant, opened the door and entered. Inside, an older man cooked behind the counter as an older woman waited on a single patron sitting in a booth toward the back end of the business.

Seeing the Senator come in, the man behind the counter hurried out to greet him.

"Senator Royce, what a pleasure. We haven't seen you for a few weeks. You must be very busy in Washington these days with the war going on."

"Good morning, Donald. Washington is a madhouse, but we intend to win this war, and win it as soon as we can."

"It looks like we have those Nazis on the run now, don't we Senator? I want this war to end so my boys can come back here. Mother and I need them to help us run this place."

"I know Donald. I have one over there too. None of us wants our boys over there."

"Well, you came in for breakfast, not to talk about work, or the war! And you have your choice of seating today, being the early bird. Pick a spot while I go grab you a cup of hot coffee. Always an honor to have you in."

"This is my favorite spot for breakfast, you know that, Donald. I've been dreaming about a cup of your coffee since I got in last night. Best coffee in Boston!"

Donald hurried off for the coffee while the Senator, still standing just inside the door, took off his coat and placed it on the wooden coat tree next to the door. He flipped his hat on the same hook, then reached inside the right pocket of his coat to retrieve a folded envelope before sitting down in a front window booth with a view of the street outside.

Donald arrived with coffee, steam rising from a thick white mug with a man size handle. "There you go Senator. Start your day with that. The usual?"

"You know me, Donald. Creature of habit. Yes Sir."

"Coming right up, Senator."

Looking over at the woman serving breakfast to the other patron, Donald yelled.

"Mother, keep this coffee full and hot for the Senator."

She looked over and waved to Senator Royce, smiling.

"Don't I always? Good morning, Senator."

Senator Royce smiled and winked at the woman.

"Good morning, Maureen."

The Senator then looked up at Donald.

"If I weren't so happily married I would have stolen Maureen from you long ago Donald."

Donald bent down close to the Senator and whispered in his ear.

"There's been a number of days over the years where I'd let you."

Both men laughed as Donald headed back behind the counter to cook the Senator's breakfast.

The Senator opened the envelope with the London postmark. It had been sitting on the table in the entry next to the front door of his house. He had failed to notice it when he arrived late last night, spotting it only as he set out for his walk to the restaurant. After he carefully pulled out two hand printed sheets, he began to read.

Dear Family,

Just a quick note. Sorry I haven't written, but things have somewhat dragged much in the last few weeks.

Still traveling with Max Gordon, and we expect to be getting over to the mainland soon. Something big is in the making here. There is a terrific buildup of manpower in England. GIs everywhere. No one knows when or where, but Hitler's army is sure to catch hell soon.

We've been instructed to not send any specific information in letters, but what I just told you can be seen by anyone here in London, and there are spies among us. I'm sure the Germans know something's coming their way and they are getting ready. They are probably just hoping they guess right as to where and when. The British have learned also that it is never wise to give a stranger too much information because that person may be the enemy. If you ask for directions, you get a response like 'it's just at the top. Can't miss it.' There are no specifics, and well, you most likely will 'miss it'.

Street signs and direction signs have been removed or changed. If the Germans ever get here, they don't want them to know where they're going.

Max and I were lucky to find a room. Some places, five or six men need to stay in one hotel room. That is, when you want to get off base.

It's been cold as ice here and we have a tiny gas heater in the corner. One of us needs to wake up every two hours to feed a shilling into it or it goes off. Before long the room inside is as cold as outside.

Every day it is the custom to give each guest two ounces of whiskey. Max and I take ours in the evening, and after enjoying our two ounces, we'll have dinner and enjoy a pint at a local pub.

We can eat anytime we're hungry, day or night. Comes from an old law written when coaches and passengers could arrive anytime and could get food and drink. Funny that they never changed the law. Max and I commandeered a couple of bicycles, which are at a premium. We sometimes pedal twenty-five miles in a day. No matter where you are in England, you will find interesting and historical sights.

Our hotel serves an excellent 'Black Market Breakfast' twice a week. Fried eggs, bacon and sausage. Items hard to come by even in our own mess hall.

I can't say Max is here all the time in the morning to have breakfast. He's quite the skirt chaser, and often shows up a bit ragged later in the day. I'm not in his category, but there are some beautiful British girls over here, and they do seem to like Americans if you know what I mean.

Overall, this is rather easy duty. We also know there are so many men in foxholes with mortars exploding around them, some finding their mark.

I'll let you know when we make the move. We're ready and biting at the bit.

I love you all and hope you are all well.

TR

CHAPTER SEVENTY-EIGHT

Burma

Mo's recon unit moved stealthily through thick growth of the jungle on a narrow path. They had rifles slung over their backs as they hacked with razor-sharp machetes each man wielded. They could hear animals and movement around them, but didn't often see creatures of the jungle. The men had been told to not worry about jungle wildlife. Animals and snakes moved quickly away when the scent of humans came near.

The four men and Thura stopped and set their packs down. Duke opened up his radio pack he carried on his back. Mo lit up a cigarette, then addressed Duke.

"CooCoo's been gone for over two hours. Radio back that we're going to sit tight for a bit. CooCoo knows not to go too far ahead."

The men heard a familiar whistle signal from the jungle. Tex looked at the others.

"Looks like our boy's back right on schedule."

CooCoo came into their midst from further up the path, spoke to Thura in Kachin, then sat on a log next to Duke. Duke reached for his cigarettes, gave one to CooCoo and lit it for him as CooCoo looked at him with a big smile.

Thura relayed CooCoo's information to Mo.

"Nothing for at least eight kilometers. CooCoo doesn't think any Japanese are anywhere near here."

"That's good," answered Mo. "Duke, let the Captain know our position. By now they should be near the clearing about six kilometers back. That's a good place for a supply drop.

Send those coordinates to HQ and see if we can get a drop tomorrow morning. If they confirm, Tex and Riley, you'll double back and join the others. We need supplies. Hurry it up, Duke. I want these guys traveling while it's still daylight."

Duke got to work on the radio.

"Got it."

Later, after Tex and Riley had left to drop back with the battalion, Mo and Duke sat on their bedrolls, while CooCoo and Thura slept. It was still light and Mo was writing in his journal when he set it down.

"Nature calls. If I'm not back in ten I'm dead."

Duke, sitting next to his rifle, barely looked up. "Mo, if they kill you, we're all toast."

While Mo was gone, Duke noticed the cover of the journal for the first time. 'Letters to Janey.' He smiled to himself. After a few minutes, Mo returned back into the small clearing from the jungle.

"Well, I lived through another dump."

"Glad to hear it."

Mo picked up the journal to start writing again when Duke asked a question.

"Hey Mo. I just happened to glance over and saw the cover of your book. I wasn't snooping and I don't want to be nosy, but you want to fill me in on Janey?"

Mo looked over at his friend.

"She's my girl back home in Springfield. I met her just before I left and we fell in love right away. I just know she's waiting for me."

"I got a girl waiting too, Mo. Been my sweetheart since we were in High School. Her name's Tawny."

"That's great, Duke."

"Yeah. She's beautiful. When I get back we're gonna have about ten kids. We both want a big family."

"I can see you with lots of kids, Duke. You're gonna be a great dad."

"Yeah, it's gonna be somethin'."

"My girl Janey only has one leg." Duke looked surprised.

"Really? What happened?"

"Had cancer real early. She was supposed to die."

"That's too bad, Mo."

"No. I said that same thing, Duke, and she stopped me dead in my tracks. She never wants anybody to feel sorry for her. She's the strongest girl I ever met. And she plays the piano and sings perfect. We'll be getting married when I get back. That's why I know I'm goin' back Duke. No way I would meet her just as I was leaving and have it turn out any other way. I'm gonna take care of that girl 'til I die, and that's gonna be when I'm good and old, not now and not in this damn jungle."

"You and me both, buddy. We got stuff to live for."

"Only thing is, Duke, I need to tell her about my Pop. I don't know if it will change how she thinks of me."

"Why? What about your Pop, Mo?"

"My father was killed because he was makin' booze during Prohibition. They found him floating in the Sangamon River north of Springfield. He had been stabbed over and over."

"Damn. I'm sorry to hear that Mo. Must have been tough on you. How old were you?"

"Maybe about four years old. I don't remember much

about my Pop, just some things. Got raised by my mom, sisters and Eddie Vernon." Both men stared ahead silently for a bit before Mo started in again.

"Eddie told us the story. He got to know our Pop pretty good before they killed him. My pop made the best booze on the north side. He only used real ingredients. He never used turpentine, fertilizer, manure, formaldehyde or lye. He didn't want to kill someone with his booze."

"We had lots of moonshiners back in Kentucky then too, Mo. They were all good fellas. That prohibition was pretty stupid."

"Yeah. Eddie said all the cops knew our Pop. They'd come by and he'd give 'em bottles to take home with them. We had two big stills set up in the two sheds in back of our house back at the alley. But even though I was only four, I still remember the trucks that would come down from upstate and load Pop's booze into the backs. There would be men with submachine guns who would get out and stand guard while they loaded. All the kids in the neighborhood loved it when they came, because the guys with the machine guns always gave us candy."

"So why did somebody kill your dad, Mo? Did you ever find out?"

"Yeah. It was a small timer who wanted protection money from my Pop to operate. Poppa wouldn't pay him. He told the guy that he didn't need protection, especially from the cops. So this guy and his gang killed my dad to make him an example to the rest of the north side."

"Bet you'd like to get your hands on that guy, huh, Mo?"

"Don't need to. That guy and his whole gang were found shot in a downtown warehouse only about a month after my Pop was buried. Word was out that the cops evened the score."

"And you think that story will make your girl think less of you, Mo? That's not going to happen. Besides, what your Pop did doesn't really have anything to do with you now."

"All my life I've had to try to be better because of what my Pop did. I know he did it for us. Eddie's told us Pop was a good man. You don't know how many times I felt like the kids in school and even the teachers were thinking I was a bad kid because of what happened to Pop."

"Well you sure as hell ain't no bad person Mo. I think you're a hell of a guy, and so do all the other guys in our outfit."

"Thanks, Duke. I think the same about you guys."

Once again both men sat silently as they stared off into the now pitch black jungle.

"Gettin' late Duke. I'll stay up for now. You get some shut-eye until Thura relieves me."

"Yeah. Gettin' late."

CHAPTER SEVENTY-NINE

Burma

The clearing in the middle of thick jungle became visible in the early morning light. The main battalion rustled all around the fringes of the clearing, close enough to take cover in the dense jungle if necessary.

Tex and Riley had their packs ready as an officer approached. Both men jumped up and saluted. The officer saluted back.

"At ease, men. Supply drop's gonna get here in about half an hour. Recon's been alerted. They're waiting in their position until you join them. I'm sending three men up with you who will help carry supplies to the others in your group, then they'll wait for us to catch up."

"Thank you, Sir."

After the officer had left, Riley looked at Tex. "Looks like we got some time to kill. I'm gonna go find me a spot to pinch off a loaf."

"Please do, big guy. And next time, please don't bother to inform me."

As the main battalion waited for supplies, the sound of an approaching airplane could be heard. The troops all looked in the direction of the big transport when they suddenly heard the engines start sputtering on the plane. They watched as the plane banked and attempted a landing in the clearing.

Riley looked up and then back over at Tex.

"Jesus, she's in trouble. He's trying to bring it in."

The plane came toward the clearing, heading toward the soft dirt. The plane barely cleared the trees, and when the wheels touched down, they dug in, flying off under the weight of the plane. The nose barreled into the ground as the propellers shattered off in all directions. The plane plowed forward, but managed to skid on its belly some ways, not flipping over, lurching forward until finally it came to a grinding halt. When the plane came to rest in a cloud of smoke and dust, men around the clearing started running toward the plane, hoping to help the crew still inside.

Soldiers scrambled in and out of the open door on the side of the transport as smoke billowed from both engines. One soldier climbed out and reported to the Captain, who was just reaching the downed plane.

"Pilot and co-pilot are both dead, Sir. Two others hurt real bad. We have them out of the plane and medics are working on them."

The Captain surveyed the wreckage. "Dammit. These are brave men. They risk everything flying these rickety old transports over the Himalayas so we can get our supplies. Do what you can for the injured and line up a burial detail for the two men who didn't make it. Have the men offload all the supplies. Then I want everyone working together to cover this plane with tree branches and brush right away. We can't have this plane spotted from the air by the Japs."

"Yes Sir. Right away, Sir."

Narration

Men and women are imperfect in many ways. Yet, in a scourge of mankind, many ascend above. For these people, their sense of decency, sincerity and concern for others enables them to overshadow their shortcomings. They fall, but will rise again. They fail, yet will succeed again.

Some leaders are put into the position of making arduous judgements which impact others, even the blameless. It is during these times when tremendous responsibility and accountability can produce heroic decisions.

CHAPTER EIGHTY
Washington DC June 6, 1944

President Roosevelt was seated behind his desk inside the oval office. In the room were the Secretary of State, the Secretary of Defense, senior advisor Harry Hopkins, Senator Royce, Congressman Tucker and several other members of Congress. Conspicuously absent was Vice President Harry Truman. Beyond the windows, in back of the President, was a dark moonless night.

The President reached into a case on his desk and took a cigarette out, put it into his cigarette holder and lit it. His face was grave and serious.

"Gentlemen, feel free to smoke. And I have some cigars if that interests any of you."

No one took up the President on his offer. The men sat in silence, anxious to find out why they had been summoned to the White House in the middle of the night. The President waited a few moments, then took a long draw on his holder before he spoke.

"You've all been my closest allies for years, well before the war began for us. That's why I asked you here at this late hour of the night, or very early hour of the morning. I suppose that depends on which way you choose to look at things. I want you all to know before anyone else, that we have just commenced the largest military offensive the

United States of America has ever undertaken. As I speak, our brave soldiers are invading the mainland of Europe, storming the beaches of Normandy."

The President paused, took another puff of his cigarette as he allowed these words to sink in to the men in front of him, then continued.

"We know these landing areas are well fortified. The Germans are dug in. They're waiting for us. We will sustain major, yet unavoidable losses. It is absolutely imperative, however, that we establish a landing area for our troops and equipment. Once we own the coast of France, we will drive the Nazis back into Germany from the west while the Russians are pushing from the East. Hitler is in a vice, Gentlemen. It is our intention to tighten that vice until we squeeze the life out of him."

The men sat silently, until Harry Hopkins began to clap, and in an instant, all of the men in the room were applauding. The President joined for only a moment, then stopped, signaling all the others to do the same.

"That appreciation is appropriate for the courage of all of our fathers, sons and brothers, who on this day, will make the greatest sacrifice for their country and their families. May God bless them and watch over them." As he took another puff from his cigarette, the President continued.

"Turning to our other front, as you all know, our troops and navy in the Pacific have gained the upper hand. We are now on the offensive. America is winning this war against Germany and Japan, gentlemen. I can't begin to tell you how proud I am to be an American today. Does anyone have any questions or input?"

"Mr. President?"

"Yes Russ?"

"From what we know, the Japanese are a completely

different foe than the Nazis. Nazis fight like mercenaries, only out for their sordid advantage. The Japanese though, are convinced they are fighting a holy war. A war of honor, in which they will not surrender. I'm afraid the war will rage in the Pacific even after we have crushed Hitler and the Nazis."

"Russ, you're absolutely correct in your assessment of our fight in the Pacific theater. I'll tell all of you one thing now, although National Security prevents me from being too descriptive. What I say must go no further than this room. We are close to perfecting a weapon which will change the way wars are fought forever. When we have defeated the Nazis and secured Europe once again, we will turn our focus and all of our forces, with our allies, to defeat Japan. Within a year, it is our hope that a land invasion of Japan will not be necessary. I pray it is not needed. If forced to invade the Japanese mainland, our military losses and civilian lives will surely be far more catastrophic than the tremendous losses that mankind will endure today."

All of the men in attendance sat silently as they pondered these words. They all understood the implications of human loss during any invasion, yet they did not, as of yet, understand the scope of the weapon which might make an invasion unnecessary. After a few moments, the President broke the silence in the room.

"We pray for our men today and in the coming times as our soldiers fight for our nation and our freedom."

President Roosevelt then sat back in his chair, and his eyes displayed his concern for the men he had sent into battle on this day. A day that no Commander in Chief should ever need to live.

CHAPTER EIGHTY-ONE

Utah Beach, Normandy France June 20, 1944

Two weeks to the day from the bloody invasion onto the shores of France, the beachhead looked nothing like it did on June the sixth.

The ocean had returned to its deep blue color, compared to the reddish tint caused by soldiers' blood which flowed during the landings.

A full military tent town had been established on the beach, which included numerous tents with large bright red crosses on the tops. The Germans had retreated from the coast, as the battle raged further into France. The sound of artillery boomed constantly as the allies forged ahead.

Hundreds of amphibious landing craft unloaded a steady stream of tanks, trucks, jeeps and troops. In one landing craft, TR and Max sat in their jeep, ready to drive onto the beach. They had spent the better part of the previous week waterproofing their vehicle in preparation for the landing. With a wrenching sound, their landing craft slammed into the submerged sandbar to a jarring halt some distance from the shoreline.

As the ramp opened and dropped into the shallow water, TR gunned the jeep down into the ocean and up onto the sand. Max, who was excited as hell as gunfire and shelling could be heard all around, yelled over to TR.

"OK TR, we're here! Our group is to join the others and de-waterproof our jeep. The Captain is going to report to the beach master for further instructions. We rendezvous north about one kilometer. Go up on the road next to the sand."

TR drove up the sand onto the dirt road above the beach and turned due north. When TR and Max reached their meeting site, others were already de-waterproofing.

"Max, let's get to work. We don't want these guys being faster than we are."

"You got it buddy."

In due time, the last jeep arrived, carrying the Captain. A sergeant driving the jeep jumped out and yelled.

"Alright! Gather around! Captain has some orders!"

The men all scrambled to form straight lines and stood at attention, saluting. The Captain finished reading some papers, then climbed out of the jeep.

"At ease, soldiers."

The Captain walked along the line of soldiers, turned and looked out over the blue water dotted with what looked like a thousand ships before he turned back to face the men. "We lost a lot of good American lives two weeks ago on this beach so we could get in this war men. There's a lot of men back in those Red Cross tents who might never make it, and if they do, they might not ever be whole again. We cannot and will not let those men down. Likewise for those soldiers up on the front lines! There will be danger. You all know that. As we follow behind the battle, there can be pockets of Germans or their sympathizers. They'll kill you if you aren't alert, soldiers, so always be ready. You don't know who to trust, so trust only your fellow soldiers. Does everyone understand me?"

"Yes Sir!" all the men yelled in unison.

"Good. We're going to bunk here tonight, on the beach.

Wear your earplugs. These blasts are going to go all night long. Tomorrow we head east to bivouac on a farm outside Isigny. There we meet up with other civil affairs detachments. Then we'll wait until we're joined by a combat unit. They'll escort us to our first destination."

The men stood silently, listening with full attention. The Captain addressed the men one more time.

"Our wait will be longer than anticipated. Our forces are stalemated at St. Lo. The damn Nazis are protected by hedgerows planted two thousand years ago by the Celts. The root banks are ten feet thick and our tanks can't penetrate them. But they will eventually. It's just a small delay. That's all for now men. Finish your work and bed down. We move at sunrise. Remember, you're in enemy territory now!"

CHAPTER EIGHTY-TWO

Burma

Recon unit had a small fire going, dense jungle all around. Mo, Tex, Duke, CooCoo and Thura sat on some long-fallen tree trunks. Tex stirred a large pot cooking directly over fire inside four big rocks. Mo worked on his journal as the others smoked cigarettes and talked.

Every man's uniform was tattered and drenched with sweat. The jungle growth was sharp and thick, and heat and humidity were one constant on the march.

Tex dipped a spoon into the pot to get a taste of his meal.

"Oh that is delicious if I do say so myself. She's ready to eat boys. Duke, let me serve you first, sir, seein's how you'll be spelling Riley from guard duty after you eat." Duke held out his tin plate as Tex heaped a couple of big spoonfuls onto it. Duke examined the food on his plate.

"Hope it tastes better'n it looks."

Tex looked at Duke and frowned.

"What? You think I'm fixin' Texas barbecue here? Just eat it."

Duke grumbled something about barbecues, then started shoveling the food into his mouth. CooCoo and Thura both held out their plates as Tex scooped food for both.

"You ready for yours Mo?"

"Nah, help yourself Tex. I'll wait for Riley to get back from standin' guard."

"OK. I'm eatin' now. I'm hungry as hell."

Tex filled a plate and eagerly ate a couple of spoonfuls before talking to Mo.

"Mo, we're almost four hundred kilometers into this jungle and besides that Jap ambush, we ain't seein' any Jap troops. Seems strange to me. Why the hell are we here do you think?"

"I know they have us headin' somewhere Tex, but I sure as hell don't know where or why. Burma's a big country, so I doubt the Japs have many troops tied up over here. Probably only a few more than we do. Most of their stuff is out in the Pacific, same as us. We're kind of forgotten soldiers over here."

"Still, Mo, day after day out here. It's gettin' to me. I keep wondering when I'm gonna feel a bullet smack into me from some strange direction."

"Hell, Tex, that's why we're recon. We're supposed to know where they are before they know about us. Remember, we're the ones hunting them, not the other way around. Don't forget, we got CooCoo workin' for us. They got nobody like him."

Tex smiled when he heard this from Mo.

"That's what I like about you Mo. That damn confidence. Shit, I think you might just get us all out of here as long as we stick with you."

"Damn right we will, Tex. But that's all of us sticking together. We're a team."

"Yeah, a team."

The men heard a whistle from about twenty yards out into the jungle darkness. In a few seconds, Riley's lumbering body came into view.

Mo looked up as Riley came into camp, not making a sound as he walked.

"Damn, Riley. I don't know how you can be so stealthy, bein' so damn big."

Riley had a sly smile on his face.

"Kinda like a jaguar at midnight, huh boys?"

Tex looked over.

"Don't be pattin' yourself on the back too hard, there, big guy. Might break your arm contorting it like that."

"Well, anyway, I'm hungry. Got any more of them vittles saved? Duke said you fellas cooked up some Texas barbecue tonight."

Tex answered. "You bet we got more. And Mo ain't ate yet either. But I hate to disappoint you. No Texas barbecue. Just plenty of Burma slop."

"That'll do just fine."

Riley grabbed his plate and fork.

"Just throw a bunch on here. I'm starvin'."

Tex dumped three giant spoonfuls on the plate, then put a smaller portion on Mo's plate when he came over after he put his writing away. Mo looked at the food on his plate.

"This Burma slop looks great tonight Tex. Good job!"

Talking stopped as the men chowed, then rinsed their plates off with water from their canteens. As he stuck his plate and fork back into his pack, Riley let out a long and humungous burp, then started talking.

"Guess it's my turn to stir up some coffee for us tonight fellas. Sure as hell glad they always make sure to drop the coffee. I think I could go without food longer'n I could coffee."

"You an' me both Riley," said Tex. "A man could go stark raving mad out here without coffee. It's about the only thing we got to remind us of normal times, besides you fellas with me."

As the men sat staring into the fire, Mo started the conversation.

"You know, I took lots of stuff for granted back home. I guess I just figured I'd be workin' at the Sangamo Electric plant in Springfield. Maybe write a few stories for the Illinois State Journal and Register if I got lucky someday. Get married, have kids. Just live life. But somehow, I think I felt trapped there in that life, forever."

"I know what you mean Mo," said Riley. "Me too. Now, here we are in the middle of nowhere just tryin' to stay alive. Crazier 'n hell if you ask me."

Tex took a big gulp of his coffee.

"It's Goddam crazy that's for sure."

Mo went on.

"I've figured out a lot of stuff while we've been here though. Really important stuff. When I get back home, I just want to be a good husband, good father, son, brother and friend. That's all that really matters."

Silence set in again as the men looked into the fire. Tex poured himself more coffee.

"As bad as things were in Texas for my family these last ten years, it was still a hell of a lot better than bein' over here."

"Same thing for us in Springfield, Tex," said Mo. "We used to have men knock on our door in Springfield. They had nothing. They'd hop off the freight trains a few blocks from our house just to try to find something to eat. My mom always fixed 'em some food and let 'em do some work for us before they moved on. She always sent the men on their way with a bag of food."

"Sounds like your Ma is a damn nice lady, Mo," said Riley.

"Yes she is. Man, I miss her. I miss everybody back there so bad. You know, right now Springfield would be just about the most beautiful place on earth. You get five miles outside of town and hit nothing but farmland. Rows and rows of corn ten feet tall. Acres of wheat fields as far as you can see."

"When we get back I want all you boys to come down to Texas and visit. Got some real fine country down there too."

"You know we will, Tex," answered Mo. "You guys are like brothers to me. We're friends for life now. Just think, Texas in the good old USA."

Everyone stopped talking, then Mo started up again.

"You boys know I got a twin brother? His name's Max. We're matching bookends. Can't hardly tell us apart."

Tex and Riley both had surprised looks on their faces, when Riley chimed in.

"Hell, there's two of you guys? What's your brother doin' now, Mo?"

"I think he's fighting Germans somewhere in Europe by now."

"Well if he's anything like you the Germans are shit outta luck," said Tex.

"Max is older than me. Came out about fifteen minutes before me, so that made me the baby of the family. An' he's the smart one of us two. I always tried to measure up to him, but just never did. Everything in school came easy to Max. I had to work extra hard just to get by."

Riley looked at Mo.

"Well, you can stop trying to keep up with him now Mo. You made your mark forever when we got ambushed. None of us will ever see anything like that again."

"Damn right," agreed Tex.

"Well, anyway," said Mo, "we were pretty much raised

by my sister Cecilia's boyfriend Eddie. Our pop was killed when we were little but Eddie was always there for us." Mo paused for a minute, then went on with his story.

"Eddie'd take us to his farm about thirty miles from Springfield. He owned it but a family around the bend farmed it for him. Then we'd go into Havana and sometimes Eddie would let us bowl. Summertime at home, we'd sit on the porch with ice cold lemonade Eddie'd just squeezed up, makin' it just right. We used to catch giant bumblebees in the front yard, trapping them in the super big red blossoms on our Hibiscus bush that was bigger than most trees. When those bumblebees would climb down deep into the flower to get the pollen, we'd close up the blossom then stick the whole flower in a mason jar. We'd do that 'til you couldn't fit any more flowers in the jar. Then we'd set the jar in the grass and take off the lid and run like hell when those cranky bumblebees came crawling out the top."

Riley and Tex both just stared into the fire when Riley spoke up.

"That sounds real nice, Mo."

"Yeah. I just didn't know how nice until now. Funny, I took Janey to see a movie called 'The Wizard of Oz' before I shipped out. The last line of the movie didn't mean much at the time. It was just another movie. But now it does. After she wakes up from a crazy dream, the little gal Dorothy can only say 'there's no place like home'. Now it means a ton."

The men all sat in silence. Tex lit up a cigarette, then took a long puff.

"I'll finish this smoke then go spell Duke."

CHAPTER EIGHTY-THREE

Dachau Germany

The vehicle barreled down the dirt road, sliding to a dusty halt next to the gate near Abraham and Aaron's barracks. The Commandant and another officer carrying a doctor's satchel were escorted by two soldiers with machine guns. As the guards on gate duty realized it was the Commandant, they quickly became stiff at attention and gave the heil salute. With only a slight wave of his right hand, the Commandant barked an order.

"Open these gates immediately!"

"Yes Sir, Herr Commandant!"

The four men hurried into the compound and went straight to the door of the Gittelsohn's room. The Commandant sternly ordered the two soldiers.

"Position yourselves outside these doors." As the two men entered, Aaron sat next to Abraham who was lying on his bunk. The Commandant and doctor went over to the bedside.

Abraham looked at the Commandant with tired, blackened eyes, but managed a weak smile.

"The art must be turned over to Aaron now. He will do a good job for you."

"We will see. The doctor will examine you to see if you have improved. Perhaps with full recovery you continue your excellent work for me, Abraham."

Abraham looked up, only able to slightly shrug his shoulders.

Aaron moved out of the chair so the doctor could sit close to Abraham.

The Commandant and Aaron walked over toward the door as the doctor examined Abraham.

"Aaron, does he do any better today?"

"No. He is weak. He cannot sit up. It is the same as it was for mother before she died."

The men stood watching the doctor, who was listening to Abraham's heart. The doctor then folded his instrument, packed his case and walked over to the two and whispered as he looked back over at Abraham.

"There is nothing I can do. The Typhus has progressed too far. One day, perhaps less. I don't know."

Aaron looked over at his father lying on the bunk. Abraham did not look at the men.

Rather, he stared straight up. The Commandant reached for the door handle and opened it, allowed the doctor to exit, then turned back to Aaron.

"Aaron. I am sorry about your father. I've come to admire him. Abraham is one of the finest men I have known."

The Commandant paused at the door, looking back at Abraham one more time before he walked out and closed the door. Aaron moved back to the bunk and sat next to his father, then picked up a cloth from a pan of water, squeezed it and wiped his father's forehead. As he did, he reached down with his other hand to clasp his father's hand. Abraham smiled weakly at his son and spoke very slowly and softly.

"I go to join Golde soon. She is waiting for me. Do not mourn for me, Aaron, but be happy."

"Father, you said to never give up."

"And I never have, my son. I am content with the life I have led. You must remember this. Time diminishes memories of pain, anguish, sorrow and fear. Do not carry them with you. Let them go."

"I love you, father."

Abraham looked up as tears streamed from his eyes down the sides of his head.

"Aaron, I have always loved you more than life itself. I will always be with you."

"I will keep you and mother in my heart, father, and I will never give up."

Aaron put his head down on his father's chest as Abraham placed his hand on Aaron's head.

CHAPTER EIGHTY-FOUR

Dachau Germany

The sun shone brilliantly in a blue sky. It was an unusually warm morning. A German truck was parked outside the open gate nearest the Gittelsohn barracks, as four German soldiers carried out the wooden box containing Abraham Gittelsohn's body from the building, followed by Aaron and Leo. As the soldiers slid the box into the back of the truck, two German vehicles came down the road. The Commandant sat in the front passenger seat of the first vehicle alongside his driver.

The second had a driver and three soldiers with machine guns. When the first vehicle had come to a halt, the Commandant motioned to Aaron.

"Aaron, come. You two ride in the back of my vehicle."

Aaron and Leo climbed into the back seat as the German guards at the gate looked on with amazement. The convoy started down the road toward Munich. As the convoy entered the Old Jewish Cemetery of Munich, Aaron and Leo marveled at a place they both thought they would never see again. As Aaron looked over at Leo, he saw tears in Leo's eyes as Leo smiled at Aaron.

The vehicles came to a place with a freshly dug gravesite and stopped. There was a large stone on the spot next to the fresh grave. The Commandant stepped out first and put his hand on the shoulder of Aaron as he pointed.

"Aaron, the grave next to where your father will rest is your mother's. Come and see it, and the monument I had placed for her. I had it carved so that no one would steal metal lettering."

The three men approached the stone. Inscribed on it was simply, 'Golde Gittelsohn. Beloved wife of Abraham and mother of Aaron'. Aaron stood silently, looking at his mother's gravesite, and tears came to his eyes. He turned to the Commandant.

"Thank you."

Standing erect with little emotion showing, the Commandant answered.

"Your mother and father deserved nothing less. I will have another stone matching this one to mark Abraham's resting place. I am going to return now to my car while my soldiers lower Abraham's burial box into the ground. Both of you pray as you will over his body, then we return to camp. My men will see to the proper burial when we have left. And one more thing, Aaron. I have made sure to direct both of their graves toward Jerusalem."

Later, when the men arrived back at the camp, the Commandant's vehicle stopped at the gate, letting Aaron and Leo get out. As the guards opened the gate, the Commandant sat looking ahead, not turning to them.

"Thank you again, Commandant," said Aaron.

Without turning around, the Commandant only raised his left hand in the air.

"You are welcome."

He then motioned his driver to drive toward his villa.

Aaron and Leo went into the compound, and as they got to Aaron's barracks, now empty save for Aaron, Leo gently grabbed Aaron by the arm.

"Aaron. I am old. Old people think about the past. The

people they knew. The things they did. But you are young. You must think about what is to come. The people you will meet and the great things you will accomplish. You always made your father and mother proud. He told me that he knew you are destined to live beyond this camp. I believe Abraham was right. Never forget that and always continue to be strong and help those you can."

Aaron gave Leo a hug as the men exchanged a kiss on each other's cheeks.

"Thank you for praying over my parents today, Leo."

Narration

How can happiness and love be present on many parts of the planet, while at the same moment, on different sides of the world, strife and hardship afflict so many? Why can a place be a bloody battlefield one moment, yet be a place of beauty and serenity before or after?

Who among men can explain? To mankind, time and space set their own rules, and produce many inequities.

In the Divine, time and space have no meaning. They have no power, because they do not exist.

CHAPTER EIGHTY-FIVE

France

The Atlantic Ocean sat calm as a lake as the sun began to rise. A warmth to the early air promised a scorching hot day ahead. The sound of artillery fire remained constant as the men in TR's and Max's detachment packed their vehicles and prepared to head out.

The Captain's vehicle came speeding down the dirt road from the direction of the tent city erected on Utah Beach. The jeep screeched to a halt and the Captain climbed out and into the men's midst.

"Alright men, listen up. We're now headed to La Haye-Pesnel. The town has been taken. Our job will be to provide gasoline and vehicles for doctors and move food supplies. We will also make sure water and sanitation are adequate. We're moving out in fifteen, so hustle it up."

As the convoy rolled down the road, TR and Max experienced their first sights and smells of the horrors of battle. Alongside the road, the convoy passed dead bodies of German and American soldiers, scenes of burning and smoking vehicles, landscape pockmarked with the aftermath of explosions as well as carcasses of dead cattle strewn about. The convoy also passed American infantry combat units on both sides of the road, marching toward the cacophony of the battle ahead.

As Max drove, TR sat shotgun with his rifle on his lap. Both men were silent as they viewed the carnage until TR spoke up.

"You know, Max, I know we have trailing units to bury the dead, but the sight of our men laying on the side of the road sickens me."

"Me too, TR. So many good men. So many fathers, sons, brothers and friends that will never go home."

The men both became quiet again, then Max continued.

"These men died so you and I can drive down this road without getting shot at. My brother Mo's somewhere fighting and I haven't so much as seen a bullet fly. It makes me feel guilty."

"We had bombs dropping in London, Max. One could have landed right on us. We're in the Army. We do what we're told. That's all there is to it."

"You're right."

When the convoy arrived at La Haye-Pesnel, the streets were empty. The jeeps drove into the central square in a place that looked as if no war existed. As the vehicles pulled in front of a building that appeared to be a city hall, two soldiers immediately climbed out of their vehicle to hoist an American flag up on the flagpole in the middle of a park-like area.

A short rotund man with a small mustache and a beret came out of the main building, followed by other men. The Captain, traveling in the third vehicle of the convoy, stepped out.

"We're Americans, sent here to restore your government and help the people."

The plump little man brightened.

"I am the mayor of La Haye-Pesnel. We welcome you. We will get word out that Americans are here. The people will come. We will put you up in rooms."

"Thank you. We're here until LeClerc's Second Armored goes to Paris. Then we will be part of that move."

"Your men will eat their meals at our restaurant while here, and be our guests. And I insist that you set up inside of our city hall to conduct your business. We will give you offices."

"The men will appreciate the meals and the use of offices will be helpful to us. Thank you."

As the men began to unload the jeeps and carry equipment into the buildings, civilians appeared in the square, with fruit and drinks for the men.

Later in the evening, TR and Max were among the contingent of American officers eating at a local restaurant. The townspeople crowded into the establishment to meet the soldiers, while the overflowing crowd stood outside of the windows of the restaurant looking in.

"TR, the people here act like we're celebrities."

"We are Max. Nazis are gone and these people have their town back."

"We're just here to get this place back on its feet. The real heroes for this village are those Americans who were lying on the sides of the road on our way here. They're the ones who gave their lives to liberate this place."

CHAPTER EIGHTY-SIX
Burma

Twenty days of hard marching through thick jungle passed since the supply plane crashed in the field. The battalion had advanced two hundred more kilometers into the interior of Burma.

Recon unit was at rest ahead of the main battalion by about two kilometers. Mo and Duke had the radio set on top of a rock formation and Mo was talking into the radio.

"Ten four. Copy. Out."

Mo turned to Duke and motioned for him to follow as the two walked over to where the others were resting on their packs, eating K-rations.

"Fellas, we've almost reached our objective. We finally have a target."

Riley looked up with a mouthful of food, trying to swallow before he talked. "Son of a bitch. It's about time. I was wonderin' if we were going to march straight through to China."

"It's a damn good thing we're finally close to the target. We're running low on food, and I haven't seen any places back there for a drop," said Tex.

Duke held up his long belt filled with bullets.

"Yeah, but we still have all of our ammo."

"Twenty-five more kilometers. We're headed for a

strategically located Japanese airfield. As long as they control it, they control the air in this whole province. We're going to take it, then give it to the Chinese."

"Hell. Now, ain't that nice of us?" said Tex. "Why the hell didn't they send the Chinese here to get it?"

Mo looked at the other men in the group, then gave a sly smile.

"Because this is a job only Americans can handle, Tex."

"Yeah, you're right about that, Mo. At the rate we're goin', we'll be on top of it by the end of tomorrow."

"No, Tex. We're going in slow. We're gonna hit 'em at sunrise in two days. The battalion is going to split in two. We're scouting for Red Group. Blue's recon unit is going out in front of them. We're gonna hit them from two sides. The airfield is surrounded by big hills and is down in a flat valley. We're coming through the jungle on both sides in cover. Any luck and we're in position with our big guns before they know we're there."

Tex finished his can of rations. "Sounds like a plan, Mo. Piece 'a cake."

"Hardly Tex. This is a heavily fortified field. We'll be outnumbered three to one."

Tex looked back at Mo with a wild look on his face.

"That all? Now I know it's gonna be a snap."

The men all shared a laugh, even as they realized the danger ahead.

"I like your attitude Tex," said Mo. "But you know how these Japs are. Crazier than hell and they don't seem to care about dyin'. We're counting on the element of surprise. It's the only way we're gonna pull this off. If they get wind of us before we're ready it ain't gonna be pretty. We need to keep those planes out of the air."

"So how are we supposed to surprise these guys with

fifteen hundred men comin' through a jungle with elephants loaded with Howitzers, Mo?" asked Riley.

"CooCoo and the other guide for Blue Group are going ahead alone. They'll tell us the positions for any guards. We're sure they'll have men up on the hills above. When we know where they are, it's up to Tex and I to take 'em out, silent. Same thing with Blue. Main force is standing down maybe a kilometer back. When we neutralize the guards, everybody moves into position. We'll control the high ground, and we should be able to keep the planes from taking off."

"I'm sure glad we got those elephants from the Kachins to carry the heavy guns. No way those tired old mules could have brought 'em this far," said Duke.

Riley looked over at Duke. "Just lucky for us the Japs screwed the Kachins. By giving us the elephants, the Kachins help us return the favor back to the Japs."

"Yeah," said Mo. "If we take this airfield, it's comin' back to bite the Japs in the ass."

CHAPTER EIGHTY-SEVEN
Letter to Janey

My Dearest Janey,

This will be the final letter in my journal. Hopefully I can give this to you myself when I get back to the good old USA. Just so that you can, you know, find out what your man has been doing since he left. And by the way, I have been behaving myself.

I think every soldier that survives this war will have a story to tell. These letters to you are my story. I never really understood what I was getting myself into when I volunteered for this particular mission, but every man here knows we're way too far in to turn back now, and our target is now two days march.

The army prepared us well for what we have done here and what we're about to do, starting when they shipped us to Canada. They had some tough and seasoned fighters train us there. I think I can tell you some of this stuff now. Those fellas were called Chindits, mostly British and some soldiers from India.

The Chindits are named after a mythical beast that Guards Buddhist Temples. I know why. They are beastly. We didn't know it at the time, but they were turning us into a long-range special operations jungle warfare unit.

Later, when we were in Hawaii, some guys would complain when we double timed it everywhere we went. We never just marched at a normal speed. Or when we would spend two hours crawling through an obstacle course or hike twenty-five miles to the top of the mountain with full field packs and weapons.

I guess I should have had some clue when every man in the battalion was issued two pairs of boots with their gear. One pair would not have done the job.

As we all sit around here tonight, after finding out today about our objective, the crew is quieter than normal. Seems like everyone here is writing a letter for back home, or at least thinking about home.

I know I am, a thousand thoughts going through my head. I've been thinking about Eddie a lot. How he taught me about his 'systematic savings'. Eddie was big on saving, but never selfish.

I remember when Max and I were little guys making money on Friday and Saturday nights working as pin-setters at the bowling alley near the fairgrounds.

Eddie would take us to the bank to put some money into our own savings account before he'd let us spend any.

And I think of you. That's the best of all. But then I realize where I am and what we're doing. Because even as I wish I could have those simple things again, I know that if I'm not aware of my surroundings and duty to the men fighting alongside me, one mistake could cost us our lives. War is a most serious business.

Coming up, in two days, we will meet an enemy not afraid of dying. We'll be engaging a Japanese force superior in number, and only cunning, deception and stealth will give us any edge to defeat them.

We're going to need and use every bit of our training. We have buried a lot of men in this jungle and I've placed as many bamboo crosses with helmets on them as I care to.

I know you are still waiting for me. It's my plan to get back. For right now, I'll take it day by day.

Love, Mo.

CHAPTER EIGHTY-EIGHT

Dachau Germany

The work crews from the camp had departed with their Nazi guards to march to the armament factory. The sick and those too frail to work were held behind in the barracks.

At mid-morning Aaron and Leo walked all of the barracks, seeing who they could help with food or medicine.

The condition of those left behind was pathetic beyond belief. Most looked like skeletons in their clothes. While the work crews were gone for the day, the weak climbed into a bunk.

With the overcrowding each night, the weak had been banished to the floors to sleep, giving up a bunk for those expected to work the factory on the following day.

As Aaron and Leo went into one barracks, one emaciated man saw them and hurried over, looking at Aaron. "You go to the officer's home, do you not?"

Aaron looked at the pitiful gaunt figure in front of him. "I have been there."

"Have you seen my daughter working in the kitchen? Klein and his men took her from my wife in the women's barracks weeks ago. They said she was working in the kitchens."

Aaron looked at the man and hesitated before he spoke. "I will look for her. What is her name?"

"Gavriella. Please see if she is being treated good."

"I will. If I find her, I'll come back and tell you."

"Thank you. You are very kind."

As Aaron and Leo continued on, Leo looked at Aaron with a distressed countenance.

"Klein has been taking the young girls for years now, Aaron, always saying the same thing. That they work in the kitchens. Then they are never seen again. I'm afraid for them."

"There are no Jewish girls working in any kitchens for any officers. They all have private German chefs."

Leo snapped.

"I knew it! Klein is the worst man. I have prayed for those girls."

CHAPTER EIGHTY-NINE

Burma

As the pitch-black night slowly gave way to soft light from the east, red recon unit moved slowly and quietly, loaded weapons and grenades on their belts. Each man had foliage attached to his helmet, their hands and faces painted in camouflage, with only the whites of their eyes barely visible in the dawn. The men each had a bayonet fixed on their rifle with another in a belt scabbard. When they reached ready position, Mo, Tex, Duke, Riley and Thura sat motionless. Any talk was a low whisper, as Mo moved his mouth close to Duke, speaking in barely audible tones.

"Radio silence until Tex and I take out the guards. CooCoo will double back here and let you know. We'll stay up on the hill. Should only take CooCoo a few minutes to make it back. He said the two he saw yesterday are a thousand meters ahead."

"OK, Mo. I wish CooCoo would get back here quick."

"He's just makin' sure it's the same as yesterday. They'll never spot CooCoo. He's invisible in this damn growth."

"Yeah."

The men heard a low whistle only loud enough for them to know CooCoo was coming in.

CooCoo emerged from the growth, the men only seeing CooCoo when only feet from the group. CooCoo squatted next to Mo as he whispered to Thura. Thura looked at Mo.

"Two men. Nothing's changed. Same lookout spot. They just replaced the guards before sunup. That's done. He's ready to take you two there."

"OK, then. It's a go."

Mo looked over at Tex.

"Ready, Tex?"

"Born ready Mo. Let's do this."

Mo motioned to CooCoo, who slowly moved into the thick jungle, followed closely by Mo and Tex.

Riley moved over next to Duke.

"There go some crazy brave sons of bitches."

As the day slowly grew lighter, the three moved stealthily along CooCoo's route, not making a sound. They reached a point where they could see the silhouettes of two Japanese soldiers standing at the edge of the trees, a clearing open behind them. The guards looked around as they stood, but the jungle was still too dark to see very far into. The Americans heard them talking to each other, laughing occasionally, with most of their attention on the airfield below.

The Americans moved silently, with the precision their training had prepared them for, as they inched closer to the guards, who were still unaware of their presence.

The two American soldiers could now hear noise and commotion from down on the airfield, as the troops below began to roust in the dawn.

Mo motioned to Tex to set their rifles on the ground. Mo pulled the bayonet out of his scabbard as Tex did the same. He pointed to one guard and to Tex. Tex nodded. Mo and Tex crouched motionless, waiting.

After a couple of minutes, Tex looked at Mo questioningly. Mo shook his head no.

A few more minutes passed, when the men heard the sound of an airplane. Mo and Tex made out a small Japanese aircraft coming in for a landing from across the valley. As it began its descent and got closer, the engine noise grew louder. The two guards turned their backs to the jungle to watch it land.

Mo looked at Tex and held up three fingers. Tex nodded. Mo dropped his fingers one at a time. When his third one dropped, both men sprinted toward the guards. Before the guards realized what was coming from behind them, each man had a bayonet in his back, with Mo and Tex reaching around to cover their mouths to muffle any screams.

Plunging their bayonets in and turning the blades, the guards collapsed backwards as the Americans dragged them back into the dense jungle. Before completely letting the bodies drop, each man yanked his bayonet from the guard's backs and finished the job by raking their knives across the fallen men's throats. Mo turned and signaled CooCoo, who had been watching from behind. CooCoo set off running to alert the rest of the recon unit.

Mo turned to Tex as he spoke in a low voice.

"Damn good work Tex."

Only a few minutes elapsed before CooCoo came running into the area where recon unit was waiting. CooCoo looked around, not seeing the men. He heard a low whistle, and Duke, Riley and Thura emerged from the jungle. CooCoo relayed to Thura what happened ahead, then Thura turned to Duke.

"Red Recon successful. Alert the main battalion."

Duke flipped on the radio as he muttered to himself, but loud enough for the other men to hear.

"Shit. Of course they were successful. We're the Goddam American Army!"

Then, into the radio.

"Red Recon. Betty Grable is secure. Get up here quick men. Over."

The men heard the response from the other end of the radio.

"Ten four. Good work Red Recon. Over."

Back on the hilltop, Mo and Tex had quickly put on the jackets of the two guards, and stood where those below could see them, but turned away from the airbase in case someone looked up from below with field glasses.

Mo whispered to Tex. "I sure as hell hope Blue Recon was successful taking out the guards on the other hill. If they didn't, we could be screwed."

"I don't know. I can't see 'em from here, but they must have, Mo. We would have heard gunfire or something from over there by now."

"Yeah, you're probably right."

After just a few minutes, the first line of soldiers, being led by CooCoo, Duke and Riley arrived and started deploying along the fringes of the jungle all along the top of the hill. Further back, men hacked frantically, clearing the way for the howitzers being pushed into position in the jungle. Machine gun crews were quickly and quietly assembling 50 caliber Browning M2s all along the line. CooCoo scrambled to the top of a tree as he looked around.

As the full complement of soldiers deployed on the top of the hill looking down on the unsuspecting Japanese soldiers below, Mo turned to Duke.

"We better get the go ahead from Blue pretty damn quick. Looks like they're getting ready to put some of those zeros in the air. If they do we're sitting ducks."

"We should hear from 'em any minute Mo," answered Duke.

Suddenly from across the valley on the opposite hillside, Red Group heard machine gun fire.

"Dammit," said Mo. "There must have been some guards they didn't get clean on the other hill." Japanese soldiers below reacted, as several hundred men streamed out of buildings with rifles and started up the opposite hillside. As Red Group watched the action, Mo signaled for the men to hold their fire, not wanting to alert the Japanese to their position.

Over the radio, Duke heard a frantic message.

"Red Recon. Blue's not in position yet. Take care of those Japs coming up the hill. We need time."

Mo nodded yes as Duke relayed the message.

"Affirmative Blue. We've got your backs."

Mo turned and once again held the troop from firing, as the signal moved quickly down the lines extending out both directions. Mo turned to Riley.

"Hold fire until I give the signal. Don't use the howitzer unless we need to. Concentrate fire on the soldiers on the hillside, not on the airfield. We don't want to damage those runways any more than we have to. Wait until they're halfway up the hill in the clear. They'll have no cover."

The men waited and watched as the Japanese climbed the steep hillside, getting closer to the top.

Mo held his hand up in the air. The men around him could hear Mo as he talked out loud to himself.

"Come on, you sons of bitches. A little further. Now!" Mo dropped his hand. "Give 'em hell!" The heavy machine guns started shelling across the canyon, cutting down Japanese soldiers who had no place to hide. The enemy on the opposite hill now realized they were being fired on from the opposite hill. Some turned and shot toward Red Group, but were firing at a force they couldn't even see. The soldiers not killed in the initial shelling on the opposite hill began to swarm back toward the airfield, trying to take cover behind anything they could find.

Heavy guns continued to blaze, as they cut down hundreds of retreating Japanese.

Mo yelled down the line in both directions to his men.

"Concentrate your fire on the airfield now. Make sure none of those planes get off the ground!"

Duke got off his radio as he smiled at Mo.

"Blue Group is getting set up on the other hill. We gave them the time they needed. In a few minutes they'll start raining down hell from their position also."

Mo ran over to the big machine guns, affectionately known as Ma Deuces.

"Fire on every plane on that field. Disable every one of 'em! Try not to destroy the runways around them."

Japanese pilots were running to their planes as ground crews below tried to get them in the air, but the machine guns from the high ground were cutting them down and blasting the planes. One pilot managed to get into his cockpit and the plane started to taxi on the runway.

Mo yelled again. "You boys better get that one before she gets in the air or it's gonna get hot up here real quick!"

All the gunners turned their attention to the slow-moving plane as it taxied. After a few direct hits, the plane veered off to the side where it blew up, eliciting cheers from the soldiers on the hilltop.

Shooting now started from the opposite hilltop from Blue Group, cutting down even more soldiers down below on the airfield.

Riley looked over at Tex.

"I'm glad Blue Group finally decided to join the party. We saved those guys' asses."

With the planes destroyed or disabled and when no Japanese soldiers moved below, the big machine guns stopped firing, as did the men in the jungles.

When the gunfire ceased, an eerie silence set in. The men looked down on an airfield of smoking airplane wreckage, the bodies of hundreds of Japanese soldiers strewn across the landscape.

From Blue Group's hillside, the Captain's voice was heard over the radio.

"Red. Damn good job. We have planes on the way that expect to be able to land here in a few hours. Have your men watch the fuel depot on the north corner of the base. If any of their men try to get to it to blow it, cut them down. We need that fuel. Everyone should stand down, but be prepared for banzai attack by their full force from below. If they don't launch an attack within twenty minutes, we're going down there ourselves using the cover of our big guns."

Mo nodded as Duke answered on the radio. "Roger. Red Group reads you Captain!"

Mo turned to Tex and Riley.

"You heard what the Captain said. Move through the men. Make sure they know the order. Tell 'em to stay on their toes. We ain't done yet."

Tex and Riley immediately moved off in different directions to spread the orders to the men.

CHAPTER NINETY

Japanese Bunker Headquarters Burma

Deep down in his bunker, the Japanese Commanding officer at the airfield stood behind a soldier working the radio. A few other officers and men waited in the room, silent and with looks of alarm and disbelief. The operator turned to the commanding officer and shook his head, as the commanding officer turned away, angry at the news he had just received.

"They cannot get more support here for three days? They tell me to take care of this with my men?"

A junior officer standing next to a large map on the wall filled with colored pins dared to speak.

"Sir, we have twenty planes inside the hangars. We can launch them."

"No. We must not launch any of our planes until we make them run out of ammunition. Did you not see what they did to the planes on the runways? They have guns on the hill and they know how to use them. That's just what they want us to do. Try to launch so they can use the rest of their ammunition on my planes! I will lose no more planes!"

The other men in the room waited to see what his order would be.

The commander paced over toward the map, simply staring at the wall. Finally, the same junior officer asked him.

"Our men are pinned down, sir. What will we do?"

The commander wheeled around with a bold look of bravura.

"Get all of the men ready. We will launch an all-out attack on both hilltops. We will overrun them!"

The younger officer again questioned his superior.

"But sir, our men have no cover. The enemy is in the jungle. We cannot even see them."

The commanding officer looked at the junior officer with an infuriated look, then yelled at him.

"We have them outnumbered! There can be no more than a handful of men on each hill. They must have been dropped from the air. No large force could have reached this far by foot. We are too deep in the jungle."

"But sir, we lost hundreds of men. If we could even get two planes off the ground we could strafe the jungle from the air and wipe them out."

"I do not expect to be second guessed by you! And I must not lose any more planes!"

The junior officer took a couple of steps backward and bowed.

"Forgive me sir. I am sure you are correct."

"Of course I am correct. It was only because they caught us off guard. We have over two thousand men. They cannot have many, and they are also probably low on ammunition. They already used up so much of it."

"Yes Sir."

"Have the men prepare quickly. Split the forces. They are hoping we will not charge them. They want us to open the hangars so they can shoot the planes. But we will overpower their positions and kill them all!"

"Yes Sir."

CHAPTER NINETY-ONE

Blue Group Burma

Up on the hilltops, the men stayed alert as they watched over the flatlands and the airfield below, still littered with bodies.

Mo sat next to Riley, not taking his eyes off the airfield. Duke was nearby as he listened to his radio.

"I sure as hell hope they decide to attack us, Riley. If we have to go running down these hillsides in the wide open, they'll pick us off like ducks in a shooting gallery. We'll lose half of the men before they hit the bottom of the hill."

"I hope so too, Mo. Captain's not gonna wait much longer though, with our planes on the way. They gotta have a place to land. We can't just sit here."

As both men stared down at the field in silence, Mo remarked to his friend.

"You know, Riley, did it occur to you that if we don't take this field, most of us will never make it back?"

"As a matter of fact, I been wondering about our chances of hiking back outta here since we set foot in Burma. It's a damn good thing our target was an airfield. Gives us a shot at gettin' home."

Duke got in his two cents worth after overhearing Mo and Riley.

"No shit men. We gotta take this field so we can hitch a

ride outta here. I'd rather try my chances in one of those old transports goin' over the Himalayas than go back through that damn jungle."

The men heard the radio crackle.

"Red Group. This is Blue Group. Come in."

Riley looked at Mo and Duke.

"Oh, oh, boys. Sounds like we're headin' down that slope, and pretty quick."

Mo grabbed the radio.

"Red here."

From the radio, Mo heard the Captain's voice. "Have the men count off down the line. One, two, one, two. Blue recon is sending a wave of the ones in ten minutes. Give us cover by your whole group. Our twos will cover also. Five minutes after our ones, you send your ones, twos still shelling for cover. When our men hit the runways, remaining men follow down the hill except for the men manning the big guns."

"Ten four, Blue."

Mo turned to Tex and Riley.

"OK. You guys heard the Captain. Go have the men count off. I want the ones and twos to know who the hell they are. It's gonna take a couple of minutes so hustle."

Both men started to move as Riley answered.

"You got it Mo."

A couple of minutes went by, and the men were prepared to cover blue when the signal was given. Mo looked at Riley.

"How much time?"

"Two minutes."

The men sat in silence, waiting for Blue Group to launch from the other side.

Tex moved over next to Mo and Riley.

"Sure feel sorry for them ones over in Blue. It's gonna

be hell moving down that hillside. Not many are going to make it."

Suddenly, from below, breaking the silence that had wrapped around the canyon since the firefight earlier, machine gun fire aimed at the two hilltops commenced. Japanese soldiers started pouring out of everywhere below, half running up the hill toward Blue Group and half toward Red's position. The Japanese fired at the front rows of the jungle, but the Americans were dug in deep, and not many bullets found their marks.

The Japanese soldiers were getting closer to the top of the hill when the big machine guns from the top exploded with fire, cutting down hundreds of the charging horde. The Howitzers started shelling opposite hillsides, wreaking havoc on the Japanese. American soldiers with rifles in the jungle joined in, killing those that weren't done in by the big guns.

The massacre continued, and no Japanese soldiers were able to get to the top of either hillside. The final waves of the banzai charge realized the force in the jungle was larger than anticipated as they got decimated. Stragglers turned and ran back toward the airfield, most getting gunned down as they retreated.

CHAPTER NINETY-TWO

Japanese Bunker Headquarters Burma

Inside the bunker, the Japanese commanding officer sat at his desk as he leaned forward with his head between his hands. The other soldiers in the room did not look at him. They only looked at each other, dumbfounded. The junior officer from earlier burst into the room.

"Their forces are much larger than expected. Our men were wiped out. I don't even know if any of the enemy were hit."

The commanding officer looked up at the other men in the room and said nothing. He stood erect and proud and went over to another door, where he opened it and entered into an adjoining room, then closed the door after him. The officer walked over to a case filled with swords in long scabbards, then carefully selected one. He held it ceremoniously with both hands in front of his chest, then moved to a rug in the center of the room.

After he knelt down on the rug, the officer gently placed the sword in front of him on the floor. He put both hands on the ground and bowed deeply, staying bowed for a few moments. He straightened up, pulled the sword out of its sheath, put the blade toward his stomach, and as both of his hands held onto the handle, he plunged the sword into his body with such force that the blade came out through his back as his body fell forward.

After a few minutes, there was a knock on the door, followed by another louder knock a few seconds later. The door opened, and the junior officer looked in to find the body lying in a pool of blood.

CHAPTER NINETY-THREE

Blue Group Burma

After the battle had subsided, the Americans waited once more at the top of the hill. After a few minutes of quiet, a Japanese soldier came out of one building with a white flag and began to wave it furiously back and forth. When he got about twenty-five yards away from the building, other soldiers started filing out with no weapons, their hands on their heads.

Over the radio, Red Group got a message from the Captain.

"Red. We're sending down our ones. Cover them in case this is a trick. Half will guard those prisoners while the other half go through the base to make sure it's clear."

"Ten four Blue," answered Mo into the headset. "We'll cover from up here."

The Captain came over the radio one more time. "When we confirm it's secure, send down Red Group ones. All twos hold position up on the hills with the bigger guns."

"Roger, Blue. We read you."

Mo turned to Tex, Riley and Duke.

"Looks like us Americans just took us an airfield, boys."

Later, down on the airfield, the Captain walked over to Mo and the others in his Group.

"Damn good job securing the high ground men. Your

cover kept the enemy from overrunning our position until we could get set."

The Captain then yelled out orders loud enough for everyone to hear.

"OK, men, work crews, double-time it! Clear this wreckage out of the way and repair any damage. We have planes in the air heading our way and we want to welcome them with open arms. You own this place now!"

The men erupted in cheers.

CHAPTER NINETY-FOUR

Granville France

Two large wooden desks with ornate carvings were inside a room on the first floor of Granville's town hall. TR sat at one, while Max was at the other. They had been in Granville for one week since leaving La Haye Pesnel as the group waited for General LeClerc to go to Paris.

Both men had stacks of paper in front of them. Townspeople sat across from each of the men, explaining their needs and various requests. Outside the room, in the vestibule, sat many more as they waited their turn.

The door into another room in back of the two men opened and an officer poked his head out.

"Lieutenants Royce and Gordon. The Captain would like a word in his office." Both men apologized to the people at their desks and asked them to wait as they headed into the back room.

TR and Max walked into the office, stopping to salute. The Captain, who was sitting behind a much larger and even more ornate desk than those in the front area, saluted back to the men.

"Come in men. Sit down."

Both men went to chairs opposite the officer, anxious to hear why they had been summoned.

"Things are well in hand here in Granville. You're two

of my best men and I'm sorry to lose you, but you're among those moving on. LeClerc's second armored has gone on ahead and reached Paris. We need help there. You've both been assigned to the eleventh Civil Affairs. Your office in Paris will be on Boulevard Voltaire. I envy you, men. Wish I was going with you, but what the hell. The army's the army, you know?"

The Captain paused for a moment with a somewhat sad look on his face before he continued.

"Anyway, you leave tonight in a convoy at twenty-two hundred hours. Finish out the day, then be ready to head out."

The Captain stood, as both men quickly stood erect and at attention. The Captain shook each man's hand.

"Best of luck to both of you. Been a pleasure to have you under my command, even if it was for only a short time. Take care of yourselves and stay sharp. There's still a hell of a lot of Nazis running around out there." Both men responded.

"Yes Sir. Thank you, Sir."

When TR and Max exited the officer's office, they turned to each other with big smiles as Max shook TR's hand.

"We're headed to Paris! So long to these little one-horse towns!"

"Yeah," said TR. "Maybe the next stop after Paris will be Berlin!"

CHAPTER NINETY-FIVE

Granville France

The weather had taken a bad turn in the evening. Rain poured. A line of jeeps with canvas tops ringed the town square. Three jeeps had headlights turned on so men in the downpour could see their way to vehicles. As they stood in a large circle, crowding in to hear final instructions, men were soaked through, their ponchos and rain caps no match for the blustery battering. The leader of the group stood in the center of the soldiers, yelling his loudest to be heard over the tempest.

"We're traveling slow. No lights allowed. Follow the vehicle in front of yours. One enlisted man will be strapped on the hood to make sure you don't run into the vehicle that's in front of you. Keep your distance but stay together. That's it. Load up!"

The men climbed into their jeeps as one poor soul sat on the hood with his back leaned against the passenger window. The lead jeep lurched ahead out of the cobblestone square, then hit the sloppy mud road just outside of the town, into the absolute pitch black of the stormy night.

Max drove with TR in the front passenger seat, where TR could only see the back of the drenched enlisted soldier, Private Ernie Chapman, sitting on the front of the jeep. Their vehicle moved at a snail's pace as it followed the vehicle in front.

"TR, I can barely make out the back of the damn jeep we're trying to follow. This is tiring as hell!"

"You're doing great Max. I can't see squat over here so I can't help much."

As the caravan crept along, the rain began pelting even more.

"Dammit. Now I can't see anything. I'm just looking out my side trying to stay on the road."

TR stuck his head out of his window as giant drops smacked against his face, then yelled to the soldier on the hood.

"Chapman, can you see the jeep in front?"

The soldier craned his head around as he yelled back.

"No Sir. Can't see anything out here."

TR pulled his head back into the jeep.

"Just stay on the road Max."

"OK, but I sure as hell don't know where we are. I can only see the road maybe five feet out."

After an incredibly long downpour, the rain began to abate. TR stuck his head back out the window.

"See 'em ahead?"

"No Sir."

TR cranked around in the seat and stuck his head out the side window looking behind their jeep, then pulled it back inside the vehicle.

"Can't see anybody in front or in back."

"OK. No sweat TR. We'll just stay on the road. We'll catch 'em eventually."

After a time, the rain stopped, but the night remained pitch black.

"Max. Maybe you should stop for a minute and get Chapman off the hood. He's not doing us any good up there, and he's looking pretty damn cold."

"Yeah, OK."

The jeep stopped as TR poked his head out the window.

"Get in the jeep, Chapman."

The man quickly jumped off the hood and climbed into the back seat, wet and shivering.

"Thanks very much Sir." As the first signs of dawn appeared, the three men realized there were no other vehicles in sight on the muddy road ahead or behind.

Max looked at TR with a bewildered, concerned look.

"Jesus, where the hell'd those other guys go?"

"I don't know Max. Better just keep on driving."

The jeep rumbled down the muddy, rutted road for a number of kilometers as all three men sat in silence, when TR finally spoke up.

"Max, you see that farm house in the distance?"

"Yeah, I think I spotted it same time as you. Got a barn there too."

Max stopped the jeep.

"Why are you stopping here Max? We need to go there and find out where we are."

"Are you kidding? There might be Nazis there. We could drive right in and get shot."

"You're right. What should we do?"

Max looked around and spied a low area below the road.

"I'll pull the jeep down into that ravine. We'll leave it here and sneak the rest of the way on foot. If it's safe, we'll get back here and move on."

"OK." When the jeep was off the road, the three men grabbed their weapons and helmets and started moving toward the buildings in a crouched down approach. As they neared, they moved cautiously in a half trot. They reached the barn.

The men hid behind the barn away from view of the house, when Max whispered.

"Stay here. I'm going to look inside the barn."

Max moved around to the barn door. He gently pulled it open, then peered inside. He came back to the other two.

"Got a donkey and two cows."

"So what now? said TR. "Storm the house?"

"Hell no! You two cover me. I'm going to sneak up and see if I can look in the windows to check the house. Doesn't look like Krauts around here. No vehicles. How would any soldiers get way out here, wherever we are? But we gotta be careful just in case."

Max ran from the barn to the side of the house where he slowly peeked in a window. He looked back toward the barn, where he saw TR's head barely visible. Max shrugged his shoulders.

Max slowly and silently moved around to the front of the house, then stepped up on the raised porch. He moved to a window to look in, then tried to open the entry door, which was locked. Once again, he turned back to the men hiding behind the barn and shrugged.

Finally, Max turned to the door and knocked loudly. A few moments elapsed when the door opened to reveal an old man and old woman, who both stared at Max in amazement. Max, in full uniform and holding an M1 carbine, searched his mind to speak in French to this couple.

"I'm an American. I'm lost."

The old man looked at his wife, then back at Max.

"Where do you want to go?"

"Paris," answered Max.

The old man looked again at his wife, then back at Max, as he pointed down the road they were on and in the very direction they were headed.

"Paris is that way."

Max looked down the direction the man pointed.

"That way, OK. Do you know if there are any Nazi soldiers close by here?"

Once again, the old man looked at his wife, then back at Mo with a quizzical look before he answered.

"We don't know. We don't like Nazis. We like Americans. Come in. We will feed you."

"I have two other men with me."

Now, as he looked around, the old man asked.

"Where are they?"

"Hiding behind the barn." As they leaned out the door to look toward the barn, the old man and his wife saw the two men's heads sticking out from behind the corner of the building. The wife finally spoke to Max.

"They don't need to hide. Have them come in too."

Max turned and motioned for TR and Private Chapman to come up to the house.

As the two men reached the area in front of the porch, Max relayed the news.

"He says Paris is ahead down the road we're on. We were headed the right direction. I just can't figure out where everybody else went if we're going the right way."

TR looked at Max, then the older man, then used his French on the two older people standing at their front door, still staring incredulously at these three American soldiers.

"Did you see Americans in jeeps come by here?"

The wife answered.

"No one went by or I would have heard them."

"We must have got out in front of them somehow, TR. But I don't know how we could have."

TR asked the old man another question.

"So we just stay on this road all the way to Paris?"

The old man and his wife both had amused looks on their faces when the old man answered.

"No. Five kilometers more is the main road. Turn right and stay on it until you reach Paris. Now, come in and eat some food." Max smiled at the old couple.

"Thank you, but we cannot. We're separated from our convoy and need to catch them if they are ahead. We need to keep moving. We are sorry to have bothered you."

The old man's wife answered.

"We like Americans."

As they turned to leave, TR and Chapman waved to the old couple.

Max shook the old man's hand before he went down the steps to leave.

"Thank you. Goodbye."

The old man and his wife waved at the three soldiers as they began to trot back to their vehicle.

When the men reached their jeep, TR took over the driving duties while Max took shotgun, Chapman sitting in back of Max. TR pulled the jeep up onto the road and gunned it as the jeep bounced down the bumpy, muddy road.

As they passed the farmhouse, the old man and his wife were still on the porch, and they waved at the three soldiers as they went by, as the soldiers returned their waves.

"We might have been their only guests in months, TR," offered Max.

"Yeah, maybe. I just hope they were telling us the truth and not sending us right to the Germans."

"I thought of that TR. But we just came from the other direction. We can't go back that way." From the back seat, Private Chapman interjected.

"Lieutenant Gordon?"

Max turned around.

"Yeah Chapman, what is it?"

"I just want to tell you Sir. What you did back there was really a brave thing."

TR looked over at Max.

"Chapman's right Max. You didn't know who was in there. Took a lot of guts man. I'm proud of you."

Max's face turned red.

"You fellas would have done the same thing. I just happened to volunteer first."

From the back seat, Chapman had the last word.

"Still ballsy, Sir."

After the jeep had traveled close to five kilometers further, Max turned to TR.

"There's a road coming up and it's got a line of American jeeps on it!"

As the men got closer to the road, TR looked at Max.

"Holy shit, Max. It's our convoy! We must've taken a shortcut and didn't even know it."

"Yeah, maybe we should've been lead jeep. We could have been in Paris by now."

As their jeep hit the highway, one of the jeeps in the convoy stopped directly in front of them. The soldier in the passenger seat yelled out the window. "Where the hell are you guys coming from?"

"We got separated during the hard rain last night. It looks like we got lucky and found a shortcut."

The man yelled back once more.

"Yeah. Great shortcut you guys. But you're right when you say you got lucky. Take a look at that."

The soldier was pointing toward a sign facing the main highway. As TR pulled into the convoy, Max and Chapman turned around to see what the sign said as Max read it out loud.

"Do not enter. Road not cleared of mines."

TR let out a shriek.

"Oh my God!"

From the back seat, Chapman spoke up.

"Somebody up there must be watching over us."

The men sat in stunned silence as they moved toward Paris.

CHAPTER NINETY-SIX
Dachau Germany

Aaron walked the barracks with Leo, recording who needed extra nourishment or medicine. With the deteriorating condition of the prisoners, Aaron and Leo were tasked with tough and heartbreaking decisions concerning who could be helped. Both men realized that when deciding which prisoners still had a chance at survival, they basically sealed the fate of the others. As they finished walking the last barracks and went out into the open, Leo put his hand on Aaron's arm.

"Aaron, what we do, we have no choice. We love every person, but only some might survive now. It is important that as many of our people live as possible, because somehow, our story must be told."

"I know Leo. The responsibility we've been given carries a great burden for us."

"Aaron, I have watched you for years in the camp. First, with your father and mother alive, and, since they have passed. You have been transformed from a strong young man to a leader of men. Your strength has given me strength, and I am an old man. You will survive this imprisonment. You will be one to do great things for our people."

"Leo, both of us shall survive. I know it must be. I feel it in my heart, the same as my father. Someday, when we leave this place, I will go to America. Will you go with me?"

"No. If that day comes, I stay in Germany. There will be much work to be done. But you will go. You must go. That is where your opportunity lies."

The men gave each other a hug and exchanged kisses to their cheeks.

"I will get this list to the Commandant, my friend. Pray and be strong."

"And you, Aaron."

As Aaron walked between rows of barracks on his way back to his room, he saw Klein and his two henchmen go into one of the women's barracks. The Germans did not see Aaron as he ducked behind one of the buildings, waiting to see what they would do. After a few minutes, the two soldiers with their machine guns came out of the building with a young Jewish girl, followed by Klein. They marched with the girl as their prisoner to the gate closest to Aaron's barracks. Aaron followed, careful to not be spotted.

When they reached the gate, the Germans on the other side opened it, allowing the four people to pass. As Klein and the others walked up the road into the German area, Aaron could hear the German guards at the gate laughing between themselves.

Aaron waited as long as he could, then went to the gate, where the guards on the other side stared at him as he stood before them. Aaron then spoke to the guards.

"I must be allowed to pass."

"No. You are not to pass today. This is not a time for you to go to the Commandant's house."

"I am to get the children ready for a special performance. The Commandant has instructed me to be there. It is important. Go ask him if you need to."

The guard looked at Aaron, then at the other guard. He then told the other guard.

"Open the gate. I don't want the Commandant angry at us. What harm can he do anyway?"

The guards opened the gate as Aaron hurried through to get close and stay within range of Klein and the others, but keeping a distance and out of sight.

Aaron moved cautiously, and did not allow Klein or his guards to see him following. As he passed the Commandant's villa, Aaron knew he was moving further into the German area than he had before.

At the farthest building of the settlement, just before an open space and forest beyond, Aaron watched as the two guards sat down in chairs outside the door as Klein forced the girl inside.

Aaron watched for only a few moments, then slipped away, back down the road, and returned to his prison.

CHAPTER NINETY-SEVEN

Springfield Illinois

Edward and Cecilia were walking down Black Avenue as they returned from a long day at the Sangamo Electric Plant. As they arrived at the steps leading to the porch, Edward stopped to check the metal mailbox affixed to a post at the base of the stairs. Edward pulled out only one envelope and looked at it.

"We have a letter from Max. It's all the way from Paris."

"Oh good, Eddie. Let's go sit on the swing and you read it to me."

"OK." They both moved to the swing, with Cecilia sitting down before Edward as he opened up the envelope and pulled out the letter. Edward meticulously pulled his glasses out of their holder, put them on, then sat on the swing next to Cecilia before starting to read.

Dear Eddie, Cecilia and Family,

We've been traveling through France for almost three months. The war is all around us. Although we're not in any actual battles, we can always hear the far-off shelling. It never seems to stop, whether it's night or day.

I've seen things no one should ever have to look at. War is hell. Hitler is like the Devil on Earth to have started this.

The front is not moving fast lately. The rains have turned roads into mud. Equipment gets bogged down. Getting supplies and ammunition to the front is the hardest part, and the army can't outrun things necessary to go forward.

On the brighter side, we have met many wonderful people who are thankful the Americans are driving the Germans back out of their country.

Some of the towns we have come through are virtually untouched by the bombing, while others are totally destroyed. They are having a power struggle here in France, and I think us Americans are the only stabilizing element in the country.

There are French militia groups who are still faithful to the Vichy government headed by Petain. They were sympathizers to the Nazis. Then there is the FFI. Communist renegades claiming to be liberators of France. There are many good Frenchmen duped into joining them thinking they are helping their country, but they are wrong.

We work with the underground French who will eventually rule France. Many here feel that the new President of France is going to be General Charles DeGaulle. He's our ally, and that's where I'm putting my money.

After all the little houses and small city halls we have been operating from, we're finally in Paris, working in plush offices of a former liquor company on Boulevard Voltaire. TR and I are quartered at a nicely furnished eight-room apartment. We've been told it had belonged to a Jewish family who departed the city.

When our convoy arrived, we drove down the famous Champs Elysees.

The Boulevard was completely empty at first, but as the jeeps moved through with our American flags on the front, people came from everywhere, swarming the boulevard and surrounding the jeeps. We couldn't move. Many brought flowers to us and the French girls all wanted to kiss an American!

We're constantly busy with all sorts who want special requests. Travel, gasoline, helping to locate missing relatives, the list goes on and on. And they all claim to have always been friends with the Americans.

We'll be on the move soon, heading toward Germany. Hitler's days are numbered. I hope you've heard from Mo by now. I know he's OK, I can just feel it. I miss all of you so, and love you all.

Take Care.

Love Max

Edward finished reading the letter, then looked over at Cecilia.

"Sounds like Max is doing just fine, Ceil."

"Yes he is Eddie. And I'm sure we're gonna hear from Mosie real soon too. Don't you worry. Those two boys can take care of themselves."

"You mean those two men."

CHAPTER NINETY-EIGHT

Dachau Germany

Aaron was in the living room listening to Commandant Hermann's children as they played a work together. When they finished, Aaron applauded them as though he were at the symphony.

"Bravo. Bravisimo! That was splendid, children!"

Both Erich and Greta smiled and blushed at the praise given them by their music teacher.

The Commandant entered the room and Aaron smiled at the children as he addressed the Commandant.

"If these two keep practicing and progressing like they are, in a few years the Hermann children will be playing in the symphony. Their musical talent is immense." This comment elicited a broad smile from the German officer as he looked at his children approvingly.

"I am so proud of both of you. And thank you Aaron for another fine lesson."

"I like teaching these two. They are such good students and eager to learn."

"Children, I need to have Aaron come into my office so we can go over some things I can do for him."

Aaron stood to follow the Commandant out of the room, then turned to the children.

"Goodbye children, until our next lesson."

Both in unison answered as Aaron was leaving.

"Goodbye Aaron."

The Commandant went to sit behind his desk, and motioned for Aaron to sit in the chair across from him. He reached into the cigarette case on the desk, took one out and lit it as he leaned back in his chair in an obvious good mood.

"So, Aaron, did you bring me your list of barracks and names today? You do so much good for your people, and it's my pleasure to help you to help them."

"Yes, Commandant. I have my list and also a special request."

Now looking intrigued, the Commandant asked Aaron.

"Very well. Let's get directly to your special request then. I'm curious, what is it?"

"Sir, with all the other suffering my people endure, there is a very bad thing happening. Lt. Klein and his two guards have been taking young girls from the barracks quite often, saying they will be working in your kitchens, then they are never seen again."

"How do you know this?"

"I was told a while back by the father of one of the girls, and Leo confirmed that many have been taken."

"Well, no young girls work in my kitchens, you know that. You have seen for yourself the many times you have been here."

"I know that Commandant."

"Then perhaps Leo and this other man are mistaken."

"No, I know it to be true."

"And how do you know this?"

"The other night as I returned to my room from walking through the barracks, I saw Lt. Klein and his men go into one of the women's barracks. After a few minutes, they came out with a very young girl."

"But you don't know why they did that."

"I do know. I followed them but they didn't see me."

Now a concerned look crossed over the Commandant's face as he asked Aaron.

"You followed them? Where?"

"To a building near the forest in your German section." The Commandant stood and paced across the room, turned away from Aaron, then turned around to face him with a stern look.

"You should not have done that."

"But he should not be taking those girls!" protested Aaron.

The Commandant had an enraged look, then turned away. He stood motionless for a few moments, then turned back around with a hopeless look.

"Aaron, I hate Klein. But there is nothing I can do."

"But you are the Commandant. Can you not stop him?"

"No. Klein's uncle is Heinrich Himmler, the Head of the SS in all of the Reich. He is a very powerful man."

"But you are powerful too. Just tell him to stop."

Commandant Hermann paused, then went over and closed the door to the office so others could not hear their conversation.

"Aaron, Klein hates me. He would like any reason to tell his uncle anything bad about me. There is already talk about the way I have helped some of your people. If I try to stop him, they will send me to the Eastern Front. And they might do harm or kill my family."

"The Nazis would kill your family?"

"Yes, Aaron, they kill anyone who does not cooperate. Hitler and the rest of his group are mad and immoral monsters. They are ruthless. They have brainwashed Germany and created their own horrible world. A world that makes mass murder necessary, and somehow the right thing to do. I could ask God to forgive me for turning my head, but how could he after what I have done? I have sold my soul so that my children may live."

"What do you mean mass murder?"

"By killing anyone who is a problem. By killing the Jews."

"Do they mean to kill all the Jews?"

The Commandant looked at Aaron with sad and guilty eyes.

"Yes. They want to kill all of the Jews, Aaron. That is why I was called to Berlin. They call it the Final Solution."

Now Aaron had an unbelieving look on his face.

"But why?"

The Commandant's face got red as he shouted at Aaron.

"Because they are Jews! Don't you understand? They want a pure Aryan Nation!"

Aaron now raised his voice to the Commandant.

"I am a Jew!"

Stunned, the Commandant lowered his voice and composed himself before he continued.

"Aaron, I knew many Jews before the Nazis took power in Germany. They were good people. Intelligent, hardworking, artistic and creative. Much better than the barbarians we Germans have become."

"Then can you not stop what you are part of? Take your family somewhere safe?"

"Aaron, I did think of it, but it is just too dangerous for us to try."

The Commandant stopped for a moment, then continued.

"Aaron, I have become fond of you. I admired your father and mother. Listen to me. Try to keep yourself alive. The Americans come from the west and the Russians come from the East. Even Hitler himself gets crazier than before. He is paranoid and does not even trust his own officers. He keeps guards around him at all times to protect himself from his own people. He lives under the ground in what they call the Fuhrerbunker."

"If the Nazis want to kill all the Jews, how will I stay alive?"

"Soon Aaron, you can be free of Dachau. Hitler underestimated the Russians and the Japanese made the same mistake with the Americans. Germany is losing this war and now every officer knows it. We have already had officers who have disappeared with their fortunes in art, jewelry and money. They run like rats before we are overrun by the Allies."

"So with all of this happening, men like Klein still get away with what they do?"

"I can do nothing now. I am sorry Aaron. You must be quiet about what I have told you here. I have told you too much. Be smart and stay alive. Please do nothing that makes me silence you. I will do what I need to do to protect my children. You must understand that."

Aaron stared upward, looked the Commandant in his eyes, then stood up, turned, and with no further words spoken, left the room.

CHAPTER NINETY-NINE

Burma

The airstrip that was under siege only hours before showed little of the signs of a battle. Bodies had been moved, and damaged planes created a twisted pile of metal in a clearing off to the north.

Crews were busy filling in smaller holes in the runway caused by the shelling. The flagpole which formerly had the flag of the rising sun waving now had two flags flying at the same time as they flapped together in the wind. The American flag and the flag of China.

Transport planes were already on the ground, and more were landing. Commandeered Japanese Zeros were getting a redo, with the emblem of the rising sun being replaced with Chinese markings. Most transport planes were Chinese, as were all the new troops. Within a short time, the area now secured, the base was to be turned over to the Chinese to continue the fight with the Japanese.

On a separate section of runway, the victorious battalion of Americans were lined up, but standing at ease, as the men awaited an address from the Captain. Mo, Duke, Riley and Tex were all together in the group, with Thura and CooCoo standing proudly between Duke and Riley.

The Captain and a few lower grade officers made their way to the front of the group, and as the Captain started to step up on a makeshift elevated platform so he could be seen, one soldier in the front started clapping, which caused the troops to shout.

"Hip Hip Hooray! Hip Hip Hooray! Hip Hip Hooray!"

All of the soldiers applauded the Captain.

The Captain smiled as he put his hands out to quiet the men. When the applause had finally abated, the Captain spoke.

"Thank you, men. We are all to be applauded, every man here. What you have done today and in these very hard months will go down in history as one of America's proudest military achievements. I want every man standing before me to know that. And as your commanding officer, it has been a privilege to have served with all of you."

All the men let out another cheer and clapped. Letting the clamor subside, as he gazed out at the men with sweat-stained, tattered and torn uniforms, tanned faces and grizzled unshaven faces, the Captain continued. "You have every right to be proud of yourselves and your fellow soldiers. And we are all proud of the men who gave their lives on our march. Heroes, every one of them, and they will never be forgotten. Never again will I ever witness the uncommon valor, courage and perseverance shown by this battalion of soldiers."

Pausing for a moment, the men remembered those fallen warriors who no longer stood with them. The Captain's face then changed to a smile.

"And I know we never had complaints from any of you."

The men laughed as they recalled some of the bitching heard along the way.

"And now, I have an announcement which it is my greatest pleasure to give. Our orders are to begin shuttling out all of the original invading forces. As you can see, this base is being taken over by our Chinese allies. That means every man here is heading back to Pearl, then straight back to the States."

All the men cheered, yelling and smiling at one another as they slapped each other's backs. The Captain motioned again for the men to quiet down.

"News of our victory here and our exploits in the jungles of Burma has reached Washington. It seems that enough of our force has died or been injured by the Japs, malaria or dysentery. General Stillwell and the President have come to the realization they have some real live heroes from the Burma theatre here. They want to keep them alive. You're going home men. Congratulations!"

Another hearty cheer went up from all. Mo turned and started shaking hands with all of the men around. Duke put his arm around CooCoo's shoulders.

"I'm gonna miss you CooCoo."

CooCoo looked at Duke, not understanding a word but feeling the affection.

Later, early in the evening, as Mo, Tex, Riley and Duke leaned against their packs eating, a young officer walked over to the four. As he approached, the men started to set down their food to stand, when the officer stopped them.

"No need to stand soldiers. Captain told me that you four are among those going out on first shuttle in the morning, Zero Seven Hundred hours. He figures that since you men put yourselves out there first all the way through this that you earned first flight out. Congratulations men."

Then, the officer looked straight at Mo.

"And it's going to be a real honor when I get to tell my kids someday that one of the men I served with in Burma was Mo Gordon."

As the officer turned to walk away, Duke addressed the officer.

"You're not the only one, Sir. Lots of us wouldn't be here if not for Mo Gordon."

The officer smiled and saluted the men as he walked away.

Mo looked around at the three men.

"Duke, we're all here. And we're goin' home. And you are all my brothers now."

Tex grabbed his tin cup and held it up to the others as they did the same. "I'll drink to that."

The men finished eating in silence, each to his own thoughts, when Mo finally spoke up.

"Men, I'm gonna head up to the top of the hill. Say a prayer for those men we've left behind on the march, and those who died today but get to go back for a proper funeral. You know, pay my last respects. You fellas want to join me?"

All the men rose instantly in agreement.

"Yes Sir, Mo."

When the men reached the top of the hill where they fought from early that morning, they looked down on the airfield. They all stood in silence, each praying in their own way. After they had been there for a few minutes, Mo asked the others.

"Fellas, can I say a prayer out loud?"

All the men nodded.

"Dear God. Accept every man into your kingdom. Forgive them for anything they may have done. For you know they've seen enough of hell already, and I think through their bravery and sacrifice that paradise should be their reward. And thank you for delivering us safely. Let us go back to our homes and families, never forgetting your mercy and blessings. Amen."

All the men stood silent for a few moments when Tex looked over at Mo, tears in his eyes.

"That was a beautiful prayer, Mo. Thank you." As the sun set beyond them in a sky with long wispy clouds, every color of the spectrum reflected around the men. Without looking at any of the men, just feasting his eyes on the sky, Duke had something to say.

"I'd a been proud to have any of those men as my best friend. Makes me real sad to know that they'll never get to do what they should have."

Mo looked over.

"I just hope that future generations never forget the ultimate sacrifice these men made for our country and for them."

"They'll remember for a while," said Riley. "But not forever."

"Guess so, Riley," answered Mo. "Otherwise we wouldn't keep getting in war after war. Been going on for thousands of years. Men just never seem to learn."

Riley now looked at the men with a serious look.

"There's always some greedy, power hungry fools ready to fight another war."

"Problem is," said Duke, "it's not those fools who fight the war. They send somebody else to fight their war."

As the men contemplated this sentence, Mo spoke up one more time.

"Well, this one's not over yet. But when it does end, and our side wins, let's hope we don't see another one in our lifetime."

CHAPTER ONE HUNDRED

St. Louis

The train crawled slowly into the station as hundreds of people waited, eager to see men they were never sure they would lay eyes on again. As the doors on the cars opened, soldiers poured from the cars, all anxiously looking for loved ones they hoped to see. Joyous and happy reunions began all around.

Mo Gordon stepped into the rail car opening with his duffel, stopping momentarily to look out over the swarm, when he spotted Carl looming over the others, a beaming smile on his face. Mo walked briskly over to the big man and shook his hand.

"Hi Mo. Welcome home."

"Hi Carl. Thanks. I can't believe I'm back."

As Mo talked, Carl could see Mo looking around the platform for someone else.

"Janey's here, and Ed and Cecilia. C'mon. I'll carry your bag."

As Carl grabbed Mo's duffel, the men made their way through the loud and happy crowd. When the crowd thinned further down the platform, Mo saw Eddie and Cecilia with Janey. Janey was standing. On two legs, without crutches. Mo turned and looked at Carl with an amazed look, as Carl smiled back at him, nodding.

Mo hurried toward the three and hugged Eddie and Cecilia at the same time as they both hugged him. He gave Cecilia a big kiss on her cheek. Eddie and Cecilia were both crying.

"Hi Eddie. Hi Cecilia. I love you both."

Eddie choked up as he answered.

"Welcome home, Mo."

Mo turned to look at Janey. Mo reached out and put his arms around her, then gave her a long kiss. He stepped back, and admired Janey as she stood there.

"Janey. No crutches."

"That's right, soldier. And I've gotten very good at walking again."

Mo hugged Janey again, as Carl patted Mo on the back. When Mo stopped hugging Janey, he stepped back once more as Janey started talking.

"And I'm driving now." Mo looked at Janey with wonder on his face.

"I can't believe it! You're walking and driving?"

"Yes. Carl bought me my own car. It's a nineteen forty-one Oldsmobile and it shifts automatically so I don't need to use two legs to drive."

Mo turned and looked at Carl.

"Carl did that for you?"

"I sure did, Mo. Bought Janey a car with Hydramatic shifting. Now you can't keep this girl home. She's driving all over the place."

Janey looked at Mo triumphantly.

"I drove the four of us down here all the way from Springfield."

"That car must've cost a pretty penny Carl."

"I've got my own radio hour up in Chicago, Mo. Five nights a week. Play music and interview guests. We have lots of famous people in Chicago now. I'm makin' pretty good money, so I could take care of my sis'. At least, until you got back."

Janey put her arms around Carl.

"Every girl should be so lucky to have a big brother like mine."

Mo looked around at all four again.

"This is the happiest day of my life. What do you hear from Max?"

Eddie saw his chance to jump in the conversation. "Max is doing great, Mo. He was in Paris the last time we got a letter. He's been writing a lot lately. The army is kicking Germany in the rear now and Max thinks they'll be in Berlin by spring."

Mo reached over and pulled Cecilia close, who was still crying.

"I just knew Max was doing good. And I can't wait to see Mama."

The smile faded from Cecilia's face, and her eyes betrayed the news she had. Mo knew instantly that something was wrong. Cecilia could barely get the words out as she told Mo.

"Mosie, Mama passed away while you were gone. We had no way to tell you. But we wouldn't have wanted to anyway."

For the first time in this joyous reunion, Mo was crestfallen, and a sad look came over his face. He was silent for a moment, then asked.

"What happened?"

Cecilia collected herself before she tried to answer.

"Mo, Mama went peacefully in her favorite chair. We found her holding onto her rosary. She said a rosary each day for you and Max."

Mo had tears welling in his eyes as he spoke.

"Now I know why I made it back here safe. I always knew Mama had a direct line to God."

Eddie put his arm around Mo's shoulder. "Mo, you will never know how proud of her boys your ma was. You both made her very happy."

"When we get back to Springfield, I want to go visit Mama. Can we go straight there? I want to say hi to her."

Cecilia gave Mo a hug.

"Of course we can. Mama will like that."

Carl picked up the duffel.

"What do you say we head home. I'll drive and Eddie can sit up front. You sit in the back in the middle between these two women Mo. I don't think either of 'em is through hugging you yet."

Mo looked over at Carl.

"That sounds like a good idea, Carl. Let's go home."

CHAPTER ONE HUNDRED ONE

Paris

TR and Max toiled in their offices on the Boulevard Voltaire, processing paperwork and requests for services, when a courier walked in, an American enlisted man.

"Lieutenants Gordon and Royce?"

"Yes soldier, what can we do for you?"

"I've been sent to drive you down to General LeClerc's HQ."

"Right now?" asked Max.

"Yes Sir."

TR sat in the front passenger seat with Max in the back.

"Wonder what's up, Max?"

"You got me. Unusual to be summoned to HQ."

When they arrived at headquarters, they went to a soldier at the front desk. The soldier checked their paperwork, then motioned to his left.

"Right through those doors, gentlemen. Colonel is expecting you."

When the men entered, the Colonel acknowledged them.

"Come in men. Don't bother sitting down. This won't take long. You've both been reassigned to Civil Affairs, Seventh Army. They're steaming toward Germany, and your skills will be needed when they reach Berlin. A convoy's heading out tomorrow morning to hook up with them. I'll have a jeep pick you up tomorrow, Zero Six Hundred hours. Be ready to go."

Both men's faces clearly showed satisfied looks upon hearing these orders as the Colonel continued.

"That's right, men. You heard me. The Seventh is moving fast. We're going to get that dirty little Nazi, Hitler. The Russians are closing fast from the other direction and it's turned into a race to see who gets there first. That's all. Congratulations. You are dismissed."

When TR and Max walked out of the building, Max's excitement was obvious.

"About time this war ends, and we're gonna be in Berlin when it does!"

CHAPTER ONE HUNDRED TWO
Washington DC April 1945

Senator Russell Royce stood on the lawn of the White House, his wife on his right while Congressman William Tucker and his wife were on his left, as President Franklin Delano Roosevelt's funeral procession passed. In a tribute to a great American, hundreds of thousands filled the streets of Washington to pay their respects. Platoons of soldiers marched in the procession and air force planes flew over in formation. It was both a sad yet proud moment for a nation which had been besieged.

The soldiers who stood at attention on the White House lawn and those all along the boulevard saluted the former Commander in Chief as the carriage was pulled slowly by six white stallions. The President's casket was covered with the American flag. Men and women wept as the President passed in front of them. They knew what he had meant to the United States of America during his terms in office.

Senator Royce leaned over to the Congressman.

"This is a sad day for me William. I greatly respected that man. I believe him to have been a man as great as we'll ever know in our lifetimes."

"He truly was, Senator. It seems so unfair for him to pass when we're so close to closing the door on this war."

"William, how many men would have over a million

people line the tracks from Warm Springs Georgia to Washington DC? The American people loved that man. They grew to trust him. We gained strength from him. Who knows? A lesser leader may have led to our demise instead of victory. America owes much to him."

"Senator, my wife and I are traveling in two days to Hyde Park when they lay the President to rest. I want to be there. Why don't we travel together?"

"William, that would be fine. When we return, we have a closed-door meeting with President Truman at the White House. It's up to him now to bring this war to a close. Germany is ours soon, but ending the war with Japan will be hell."

"I'll send a car to pick you up on the morning we go. Say ten?"

"The wife and I will be ready, William. Thank you."

CHAPTER ONE HUNDRED THREE

Washington DC

As long-time allies of President Roosevelt sat in the large White House meeting room waiting for President Harry Truman to come in, the men focused on the empty chair in the center of the long table which was formerly occupied by the Commander in Chief. The man who had occupied it for almost fifteen years would never sit in it again.

The doors opened, and in strode the newly sworn President, Harry Truman. He walked around the table and shook hands with those he passed, exchanging some small talk with some.

When Truman reached the empty chair, he did not sit immediately. Instead, he stood behind the chair with both hands on it, and looked around the room at all the men before he began.

"Thank you all for coming today. You are indeed a special group. You were all with President Roosevelt. You supported him through the toughest of times, even when it was not popular to do so. For that, you have my admiration. That's why I want to start this meeting standing behind this chair. Because I too stood behind President Roosevelt. He was a great man. I know I will never be able to be President Franklin Delano Roosevelt. I will have to be content to simply be President Harry Truman."

Stopping for a moment, the President turned a wry smile to the men before him.

"And I'm sorry to say, you will also have to be content with President Harry Truman!"

The men laughed at the President's remark, which served to loosen the mood.

"As all of you, it sorrows me that President Roosevelt did not live to see Hitler meet his fate. But I do take much solace in knowing he was confident that ultimate victory would soon be in hand."

The President paused, looking the men squarely in their eyes as he surveyed the room once more. Harry Truman looked more Presidential with every word.

"President Roosevelt rests at peace, because he knew he had successfully guided America through the most critical fifteen year span this nation has ever had to endure. He was the leader and strength this nation needed in its darkest moments. And for that, gentlemen, we may all thank God. We have risen to the challenges, men, and as a result of this, we are now the strongest nation on earth."

With that, everyone stood and applauded loudly. After a few moments, President Truman held up his arms to quiet the applause.

"Now Gentlemen, we must get back to work. This war is not over. Our men are not home. It is our job and the job of our great American military to bring them back. And it will also be our job to work together here in Washington to make sure our nation is ready for those men when they return. We must, we can and we will move into an era of great prosperity when this war has ended. And the soldiers who return will all be a part of that great prosperity."

With that, President Truman pulled the empty chair out and sat down, then pulled himself up to the table.

"I have items on today's agenda which we shall now go over."

Senator Royce looked over at Congressman Tucker, a smile on his face as he nodded to his friend. The men in the room were now secure, feeling that a good man was in charge.

Narration

All of evil will be put asunder. Some scores must wait until the reckoning. Others shall be settled on earth. Wickedness may run, but it can never hide.

CHAPTER ONE HUNDRED FOUR

Dachau Germany

As the morning dawned, Aaron slept on his bunk when his door opened. Two Nazi guards with machine guns looked in as Aaron rolled over to see the men standing at the door.

"The Commandant wants to see you. Come with us right now."

Without a word, Aaron stood, dressed quickly, and went with the men.

As Aaron arrived at the villa, he was surprised to see the Commandant standing in the street waiting. He noticed the Commandant had his sidearm Luger on his hip.

"Commandant, the guards made it sound important. Are the children alright?"

"They are fine, Aaron."

Then the Commandant addressed the two German soldiers.

"You two are dismissed. Leave us alone."

"Yes, Herr Commandant." The guards moved down the road back toward the camp.

"What is it, Sir?"

"Aaron, the allies are closing in on Germany. They will reach us soon."

"What does that have to do with me?"

"I sent for Lt. Klein. No one can find him or the two

men he always has with him. I want you to take me where you saw them take the girl. I will deal with Klein now."

"Yes, I will show you."

Aaron led the Commandant as they started on foot in the direction of Klein's private building.

Approaching the far reaches of the camp, the Commandant saw the two guards sitting next to the door of the building.

The Commandant walked briskly straight toward them. Seeing the Commandant, they both instinctively jumped to their feet, giving the heil salute. Their weapons were left leaning against the building. The Commandant did not return their salute, instead pulling the flap of his holster as he placed his hand on his weapon.

"Where is Klein?"

The guards looked at each other nervously, then glanced down at their weapons. "We do not know, Commandant."

"You're lying. He's inside. I'm going in!"

One of the soldiers pleaded with the Commandant.

"Commandant, you don't want to go in."

As the other guard bent down to retrieve his machine gun, the Commandant quickly pulled his Luger pistol. Without hesitation, the Commandant shot both men directly in the chest, then turned and kicked the door in. He entered the room as Aaron followed close behind.

Hearing the shots, Klein had jumped up off the bed, and was trying to put on his pants, as the Commandant trained his pistol on him.

A young nude girl with purple bruises on her face, arms and back curled up, as she attempted to cover her nakedness.

"Klein, you pig. You are an animal. Worse than an animal. Move over against the wall now!"

"Aaron, put a blanket around this girl. Take her outside and go down the road and wait for me. Do it!"

Aaron rushed over to the bed, yanked off the blanket, then wrapped it around the girl as he helped her up. He quickly took her out the door, leaving the Commandant alone with her attacker.

Klein looked at the Commandant with a sneer.

"You are a traitor to the Reich. You love the Jews. My uncle shall hear about you and what you do!"

"He may find out, but it will not be from you, pig!" The Commandant took aim and shot Klein directly in the scrotum. Klein screamed and grabbed for his groin as he dropped. Blood poured through his hands. As Klein writhed on the ground crying in agony, the Commandant slowly strode over to the man on the floor, then took aim at his skull.

"You and I shall meet again in Hell for what we have done. But you will go first."

The Commandant put two shots into Klein's head. The screaming subsided. The room was quiet, save the boots of the Commandant on the raised wood floor as he walked out, not looking back.

CHAPTER ONE HUNDRED FIVE

Springfield Illinois

Edward Vernon's car wheeled up to the curb. Mo hopped out, in full uniform, and moved briskly to the front door of the Ryan house and knocked.

As the entry door opened inside the screen, Mo smiled at Fern Ryan, Janey's mom.

"Well, Mo Gordon. God Bless You. Come on in."

Mo pulled open the screen and came in, then gave Fern a big hug.

"Great to see you again Mrs. Ryan. You look even younger and prettier than last time I was here."

"Oh, you cut that out. Where did you learn to butter up like that?"

"I always practice my buttering up! But with you I don't need to kid."

"Mo, you've turned yourself from a young soldier the first time you were here into a man. I can see it in your eyes."

"Well, Ma'am. After I left here, life got very serious."

"Life is always that way, Mo, always has been. I can only imagine how serious being in war was. But now you can start living a more normal life."

"Yes Ma'am. And appreciating it too!"

Now, Fern lowered her voice and glanced around to make sure Janey wasn't in the room yet.

"I can tell you there sure was one young lady that's had you on her mind every day you were gone."

"I was bent on getting back here to her, Mrs. Ryan."

Janey entered the room wearing a flowery pink dress that went below the knees, which successfully hid the knee joint of her prosthetic leg.

"Hi Mo."

"Hi Janey. Ready to go on our date?"

"Yes. Where are we going tonight?"

"Well, I promise we won't do this every date, but since I left, I've been reliving our first date over and over in my mind. I want to do it again, only this time for real. Movies at the Orpheum, then burgers and shakes. OK?"

"I can't think of anything I'd rather do tonight with a handsome soldier like yourself."

"Great. Mrs. Ryan, I'll get Janey home early, I promise."

"Well, I'm turning in early. I won't know what time you kids get in. Just go have a wonderful time. This is such a happy day for me, Mo. Now go on, you two."

Janey gave her mom a kiss on the cheek.

"See you later, Mama."

After the movie, Mo and Janey sat in the car eating their food and talking.

"So Janey, it's just you and your ma still living together?"

"Yes Mo. Just me and Mama."

"Have you ever thought about the day you might move out?"

"Well, not really. Until recently maybe."

Mo's eyes lit up.

"Really? You thought of it recently?"

"Mo Gordon, what are you getting at? Is something on your mind?"

Mo hesitated, then took a long drink from his milk shake.

"Well, I know we haven't been together very long, but, I just know you're the only woman I ever want to be with. I love you, Janey. Would you marry me?"

Janey looked at Mo with worshipping eyes, and tears started forming.

"Mo, it's not true we haven't been together very long. We might have been separated, but we've been together since the first night we met. I've loved you from the first time you kissed me. I knew you were going to come back, and that we would get married. Of course I will marry you!"

Mo leaned over and gave Janey a long kiss, then leaned back in his seat as he looked straight out the front window into the darkness outside.

"You don't know how many times I thought about this moment out in those jungles, and I'm finally here. It's just like I dreamed it would be."

"Mo, I can't honestly say I saw us having burgers and shakes before you would ask me to get married, but this is just as romantic as anything I came up with."

"What will your mom think? I mean, I'll be taking you away from her."

"My mama loves you, Mo. She's going to be thrilled. And Carl thinks you're the end all, and that's saying something for my big brother."

Mo smiled.

"Yeah, I want to keep Carl on my good side. Janey, I have some money saved, but not much. We'll need to rent to start. Someday we'll buy our own house. Would you mind living at our place with Edward and Cecilia until we have more money? It's a big house and we'd be away from those two."

"I'm OK with that Mo. I think the world of Eddie and Cecilia. But do you think they would be OK with that?"

"Oh yeah, I already talked with them."

"Really? What if I had said no?"

"I didn't think of that possibility."

"I make pretty good money playing at the club, Mo. My tips are usually more than my wages."

"Well, as soon as the war ends and I get released, I'll get a job. We'll do just fine."

"Do you still want to work at Sangamo, like Eddie?"

"No. I'm going to try to hook on at the Illinois Journal and Register. I want to be a writer, and I'm going for it. That's what I really want to be."

"Well, I think you'll be a great writer Mo. We may just have to clean up your diction a little, maybe a few less contractions."

"You know, when I try, I can speak and write in a proper manner, Miss. It's just when you're marching through jungles in Burma with two thousand sweaty, smelly men your speech and writing can tend to get a little sloppy, if you know what I mean."

Janey just looked over at Mo, smiled and shook her head.

"I just can't imagine what you did over there, Mo."

Mo hesitated, then smiled.

"I'm just glad it's done. I don't think I'd have it in me to do it again."

"You'll never need to."

After a few more seconds, Mo asked.

"Janey, do you want children?"

"Of course I do silly. But maybe we can wait a little to have our first baby."

"Yeah OK. But not too long."

Janey rolled her eyes.

"Oh Brother!"

Eastern France

The American military convoy stretched for miles as it wound its way through the open European countryside. Jeeps and trucks loaded with soldiers moved eastward. Weather was favorable for fast movement, being mild and sunny.

TR and Max were in one jeep, TR driving. Both men wore full combat gear, while Max had a carbine across his lap. Another rifle sat upright between the two men.

"Well TR, one thing about this war. You never know what the hell you're doing or where you'll end up. Here we think we're going to join up with the Seventh headed straight for Berlin and the next damn thing you know we're changing course for a prisoner of war camp outside of Munich."

"Yeah, Max. At least they think it's a POW camp. Recon reports say it looks like a hell of a big prison camp from the air. What else could it be?"

"We're following the troops right in TR. There's not much resistance. Germans are running back to Berlin to cluster around their Fuhrer, but it's not going to do them any good."

"I want to fry that little scumbag's ass, Max."

"You and every other GI in Europe."

TR stretched up over the windshield as he held onto the steering wheel, yelling out loudly.

"We're comin' to get you Hitler!"

TR sat down as the men sat in silence for only a bit as they moved along the road. Two soldiers with faces brown from the dust of the vehicles in front of them.

"TR. Have you thought about what you're gonna do after the war ends?"

"Yeah, Max, I have. I've decided I'm going back to work for Congressman William Tucker from New York, but it will be in Washington most of the time. I want to go into politics. Someday I could be in Congress, maybe the Senate."

"Oh yeah? Well, you have the pedigree for it. And now with your military record? You're a shoo-in, baby. Hell, as far as I can tell, you're squeaky clean, TR. No baggage."

"Max, I don't think all of our politicians in Washington are squeaky clean, but the ones I've met seem like good men."

"Probably because your dad the Senator is a stand-up guy, TR. Birds of a feather flock together you know."

"Yeah. I look up to my dad. He's a helluva guy."

Both men sat for another moment when TR started up again.

"OK, so now you tell me your plans, Max. I let you in on mine."

"I like being in this man's army. I'm going for Judge Advocate General's Corp."

TR looked over.

"JAG? Really? Yeah, I can see that. You'd be really good there, Max. Maybe you can end up in Washington. That's where all the action is."

"Wouldn't be bad. If you get to be a Senator, maybe you can help put me there?"

"Not so fast, Max. I'd have to win a couple of elections 'til I get to Senator."

"Those elections are going to be landslides. Mark my word."

As he studied the landscape as he drove, TR remarked to Max.

"We go through places that have been blown to shreds, really scorched. Then we go twenty kilometers through areas completely untouched. Hard to figure, huh Max?"

"Yeah. It's just good to see both sides couldn't make enough bombs to blow up every square mile of Europe."

Silence set in again as both men stared ahead, moving toward their objective, a Nazi camp outside Munich.

CHAPTER ONE HUNDRED SEVEN
Dachau Germany Morning April 29, 1945

Nazis herded Jews into trucks as fast as they could push them, but most prisoners looked and moved like walking dead. Amid the chaos, the din of shelling and explosions getting closer overshadowed everything.

A Nazi officer yelled at his men.

"Hurry, Hurry! Get them in the trucks. We need to move these prisoners out of here!"

The soldiers continued to push and beat prisoners, but it did no good, as they were too physically weak to move faster.

Another officer hurried over to the first officer who was yelling orders.

"We will never get all of them out in time. The Americans are too close. There are too many prisoners. We must leave now and get to Berlin. Leave these Jews. Do you want to get caught here and be machine gunned by Americans?"

The first officer looked at the other man, then at the lines of prisoners still to be loaded into the trucks. He thought for a moment, as the sound of artillery fire got louder.

"You are right. Give the order to the men to get ready to leave. Lock the gates. The rest stay here. Instruct some guards to stay in the towers to keep them inside until we are gone."

Further down the road, in the Nazi German section of Dachau, officers frantically loaded whatever they could salvage into trucks as their families sat in vehicles waiting to leave. All were dressed in civilian clothes, not military uniforms.

The Commandant stood next to his vehicle with a soldier in the driver's seat. His wife and two children were in the back seat. Two soldiers with machine guns stood guard next to the car. The Commandant instructed his driver.

"Wait here for me. I will be right back."

Then he ran back into the house. As he entered the living room, Aaron was waiting for him.

"Aaron, I must leave now with my family to go to Munich. I have a house there. I sent for you because if I did not, my men would have taken you away with the others."

Aaron looked at the Commandant.

"To be killed?"

"Yes, to be killed. Now listen to me. I must leave my artwork behind. I have money, but we cannot travel freely with the art. Aaron, stay with the art. I will hide you so my soldiers do not find you or the artwork. Come with me quickly."

The Commandant led Aaron into his office where he went over to the large bookcase on one wall behind the desk and pulled on one end of it. The entire bookcase rolled out, exposing a hidden room filled with paintings on shelves and in slots.

"Hide in here. If my men come into the house do not make a sound. They will take you away in the trucks if they find you, or kill you right here."

"How long will I need to stay in here?"

"It won't be long. The Americans are coming. There is a little hole behind the books here where you can see the room but they cannot see you. When Americans get here, push the wall to get out. Hopefully good Americans find you and will not harm you. I cannot take you with us where we are going. Will you know what Americans sound like?"

"Yes. I was taught the English by my father."

"Very well. Goodbye Aaron."

"Goodbye, Commandant. I hope the children will be alright. And, thank you."

"Go in. I will close the wall. Be silent now."

The Commandant ran out to the waiting car and quickly climbed into the front seat next to the driver as the car sped off, as the sounds of intense firefighting neared and the ground reverberated from explosions.

CHAPTER ONE HUNDRED EIGHT

Dachau Germany Late Afternoon April 29, 1945

With much of Max's and TR's convoy already parked on the roads surrounding the grounds of Dachau, their jeep pulled into the area. A group of Nazi soldiers that did not escape in time sat cross-legged in the dirt as American soldiers guarded them. The bloodied bodies of dead Nazis killed in the recent final fire-fight were scattered about.

The gates to Dachau had been opened, allowing the walking skeletons to come out. Medics helped those they could, while others wandered like zombies down the road toward Munich.

"Oh my God, Max. I could never imagine anything like this. How could they do this?"

"I don't know, TR. What we're seeing can't be explained. It's inhuman. I can't believe my own eyes." As TR and Max stepped out of their vehicle, they heard screaming over where the prisoners were being held captive. One American soldier had totally lost his composure and had his rifle aimed at the Nazis sitting on the ground.

"You sons of bitches. You should all be dead for what you've done here! God damn you!"

As he stood there, crying uncontrollably, trying to make himself pull the trigger, an American officer behind him yelled.

"Soldier! Stand down! Lower your weapon! Don't ruin your life by killing them! Lower your weapon! Now!"

The soldier looked over, lowered his weapon and turned away, sobbing, overwhelmed by the horror he was seeing.

TR looked over at Max.

"You know Max. I'd find it hard to hold it against that guy if he had pulled the trigger."

"I know what you mean. I feel the same. Who could have imagined the Nazis would be capable of this kind of evil?"

"I'll tell you one thing Max. If this is the kind of sick world the Nazis were planning on shoving down everybody's throat, then not one of our soldiers in this war has died in vain. They just weren't fully aware of the noble cause they fought for."

An officer came over to Max and TR.

"Lieutenants Gordon, Royce. Captain would like you to report to him. He's about a half kilometer down this road where the Germans lived." TR and Max climbed back in their jeep and rumbled down the dirt road that soon turned to cobblestone as they neared their destination.

A few officers surrounded the Captain, and thirty or so GIs with carbines stood by.

"OK, men, listen up."

As the Captain started speaking, a jeep screamed into their midst and came to a screeching halt, dust flying. A junior officer jumped out, sweating, his face white like he had just seen a ghost. He ran over to where the Captain was standing, completely out of breath.

"Captain, Sir."

The Captain, who could see the urgency in the soldier's face, stopped what he was saying.

"What's going on soldier?"

"Sir, on the train tracks, we found, about fifty cattle cars full of, full of corpses, Sir. Bodies, just piled on top of bodies. They all looked like skeletons. It was horrible. There must be over a thousand bodies, Sir."

The men standing there had varying degrees of looks, ranging from shock, disgust and disbelief. The Captain, momentarily taken aback, stood speechless. Finally, righting himself out of his shocked state, he spoke.

"Jesus Christ help us. What the hell was going on in this place? This was just a damn death camp."

Then, he looked at the men close by around him, including TR and Max. "We need to know if there are any more of these Nazi bastards hiding around here. I want two officers and six GIs per detail. Let's make sure this goddam area is clear of any Nazis. Check each house. Be thorough, but be careful. If you find any Nazis, you have my permission to shoot them when... if they try to escape."

All the men answered in unison.

"Yes Sir."

As TR and Max and the six GIs assigned to them exited the house next to the Commandant's villa, they approached the nicest and largest building on the street. Every man carried a rifle at the ready. As they ran up to the front door, two men stood at the side as one man tried to push the door open, only to find out it was locked. Stepping back, one soldier blasted the doorknob and kicked the door in. The men proceeded as though hostiles were waiting. After hearing the first three soldiers in the building yelling 'clear', Max and TR went in.

As the other six went silently through the house, TR and Max looked around at the nicest home they had been in yet in this camp.

"Max, this must be where boss man lived."

"Tell me about it. This guy was living the high life."

Soon, the other soldiers came back into the main room, where one of the soldiers reported.

"The house is clear."

"Very good. Lieutenant Royce and I are going to check this place out ourselves for a few minutes. You and the rest of the men wait outside and stand down."

"Yes Sir."

As they walked through the house cautiously in case a hostile was missed, TR and Max kept their weapons ready. As they entered the Commandant's office, they saw his magnificent desk, large filled bookcases and artwork hanging on the walls.

"Look at this place, TR. This guy's living in luxury while they're starving and killing prisoners a few hundred meters down the road."

"Yeah Max, and if this Death Factory's been here since the war started, you can imagine how many people died in the last five years."

Max shook his head.

"I don't even want to think about it."

Aaron was silent behind the bookcase as he hid, but when he heard Max and TR speaking, he knew they were Americans, and slowly pushed on the wall, making it move. Startled, Max and TR both moved away and trained their weapons on the opening, ready to shoot. Aaron stepped into view.

Seeing him first, TR shouted to Max.

"Don't shoot Max. This guy's not a Nazi."

Then, he directed his voice at Aaron.

"Who are you? Is anyone else in there?"

"I am Aaron Gittelsohn. I am the only one left." Aaron pushed the bookcase all the way open, revealing the massive collection of artworks.

Max moved forward into the hidden room looking around while TR kept his rifle trained on Aaron.

"What the hell? Will you look at this?"

Max turned back to Aaron.

"Any more hidden rooms?"

"No, only this one."

Then Max asked Aaron.

"Do you know if these are real? Are they valuable?"

Aaron looked back over the cache as he answered.

"They are all original masterpieces worth a fortune."

TR then interjected.

"Max, we've heard from so many of those along the way that the Germans took everything of value. The head man had his own big chunk stashed right here. Just ran like a rat and couldn't take it with him."

"Now what should we do, TR?"

"We close up the wall and get this guy outta here. Then we go tell the Captain."

"Yeah, OK." Max pushed the bookcase wall back in place while TR still watched Aaron, keeping his rifle trained on him. TR glared at Aaron.

"You come with us."

As they walked out the front door, the six soldiers out front all jumped to alertness upon seeing Aaron, as the earlier reporting soldier spoke.

"Lieutenants, that house was clean. I don't know how we missed him."

"Don't worry men," said TR. "He had a helluva special hiding place. Wasn't your fault."

Max gave the men an order.

"I want three of you to guard the back of this building and three stay out front. Nobody goes in there until we get back with the Captain. Got it?"

"Yes Sir."

TR and Max marched Aaron in front of them like a prisoner as they moved toward the street where they left the Captain. As they arrived at the spot, the Captain was no longer there, just soldiers milling around three jeeps. One of the soldiers saw TR and Max approaching, their rifles trained on Aaron.

"You found a Nazi hiding, Lieutenants?"

Max answered.

"We don't think he's a Nazi. Where's Captain?"

"He's back at the main gate to this hell hole, Sir."

"OK. We're taking this guy to the Captain." The men ordered Aaron into the passenger seat of a jeep as TR sat behind him, the rifle to Aaron's head as Max got in the driver's seat.

TR from the back seat warned Aaron.

"Try anything funny, I shoot you!"

Aaron sat calmly and silently as he stared straight ahead.

As Max pulled out, TR started talking from the back seat.

"This guy's a little thin, but not emaciated like the others. He looks healthy even."

Then addressing Aaron, TR asked him.

"Why don't you look like the others? Why were you in there? Did the head man keep you as his pretty boy? Was he a weirdo?"

With no emotion, Aaron answered.

"I taught the Commandant's children to play the violin."

After all he had witnessed since arriving at Dachau, with sarcasm in his voice, TR continued.

"Yeah, right. Max, if this guy was a Nazi collaborator, all we've got to do is stick him with the other prisoners. Even though they're skinny and weak, they'll still tear him apart."

Aaron answered calmly.

"You may think what you want. I did nothing wrong."

Max looked over with a smirk. "We'll see about that. Let's take him to the prisoners, TR, before we go get the Captain."

"Ten four, Max."

As the jeep pulled up in front of where the masses of prisoners were being fed and cared for, TR ordered Aaron.

"Get out!"

Aaron stepped out of the jeep. Before TR could climb out of the back seat, Leo, who was with a group of now liberated prisoners, caught sight of Aaron and ran over to him, hugging and kissing him on the cheek.

"Aaron, I give thanks you are alive. We were worried the Nazis took you away in the trucks with the others."

Max looked at the joyous old man.

"You know this man? He was not a Nazi collaborator?"

"Oh, no, no! If not for Aaron and his parents Abraham and Golde, many more would have died."

Leo turned back toward the prisoners and pointed, then continued.

"Many who you see here owe them their lives. Through their work for the Commandant, they were able to bargain for food and medicine for others. Never did they take for themselves, only for those who needed it most."

Max looked over at TR.

"We had this guy pegged all wrong, TR. He's actually kind of a hero." TR lowered his weapon as Aaron looked at him, a serious, yet weary and sad look.

"Aaron, I'm sorry."

Aaron looked at both men before he answered.

"I understand why you thought what you did."

Max then asked Aaron.

"Do you know anything about that stuff we found back there?"

"I know everything about it."

"Then you're going with us to see the Captain, Aaron. Get back in the jeep. He's gotta see what we found."

Aaron hugged Leo and smiled at the now free man.

"Leo, now we shall live again. The time has come as my father foresaw. Thank you for all of you have done."

"You are the one to be thanked, Aaron."

Leo hugged Aaron once more and kissed him on both cheeks.

"Now go with these two soldiers. I will never forget you, young man. I love you."

"And I you, Leo", as Aaron got back in the jeep.

After they located the Captain, the three men led him into the Commandant's office. As he looked around, the Captain asked the men. "OK men. You have my curiosity. What exactly is it that was so important I come here to see?"

TR looked over at Aaron.

"Aaron, show the Captain where you were hiding when we searched this house."

Aaron went over to the bookcase and pulled on it, opening it up to reveal the massive collection of art. As the Captain saw the bookcase roll back, he stood, stunned at the sight.

"Oh my God."

He walked into the room, looking everything over.

"This is real? These are original paintings?"

Aaron stood beside him and pointed all around.

"Every piece you see is a priceless work of art from many of the masters. My father was in charge of the Commandant's collection until he died in the camp, then I took over. My father was a learned historian of art, and taught me also."

The Captain surveyed the room, not saying a word, then turned to Max and TR.

"Gentlemen, you've just pulled off a major coup. You just uncovered as much Nazi loot as hundreds of MFAA agents."

The Captain walked about, looking at the masterpieces, then turned back to the three men again.

"Lieutenants, this accomplishment by you two and Aaron will be talked about for years, maybe decades. Hell, I might even be promoted because of you two." Then, walking out of the room, the Captain continued.

"I'm going to report this to HQ in Paris. This is an incredible find. Lieutenant Gordon, come with me. Lieutenant Royce, stay here with Aaron until we get back."

"Yes Sir."

The Captain and Max left the house.

When they had left, TR started talking with Aaron.

"You know Aaron, that all of this was stolen from others."

"Yes. The Commandant also had money and jewelry in his satchel. He took that with him. That was also taken from others by the Nazis."

TR shook his head.

"These damn Nazis were killing people so they could rob them. People worked their whole life for things like this and then it was all just taken."

"The Commandant told me the Germans wanted to create a pure race. They wanted an Aryan Nation. They were willing to kill to do it."

"What was the deal with this Commandant you talk about? Why did he save you before he left?"

"The Commandant was forced to work for Hitler. He told me they would kill his family if he refused. He tried to save his children. He did evil things, but he was not an evil person."

TR looked at Aaron, not saying a word while he thought about what Aaron said. "After what he did to so many people, and seeing the death that was all around, I don't know how you can give him any credit, Aaron. Good people wouldn't sell out their morals and do what he did, even to save their children."

"Perhaps, but I think unless you were put in that position, you don't really know what you would do."

The Captain and Max came back into the house and the Captain relayed his information.

"HQ wants everything brought back to Paris. We need to move this now. They don't want Russians to roll in here and try to lay claim to any of it."

Max stood next to TR as the Captain continued.

"I'm sending you two back to Paris with the artwork. A full detail will be assembled to make a small convoy. Two trucks with the art and seven jeeps escorting. Each truck will have two men and the jeeps will each have four soldiers."

TR then quizzed the Captain.

"Then we're not going to Berlin from here?"

"No Lieutenant. This is much too important. I need you both to document the art as it's loaded into the trucks. Every painting must be accounted for."

The Captain addressed Aaron.

"Aaron, will you help my men to identify and label this artwork."

"Yes. I don't want the Nazis to get these paintings."

A slight smile crept over the Captain's face. "Aaron, the

Nazis are finished. We just don't want the Russians to get hold of them."

Aaron then added.

"Then not only the works in this room, but every painting hanging in this villa should go. They are all masterpieces."

"Alright men, get started. I'm sending the convoy here now. We need this packed and on the road back to Paris by sunrise tomorrow."

Max answered.

"Yes sir, we're on it. Right away."

As the Captain walked to the door, he turned back around.

"Two things, men. I will be alerting our trailing forces heading this way to give the convoy right of way on the roads. And remember this. There are still rogue Nazi snipers out there, roaming the countryside. They work alone and they're deadly. Keep your eyes open. This war's not over yet."

"Yes Sir."

Both men saluted as the Captain left the room. When the Captain had left, TR asked Max.

"Hey Max. I didn't want to act stupid in front of the Captain and you acted like you knew what he was talking about. What the hell is the MFAA anyway?"

Max had a surprised look.

"Why TR! That report came across our desks when we were back in DC working on the army manual for Major Brandwyn."

"OK then," sputtered TR, "I got it. Just because I don't read every piece of paper that comes at us like you do. What is it?"

"It stands for Monuments, Fine Arts and Archives. They're actually a part of our Civil Affairs and Military

Government Division. They started back in forty-three. Their whole job is to search for Nazi plunder."

"Wow, then the Captain's right. Because of Aaron opening that case when we were here, we bumbled into a big deal."

"A really big deal, TR. Think about it. Can't hurt you becoming a Senator!"

"We'll see about that Max. OK, let's get to work on this stuff and get on the road."

"One more thing TR."

"What's that, Max?"

"Captain's a stand-up guy. I heard his radio transmission to HQ. He gave all the credit for this find to the three of us in this room."

CHAPTER ONE HUNDRED NINE

German Countryside

The sun was rising behind the convoy as it moved westward away from Dachau. Three jeeps in front, followed by two trucks laden with artwork, while four jeeps brought up the rear. The day was warming quickly and the sky was crystal blue.

In the lead jeep, an enlisted soldier drove, as TR sat in the front passenger seat. Max and Aaron sat in the back seats. All the men wore helmets with rifles at the ready, except for Aaron, who sat silently, his violin case next to him on the seat.

The jeep moved down the road, bumping along, the driver needing to swerve occasionally to avoid big potholes and ruts in the road.

TR turned around in his seat to talk to the men in the back. "Well Max, we almost caught up to the action, and here we are headed back to Paris."

"Go figure, but who could have seen this turn of events coming at us?"

Then, looking at Aaron, TR continued.

"Aaron, how long were you in the camp?"

"Five years. I thought I would die in the camp like my mother and father, and so many others."

Max turned to Aaron.

"Aaron, there's no words to describe what went on there. The Nazis were like devils on Earth. I think Hitler is Satan himself. How an entire nation could do what they did, I will never understand."

"Germany was poor. They have always hated the Jews. The people let themselves get brainwashed because a leader emerged who told them he would solve all their problems and take care of them. Germany was only told information Hitler wanted them to hear. My father told me this and many other things in the five years we lived in one room."

Aaron paused for a few seconds, then finished.

"Now it is over."

"Aaron," asked TR. "What happened to your parents in the camp?"

"They both died from Typhus, but not like the others in the camp. The Commandant admired my father and mother, and had them both buried in Munich. He even put headstones for each." TR turned back around as the jeep moved along on the road, the four men sitting in silence.

After riding on for some time, TR looked over at the soldier driving.

"You're doing a great job dodging the potholes. Clear sailing so far."

The driver looked over at TR with a smile.

"Yes Sir. And that's the way we want it!"

CHAPTER ONE HUNDRED TEN

German Forest

Fifteen kilometers ahead of the convoy, open rolling countryside gave way to a forested area which rolled right down next to the road.

At the edge of the treeline was a giant oak with full foliage, a German sniper perched in the crook of the tree. The marksman blended perfectly, his camouflage uniform and painted face making him nearly invisible. He straddled comfortably on one of the fat horizontal limbs in the center of the tree. As he surveyed the countryside, he patiently eyed the road which stretched to the east.

Peering off in the distance, he could see dust rising from the road, with no vehicles yet visible. The sniper peered through his scope as he calibrated it onto the road.

As the convoy rolled west along the still open countryside, TR turned back around.

"Aaron, after we pass off the artwork in Paris, do you want to go back to Munich? We can make sure the army gets you home."

"I will never return to Germany. There is nothing for me there now. It is my dream and the dream of my father for me to go to America. There I will start a new life."

Max looked at Aaron, then TR.

"What do you think, TR? After all that Aaron has done

for us to save this art, and for what he did for the prisoners in that camp, we should be able to do something."

"Hell yes we can Max. Aaron, consider it done. My father can help us. We'll get you to America, and when we do, we'll help you get settled."

Aaron looked at both men, and the first smile they had seen came over his face.

"You are both very kind. Thank you."

Off in the distance, the convoy now came into the sniper's view, still almost five kilometers away. The marksman took out a small telescope and opened it to view the approaching vehicles. Seeing the four men in the lead jeep, he calmly closed the instrument, then situated himself behind his rifle. He slowly adjusted the crosshairs on the rifle's scope as the first jeep came clearer into view.

Through the scope, he trained first on the driver, then on TR in the front seat. He moved the view to the back seat taking a bead on Max, then moved it onto Aaron's chest, the only rider in the jeep not in a uniform. He rolled back onto Max, then back to Aaron. The crosshairs stayed on Aaron's chest as the jeep drew closer. The sniper's finger began to slowly squeeze the trigger.

Just at that moment, the driver saw a large pothole in the road and swerved to avoid it. A single shot rang out, the bullet piercing the jeep just between Max and Aaron. Max looked at the gash in the seat back next to him and screamed.

"Holy hell, somebody's shooting at us! Get down!"

The driver gunned the jeep forward, swerving as TR ducked and Max lunged over to push Aaron down, getting on top of him. As another shot rang out, Max let out an ugly grunt and slumped over Aaron, blood spurting out the back of Max's shirt. TR turned around and saw Max.

"Jesus. Max! Max!"

The driver slammed on the brakes, bringing the jeep to a stop, with the driver and TR bailing out. The two of them dragged Max's body out of the vehicle, putting him on the ground behind the jeep. Aaron jumped out and crouched with the other three. Max was conscious, but beads of sweat already had started forming on his head as he looked up at TR.

The two jeeps behind the lead vehicle raced past the stopped jeep, zigzagging furiously until they reached the edge of the forest. Soldiers jumped out and fanned into the forest as they searched for the sniper.

TR tore off part of Max's shirt to see the wound, then stuffed the shirt into the hole in Max's shoulder left by the bullet.

"Hang in there, Max. We'll stop this bleeding and get you to a medic." The distinctive sound of a Browning Automatic Rifle came from the woods ahead, then silence, as TR looked at Aaron.

"I need to go ahead and see what happened. Push on this to stop the bleeding."

Aaron reached over to push against Max's wound, taking over for TR.

"Max saved my life."

TR started sprinting zigzag toward the other two jeeps positions, but no more bullets came his way. After a few minutes, TR came running back to the jeep.

"They got him. One son of a bitch in a tree. Let's get Max into the back seat. Medics are in the next town ten kilometers from here. We've got to step on it. He's losing too much blood!"

CHAPTER ONE HUNDRED ELEVEN

Washington DC

Senator Russell Royce and Congressman William Tucker were seated in the White House meeting room with many of the same men who attended President Truman's first meeting some months before, just after President Roosevelt's funeral. As they waited for the President to arrive, they had no knowledge of why they had been summoned to the White House. After a few minutes, with everyone seated, President Truman entered the room accompanied by his Secretary of State and close advisors. Before any members had a chance to stand, Truman gestured for everyone to stay seated, then walked directly over to his chair.

"Thank you for coming. I have an important announcement, and I want you all to hear this directly from me. A few of you may know, the United States has been developing a tremendous weapon. This is something even I did not find out about from President Roosevelt. Only after I took the oath of office was I privy to the ongoing 'Manhattan Project'. There is no reason to keep this secret any longer Gentlemen, because the world will know very soon. It seems that a quiet unassuming Senator from Missouri, yours truly, has been put in charge of a weapon of unprecedented force. We have developed the most powerful bomb ever created. It is a uranium atomic bomb."

No man in the room spoke. The President had the floor. All eyes were on the President, and every man in the room was intent and serious as they listened.

"We won the war in Europe, and it was a great victory. But for months now in the Pacific and Asia, the Japanese fight us doggedly. Their pride, perhaps even stupidity, prevent this war from ending. They know they are losing, and that we and our allies will ultimately prevail, yet our men are still being killed over there. It is simply not acceptable any more. Therefore, I want you to know that I have listened and pondered. In the end, based on the advice of my advisors, both military and civilian, I have made a determination. Any attempt to invade the mainland of Japan will result in horrific American military casualties, as well as Japanese military and civilians dying. We cannot and will not accept the invasion option. Our nation is wearied of war. So, given the options, I have directed the military to utilize our newest weapon. Many will condemn this decision. It will be debated for decades. The responsibility stops, however, at my desk. The truth is, gentlemen, Hirohito has ordered civilians to kill themselves rather than be taken alive. Japanese propaganda has convinced Japanese civilians that if captured, our men will rape or murder them. The worst lie they have spread among their people is that to become a United States Marine it is necessary for the soldiers to murder their own parents. To sum it up, Japanese civilians will perish by the tens of thousands with our bombing strike. The collateral damage is inevitable. The truth be told, however, is that we will be saving millions of lives by not sending in a land and air invasion force. Men, we're damned if we do and damned if we don't."

The President then paused before continuing.

"That being said, as I speak to you here in our nation's

capital, we have a B-29 Bomber in the air with an atomic bomb targeting Hiroshima Japan. If this mission is successful, we hope and pray the Japanese will accept terms of surrender. This attack should force the end to the most destructive war in history. Gentlemen, at this point, we pray this mission works to perfection, our brave crew comes home safely, and that the rest of American troops are not far behind them. It's time this war stops. You will all be kept up to speed on our mission today. Thank you all, and may God Bless this United States of America."

With that the President rose, every other man in the room standing with him. The President left the room without another word, followed by those who entered with him.

After the President's departure, chatter began among those left in the room.

Senator Royce looked at the Congressman standing next to him.

"I'd say that quiet Senator from Missouri makes a pretty damn good President, William."

"I agree, Senator. And that's saying something, considering the man he just followed."

CHAPTER ONE HUNDRED TWELVE

New York Harbor

Swarms of families waited anxiously for homecoming soldiers to disembark from troopship Queen Elizabeth on a weather perfect late September afternoon.

As the gangplank opened, soldiers rushed down, looking for loved ones. Others walked solemnly, knowing no one waited, only that it would be up to them to wire home via western union to let family know when to expect them. Still other soldiers made their way to a bus or train station, simply to show up where they were going.

Most disembarking men's faces showed joy and happiness, while some seemed lost and morose. Nowhere to go and not knowing what to do.

Senator Royce and family waited in the special cordoned off area. They scanned the decks near the gangplank, hoping to catch sight of TR, when the Senator's wife spoke. "How will we ever see TR? I've never seen so many soldiers, Russell."

"This may take a bit, dear. Eisenhower's crammed over fifteen thousand troops on this crossing. The men are in a hurry to get home."

Just then, TR's sister pointed and yelled out.

"Look. There he is! It's TR!"

As he moved slowly along the rail approaching the gangplank, TR could be seen. His duffel was slung over his shoulder as he looked out at the sea of humanity below him on the dock. As he searched for his family, he spotted his little sister as she jumped up and down frantically, flailing with both arms.

The family could see TR's smile all the way from where they stood. TR reached to his left and brought another young man, not in uniform, to the rail and pointed down to his family, then waved.

As the Senator and TR's mom waved, the Senator leaned over to his wife.

"That young man must be the Jewish boy they rescued from the Nazi prison. I pulled some strings to get him on the transport."

As the men neared the gangplank, another soldier arrived at the rail, his arm in a sling. TR pointed again down to the family, as Max looked down on the dock.

When the three men reached the dock and made their way through the melee of happy reunions, they entered the cordoned area. TR headed immediately to his mom and gave her a big hug and kiss on her cheek as his sisters clamored around, hugging him from behind. As TR greeted his mom, Max and Aaron watched the family joy. TR then turned and gave his Dad a handshake, then pulled him into a hug.

"Welcome home, son."

"Thanks Dad. I missed all of you. It's good to be back on good old American soil."

TR turned around to Max and Aaron.

"Everybody, this is Max Gordon and Aaron Gittelsohn. Aaron helped us recover the art treasure and identify the pieces. He's a walking textbook when it comes to art."

The Senator shook hands with Aaron first.

"Welcome Aaron. I want you to know that I've made some arrangements for you here in America to help you get settled."

"Thank you, Sir. I'm very happy to be in America."

The Senator shook hands with Max, grabbing the hand not in the sling.

"Max, I feel like I know you already. TR's told us so much about you in his letters."

"Thanks Senator. I hope he only told you the good stuff."

"Absolutely. Everything was quite complimentary. And it's an honor to meet you knowing that in addition to being responsible for recovery of the artwork, you're a hero. Throwing yourself in front of a bullet while covering this other young man? Not many would do such a thing."

Max responded with a sheepish, humble look.

"Senator, I can't say I was planning on taking a bullet. Getting shot hurts way too much. It just turned out that way. These fellas saved my life when I was shot by stopping the bleeding and getting me to the medics."

"Nevertheless, Max, it was a very brave thing you did."

"Thank you, Senator."

"And Aaron, your story of being in the Nazi camp for so many years and now coming to America is front page news here. It's in all the newspapers. Your help and expertise with the recovery of the art found at the camp has my office fielding inquiries about you from some of America's most prestigious art museums."

Aaron just smiled and acknowledged the warmth and acceptance that this prominent American family offered.

"Thank you, Sir. TR and Max have been very kind to me. I'm glad and very lucky it was them when I opened the bookcase. The right people were sent at the right time."

TR put his hand on Aaron's shoulder.

"It was meant to be, Aaron."

The Senator's face beamed with happiness with the safe return of his son, being surrounded by his entire family.

"Well I want all three of you young men to know how humbled we are to stand here with you, and we're very proud."

TR cracked a sly smile when he responded.

"Spoken like a true Washington politician!"

Then, quickly, he put his arm around his dad and laughed.

"Only kidding Dad. Well, maybe halfway kidding."

The Senator, looked up at his tall, handsome son with a smile.

"Well I'm too damn happy to see you to get mad at you!"

The Senator looked at Max.

"I have news for all of you, especially Max. Max's twin Mo was a big hero in Burma."

Max interjected.

"Yes Sir. Word gets around quick in the army. Everyone's heard about Mo's story when his battalion was surprised by the Japs in the jungle. But it doesn't surprise me that my brother would do that. He's always had more guts than anybody. Now it's made him kind of a celebrity."

"That's right, Max," said the Senator. "And the President has taken notice. Mo is on his way to Washington right now for a black-tie dinner at the White House, and you three are also going to be guests of honor."

The three men had surprised looks, while Max's eyes lit up.

"Mo's on his way to Washington and we get to go to the White House?"

The Senator gave Max a pat on the back.

"Max, you're not just going. You three will be honored

there for what you did. And the President is anxious to meet Aaron."

"Wow, how about that TR?"

The Senator went on.

"Staff has informed me that not only is the military awarding a bronze star to every member of Mo's battalion, but Mo is going to be the recipient of our country's Congressional Medal of Honor. And you will be receiving your purple heart, Max. Straight from the President himself."

The Senator then looked over at TR.

"How about these Gordon twins?"

"I'd say they were like two peas in a pod, Dad."

The Senator continued talking.

"Max, seems Mo wouldn't make the trip to Washington for dinner with the President unless they invited three other members of his unit from Burma."

"Yeah, that definitely sounds like my brother, Senator. Sharing the praise and awards."

"Well, it's going to be a grand event to honor American heroes! Now, why don't you three let me take you for a big fat steak dinner? Then you can all relax in your own hotel rooms tonight before we drive to DC tomorrow. I've made all the arrangements."

Max looked over at TR with an amazed look, then back at Aaron before responding. "Senator Royce, TR told me about his dad, but you are way better in person. Thank you, Sir."

"It's my pleasure, Max. It's a great day."

CHAPTER ONE HUNDRED THIRTEEN
Washington DC

TR and Max waited on the platform as the train pulled into the depot. Military uniforms were everywhere as America basked in the glow of winning the war. Mo and Janey were two of the first people to appear at the top of the steps on the train. Mo stepped down first, then reached up to help Janey as she carefully stepped down one step at a time, rather skillfully with her new artificial leg.

Max and TR hurried to where Mo and Janey stood.

"Mo, are you a sight for sore eyes. Good to see you brother!"

Max put his good arm around Mo and the brothers hugged. Max then hugged Janey.

"Look at you, girl! No more crutches! And you're more beautiful than ever!"

"Hi Max. Thank you for the nice compliment. There will be no more crutches ever for this girl."

"Mo, Janey, this is TR Royce. We've become the best of friends. Went through the entire war together."

TR shook Mo's hand, then Janey's.

"Hi Mo. Hi Janey."

TR did a double take of Max, then Mo, then shook his head.

"Mo, Max told me you guys were identical, but I can't

believe my eyes. You two can't be told apart. How the heck did you ever decide between these two, Janey? Max told me you met both guys the same night."

"It was tough, TR, but Mo swept me off my feet. Or maybe I should say he swept me off my foot."

All four laughed at Janey's comment poking fun at her own disability.

Mo checked out Max's arm, still in a sling.

"How's the arm, Max?"

"Bullet went clean through and missed the bones. I got lucky. TR and Aaron kept me from bleeding to death until we got to the medics in the next town. I'll be fine in no time, just some nasty scars."

"More like badges of honor if you ask me, Max," said TR.

"I guess something was bound to happen to one of us in Europe while Mo was taking it easy over there in Burma."

"Yeah. I marched eight hundred miles through the jungle and only got a little scar on my face," laughed Mo. "Just a walk in the park."

Mo continued.

"So here we are in Washington DC, and we're all going to the White House. Who could've known? From the jungles for me and a German concentration camp for you guys, and a few months later we get to meet the President! And I can't wait for you to meet the three greatest guys ever who went through Burma with me. They're the best."

"I'll bet they are Mo," said Max. "I can't wait to meet those fellas."

"Well listen you three," chimed TR. "My dad has suites booked for all of us at the Hay-Adams. Best place in Washington. We're going to meet everybody at the hotel. Dad has people set to meet all three of your crew, Mo, when they get in. Meanwhile, let's all go to the hotel and have a drink while we wait for them. This deserves a celebration. And you two can meet Aaron, the young man who helped us recover the art from the camp. He spent five years there in that prison."

"That sounds like a great idea!" said Max, as he extended his good arm for Janey to hold onto.

"Mo, let me escort your beautiful gal to the car." Janey grabbed Max's arm.

"Thank you soldier. Such a gentleman."

Washington DC

The bar in the Hay-Adams was packed. Civilians dressed to the nines and officers and soldiers in immaculately pressed uniforms created a room filled with loud and happy conversations.

Amidst the elegant surroundings, a large seating area had the Senator and his wife, TR, Max, Aaron, Mo and Janey, along with three empty chairs at the table.

"There they are!" exclaimed Mo, as he looked over, pointing toward the entrance.

Standing together, Duke, Riley and Tex scanned the room as they tried to spot the party they were to join. Mo stood up, waving his arms to get the attention of the three men.

When the three reached the table, Mo gave hugs to each of them, then turned back to his party. "I want you all to meet three of the best and bravest men in America, Duke Marlow, Riley Meadows and Tex Bowlin."

After the men exchanged handshakes and greetings, the three took turns introducing themselves to the women seated at the table.

The Senator could not hide his delight as he hosted this group of real American heroes.

"Gentlemen, sit down and join our celebration. Your

money is no good while you're in the Capital. I'm your host, so let's get you some drinks."

The Senator held up his hand to summon a server, who hustled over to the table immediately. After the men had ordered and everyone settled in, conversations between those sitting near each other started all around.

As the three newcomers were served their drinks, Tex, sitting across from Mo, looked around at the room he was in, and marvelled out loud.

"You've done it again, Mo. Doesn't matter whether we're in a jungle or Washington DC, you never cease to amaze. I couldn't believe it when I got the call we were invited to come here."

Mo looked at all three of the men who he had marched through hell with.

"None of us would be here today if we didn't work perfect as a team back in those jungles, Tex. No way I'm going to get an award without you three with me."

Duke, who could pass for a Hollywood leading man in his uniform, looked around the table, then straight at Max.

"Max. Not one of us would be here today if it wasn't for your twin brother. And you know he's a little crazy, don't you? Nobody in their right mind would have done what he did." Max gave an admiring look at his twin.

"I don't know about crazy, but he's sure never backed down from anybody, and I should know."

Mo looked to change the subject away from his exploits, interjecting before Max could say anything more.

"You know, you fellas clean up real nice. I've never seen you three looking so natty."

Then, looking over at Riley, huge and buffed in his uniform, Mo continued.

"Janey, I told you about Riley. Can you imagine getting

this guy in the ring with your brother Carl? It would be a battle of the giants."

Riley looked at Mo with his big smile.

"Aw, Mo, I'm just a gentle soul. I finally get back here and you want to put me in the ring?"

Everybody at the table erupted into laughter.

As the conversations continued, TR leaned over to Max.

"I like this a lot better than the Savoy, Max."

"Yeah, me too, TR. And I'm sure the menu has better choices for our dinner. But it's sure not as cheap as the ten shillings!"

"No worries. Dad's got us covered!"

As he quietly enjoyed the get together, Aaron sat amid the group, but it was easy for all to see he was feeling foreign to his new life. Janey, sitting next to him, noticed his shyness and started a conversation.

"Aaron, Max tells me you play the violin."

"Yes. I taught the Camp Commandant's children the violin while my family was in the camp. It is part of the reason we were spared suffering which others endured."

"I'm so sorry, Aaron. But you're here now." Janey had a slight pause as she tried to imagine what Aaron must have endured, then continued. "You know, Aaron, I play the piano. You and I have a love of music in common. I saw a grand piano in the ballroom when we went by. And I can't help but notice you brought your violin case with you."

"Yes. The Commandant gave me a beautiful instrument. I brought it with me from the camp. I keep it with me."

"Maybe they'll let me play the piano in the ballroom and you and I can play something together?"

"I would like that very much, Janey."

Overhearing this conversation, the Senator jumped in.

"Janey, Aaron, when we're through celebrating here,

would you allow us all to come and listen while you play? The manager here is an old and good friend of mine. He'll be only too happy to let us use the ballroom."

As she looked over at Aaron, then back at the Senator with her beautiful smile, Janey answered for them both.

"Senator, I'm sure we would both be delighted if everyone came to continue the celebration."

CHAPTER ONE HUNDRED FIFTEEN

Washington DC

Tables in the Grand Ballroom of the White House were filled with the nation's elite. Servers in white uniforms moved about the VIPs at the black-tie ceremony as they served champagne and carried silver trays with exquisitely prepared and presented hors d'oeuvres.

Senator Royce and Congressman Tucker, with their wives, were situated at a table toward the front of the room.

A long table had been set up on an elevated area at the front of the room. President Truman and his wife Bess were seated in the center. To their left sat the Vice President and his wife as well as members of the cabinet and their wives. To his right was Mo Gordon, Janey, Duke, Riley, Tex, then TR, Max and Aaron, with the soldiers looking handsome in immaculately pressed full dress uniform. The President leaned across his wife, as he spoke to the Vice President, laughing about something. He then straightened up in his chair and grabbed a spoon, as he looked over the gathering of people chatting at their tables.

The President began gently tapping his wine glass with his spoon, a big smile on his face, and within only a few seconds, the room fell silent as all eyes looked to the front.

President Truman stood, slowly and deliberately, then turned to look over at those seated on his right, before beginning to address the crowd in front of him.

"We are all privileged to be here tonight with our honored guests. These men to my right represent the millions of our soldiers who so gallantly fought for our freedom."

Once again, he turned his attention back over toward the assembled soldiers next to him.

"America, and all of its citizens owe you and so many others for your sacrifices and courage. We honor those fallen soldiers lost in battle, and are committed to always remember them. However, tonight we celebrate those who have come home, heroes, every one. Thanks to men such as you, our nation can now move forward into an era of unprecedented peace and prosperity."

The President began clapping, as all in attendance rose to their feet, including Janey and Aaron, giving the soldiers a long, standing ovation.

After everyone took their seats, the President, who still stood, continued.

"As I name you, would you please stand? We have the son of our distinguished Senator Russell Royce from Massachusetts, TR Royce. We also have Max Gordon. And, as a guest tonight, Aaron Gittelsohn, a survivor from one of Germany's harsh concentration camps in Dachau, outside of Munich."

The three men all stood as they were called. When the last of the three had risen, the crowd issued another round of applause. The President then addressed the men.

"Aaron, I've heard the story about the heroic actions of your family while held as prisoners by the Nazis. Our nation gives you our condolences for the passing of both your mother and father while they were held in the camp."

Aaron looked over at the American President as he nodded acknowledgement humbly, before the President continued.

"Aaron and his father were responsible for saving many

lives while in the camp. Aaron, I can only thank God that America and its allies were able to put an end to the senseless and grotesque genocide committed by the Nazis."

The crowd applauded again.

"Aaron, are there any words you could share with us tonight that might give us insight into how you persevered? The strength and will to survive all those years?"

Aaron looked at the President, then around the room.

"My people had no choices. Nazis came with machine guns and took us all. They shot those who struggled against them, or worse. My father was a wise man. He told me often that although the Nazis made him physically captive, they could never control his mind, his heart or his soul. My parents acted with courage, faith and high morals. I made a promise to both of them to never give up hope. If we lose hope for the future, we will have no future. We will have nothing to live for."

Aaron stopped speaking, the room completely silent for a few moments. Finally, the President spoke, with real tears showing in his eyes.

"So well said young man. May I welcome you to America. I am sure your future here will be an excellent one. Thank you."

The crowd remained silent as the President continued.

"Let all of us here tonight pray that we never again allow these kinds of atrocities to take place. Evil such as this should never be tolerated. If the lessons we have learned are ever forgotten or denied, we should be ashamed. The world should be ashamed to ever turn a blind eye toward this kind of atrocity."

The President looked back toward Aaron as he finished, as Aaron nodded again. Max reached over and put his hand on Aaron's shoulder. The President went on.

"TR Royce and Max Gordon, traveling as part of the Seventh Army when it liberated the Dachau concentration camp, were responsible for finding one of the largest caches of stolen artwork in Germany. Along with Aaron, they headed a convoy from Dachau to Paris with the recovered Nazi loot. And note that Lieutenant Gordon is still recovering from a Nazi sniper's bullet while he was shielding Aaron from fire. I will be bestowing Max a purple heart at a ceremony tomorrow."

The crowd applauded again.

"TR, Max, your country thanks you, as do I."

The crowd applauded once more, along with the President. The three men acknowledged the crowd, then proceeded to sit.

The President looked back over toward the men. "Lieutenant Gordon, would you please stand back up?"

Somewhat bewildered, Max rose by himself.

"I understand that you have chosen to stay in the army, and you are entering into the Judge Advocate General's Corp. Is that your plan young man?"

Max looked over at the President, and with a shy smile, answered.

"Yes, Mr. President."

The President walked over to where Max stood.

"Well, in that case, from here on, you will be addressed as Captain Gordon. Congratulations soldier!"

The President extended his hand to shake Max's good hand, the other arm in the sling.

The President walked back to the center as the crowd applauded loudly while the other soldiers on the dais all congratulated Max, TR slapping him on the back.

As the applause stopped, the President looked back over the crowd.

"And while we had heroes in Europe, we also had heroes in many other parts of the world. Please stand as I call your names, soldiers. Mo Gordon, Duke Marlow, Riley Meadows and Tex Bowlin."

The President stopped momentarily, then turned to the crowd with a big smile.

"I'm sure by now, you've all noticed something up here on this stage. Probably for the first time in the history of the White House, we not only have two soldiers from the same family at the same time being honored for heroism, they just happen to be very identical twins!"

The President looked over at the man next to him, then at Max further down the table.

"Your mother must have been very proud of both of you young men. You make us all proud. Mo, tomorrow, I will be presenting you with America's highest military decoration, The Congressional Medal of Honor. Congratulations."

Everyone rose in unison to a standing ovation as the President shook Mo's hand. When they had finished clapping and seated themselves, the President continued.

"Mo, you distinguished yourself at the risk of your own life above and beyond the call of duty in action against an enemy of the United States. It is a rare thing indeed. And I've been told, Mr. Gordon, when you were asked to come to Washington to accept the honor, you would not make the trip unless we included Riley, Tex and Duke. Is that the case?"

"Yes Sir, Mr. President. I wouldn't be here tonight if not for these three men who marched with me in those jungles, and every other man who marched with us. We left a lot of men just as good as we are over there, Mr. President."

"Yes, you did, Mr. Gordon. Thank God for the good men who did come back."

The crowd once again erupted into spontaneous applause. When it had quieted, the President continued.

"Mo, when you made the decision to put your life on the line, charging into machine gun fire, what were you thinking about?"

"Mr. President, sometimes during the Circumstances of War, there is no decision to be made. You react. You do what you must. You try to do what is right."

"Young man, circumstances can create heroes, and that is certainly the case here. Thank You." The President shook Mo's hand again as the crowd applauded. The President moved down the table as he shook each man's hand. When he returned to his spot in the center, and before he sat down, the President spoke one more time.

"I have one more announcement before dinner is served. I understand that after dessert we have a very special treat for everyone. Mo Gordon's fiancé, Janey Ryan, and another of our honored guests, Aaron Gittelsohn, will perform a musical number for us. I for one can hardly wait, so let's get on with our dinner."

With that, the President sat, then turned to start a conversation with Mo and Janey, as the food began arriving, brought in by multiples of servers.

Later, as the crowd enjoyed dessert, a grand piano was wheeled into the room from a side door, with a violin placed on a stand next to it. A microphone was then set on top of the piano. Mo stood and gave his hand to Janey as she stood, then walked her down the two steps and over to the piano as Aaron followed them.

Janey took her place on the bench as Aaron picked up his violin and bow. Janey looked at Aaron and smiled, as did Aaron, nodding to her. Janey then pulled the microphone over and in a clear, confident and professional manner which belied her young age, addressed the White House VIP crowd, the President and his wife.

"Good evening, ladies and gentlemen. I was introduced to Aaron last night, and we immediately realized we had a common bond, music. We had some time this afternoon, and we rehearsed a bit on a lovely and famous musical piece. It is our great pleasure to be able to perform this piece for you. Aaron told me that this song helped save his life in Dachau, when he was ordered to play it for the Camp Commandant. We now present to you, 'Claire de Lune', by Claude DeBussy."

Janey started softly with a lush concert quality piano introduction, then was joined by Aaron as he lifted his bow to play his violin beautifully, as they captivated the audience.

CHAPTER ONE HUNDRED SIXTEEN

Springfield Illinois

Edward, Cecilia, Mo and Max sat on the front porch of the house on Black Avenue. Mo and Max were dressed in civvies, and the three men all had a bottle of beer.

"Plenty of times in Burma I sure wished I was back here with you guys. How about it, Max? You had to have been as homesick as I was."

"Was I ever, Mo. Even though it was a hell of an adventure, I missed home."

"Well fellas, you're back and in one piece, both of you," said Eddie.

"Eddie, any word about Tommy Kelso? Do you know if he's back in town yet?"

Edward put his beer down on one knee.

"Mo, Tommy was killed in action."

"Oh no. Dammit. Do you know where he was?"

"Tommy was in the first wave of troops that stormed the beaches during the big invasion of Normandy. They said Tommy was trying to drag a wounded soldier up the beach when he was killed."

Max's face turned white as he heard about Tommy Kelso.

"That means Tommy was one of the men who died taking that beachhead so that we'd have a landing spot. TR and I drove up those beaches two weeks after the invasion. Damn."

"Ceil and I went to the service for Tommy a couple of months ago. Tom's mother and father were so proud of their son. Now it's just the two of them."

Mo and Max sat silently when Mo finally spoke.

"Damn. Seems like just yesterday Tommy and I were rollin' around in the street punching each other in front of the White's house and now he's gone."

Cecilia had tears in her eyes as she looked at Mo.

"I still remember your puffy little red face coming into the living room."

"So do I," said Edward.

Max looked at Mo.

"You never did get in much trouble by Momma that time Mo."

"Nah. Guess I didn't."

All four sat silently again, as they looked out at the front lawn for a few moments, when Edward spoke up. "Well, you're both headed out for new experiences. I'm going to miss these two, Ceil."

"Eddie, we knew they were going to fly the coop when they got back. It just gives us an excuse to go visit the boys."

"Yeah. Just, it's gonna be real quiet around here again. I was hoping maybe these two stick around for a while when they got back."

"Eddie, Mo and I will be living pretty close to each other, him in New York and me in Washington DC. You two can see us both with just a couple days train ride."

"I know Max. And I'm glad for both of you with your new opportunities."

"I knew I'd get into JAG, but it was TR's dad who made sure I'd be based in Washington. It's where all the action is.

And anyway, I'm sure TR will be elected to something in not too long."

Mo then got in the conversation.

"Eddie, I almost ended up staying here in Springfield. I was just planning on trying to hook on at the Journal and Register as a writer. Janey would have worked around here playing the piano, we'd have kids, you know, the normal stuff. But the opportunity to work for the New York Times as a writer came out of nowhere."

"Not nowhere, Mo," said Max. "First of all, you guys, Mo comes back a real hero, Medal of Honor. He's a full-blown poster boy. Mo's a national celebrity. Then, after dinner at the White House, the Editor of the New York Times comes up to Mo and asks for an interview. The next afternoon at the Hay-Adams when he asks Mo what his plans are, Mo says he wants to write for a newspaper. Bang! He offers Mo a job on the spot! Mo's a real feather in that paper's cap if you ask me."

"Max has it right. That's just the way it happened," said Mo. "And when I told Janey about the job offer, she told me she always wanted to go to New York. She's always wanted to see if she could make it big on the biggest stage. And she will. She's thrilled, but her mom is a little sad just like you guys. But we won't be going until after the wedding."

Cecilia stood from her chair and went to sit on the swing with Eddie as she put her arm around his shoulders.

"You boys should never make these big decisions on what you think us older folks want. You do what's right for your futures and what makes you happy. Isn't that right, Eddie?"

"Of course it is Ceil. We always want what's best for these two. But we're coming to visit you fellas a bunch, so get used to it."

"You know it, Eddie. Just think, when you get to New York or Washington DC, you have a place to stay for free and a great guide to show you around. Right Max?"

"Absolutely brother!"

Everyone sat in silence again for a few seconds, with the men all taking a big swig of their beers, when Max started talking again.

"Eddie, remember the last time I was here before I took off for duty? I asked you if there was something special you would do with Mo and I when we got back."

"I don't just remember it Max. I was kinda waiting for you to bring it up."

"Well, how about it?"

Eddie got up from his chair.

"Ceil, I'm gonna take these two out for a bit. We won't be too late. Kind of a man thing."

"Well, I sure don't want to stand in the way of your 'man thing' with these two. You just go right ahead but I'll expect a full report when you get back."

"Yes Ma'am. C'mon you two."

Mo looked stumped.

"Where we going?"

"Just hop in the car and don't ask questions, Mo. You'll find out soon enough where Eddie's taking us," said Max as he stood and set his bottle on the porch railing.

Later, as Eddie's car traveled north, then turned onto a familiar road, Mo looked over at Eddie from the passenger seat, then behind him at Max with a smile on his face.

"I think I figured out where we're headed men."

After about forty-five minutes of driving and lots of small talk, Eddie pulled off the highway, down a long paved road, then onto a dirt road, where he stopped at the edge of a field.

Eddie, Mo and Max got out and walked onto a slight rise on Eddie's farm. With Max on one side and Mo on the other, Eddie stood in the middle as the three men looked out over the crops spreading out in front of them.

Tall corn on one side, ten feet tall at least. On the other side was a lush field of wheat, tops bending with the wind as ripples of gold washed across the top.

The three men just stood there, looking out over the fields, as a warm wind blew the crops back and forth. Mo looked over at Max as a small tear started in his eyes.

"Thanks Max. Thanks Eddie. This is the most beautiful thing ever!"

Eddie put his arms around the shoulders of each man, as he took in the moment, tears in his eyes and a smile on his face.

"Best crop I've ever had boys. Best ever."

Narration

There has always been one constant battle on Earth. Good versus Evil. Just when it has appeared evil will win, men and women have done something so selfless and so heroic that they have totally redeemed themselves. By doing so, they have pulled humanity out of the darkness, and back into the light.

The force of one soul that strives for divinity has more power than the thousands that fall into darkness. However, the forces of darkness will not be deterred, and they work tirelessly to turn more to their side.

During this war, the light dimmed, and when it appeared ready to flicker, to be diminished completely, the bravery and heroism which was exhibited brought light. Only the living control the intensity of the luminescence, so it follows, when there are not enough souls reaching for perfection to overpower the evil, then, it will finally be ..

THE END